CHILDREN of USEYI

Moses Ose Utomi

atheneum

New York   Amsterdam/Antwerp   London
Toronto   Sydney   New Delhi

atheneum

An imprint of Simon & Schuster Children's Publishing Division
1230 Avenue of the Americas, New York, New York 10020

Text © 2025 by Moses Ose Utomi
Jacket illustration © 2025 by Laylie Frazier
Jacket design by Greg Stadnyk

For information about special discounts for bulk purchases, please contact Simon & Schuster Special Sales at 1-866-506-1949 or business@simonandschuster.com.
The Simon & Schuster Speakers Bureau can bring authors to your live event. For more information or to book an event, contact the Simon & Schuster Speakers Bureau at 1-866-248-3049 or visit our website at www.simonspeakers.com.
Interior design by Irene Metaxatos
The text for this book was set in Modum.
Manufactured in the United States of America
First Edition
10 9 8 7 6 5 4 3 2 1
Library of Congress Cataloging-in-Publication Data
Names: Utomi, Moses Ose, author.
Title: Children of Useyi / Moses Ose Utomi.
Description: First edition. | New York : Atheneum Books for Young Readers, 2025. | Series: Sisters of the mud ; book 2 | Audience term: Preteens | Audience: Ages 12 and up. | Summary: The elite group of girl warriors from the Mud Fam, who excel in the sport of Bowing, face new challenges and threats when a mysterious man claiming to come from the gods arrives and initiates a dangerous tournament.
Identifiers: LCCN 2024014832 | ISBN 9781665949910 (hardcover) | ISBN 9781665949934 (ebook)
Subjects: CYAC: Contests—Fiction. | Hand-to-hand fighting—Fiction. | Black people—Fiction. | Feminism—Fiction. | Africa—Fiction. | Fantasy. | LCGFT: Fantasy fiction. | Novels.
Classification: LCC PZ7.1.U88 Ch 2025 | DDC [Fic]—dc23
LC record available at https://lccn.loc.gov/2024014832

To my sister,
Ijenerumhen Joy Utomi,
who was blessed with the
skin of the gods

To my niece
Elysia Ijenerumhen Utomi,
the First of the First

And to my niece and goddaughter,
Noelle Ivie Helena Hartmann,
who makes every day a good day

Na North

Na West   Na East

Na Isle

Na South

Na River

Na Vine

Na Creek

Grand Temple

Na Mud

Antie Yaya's

Na Rock

Na Sand

N

W   E

S

CHILDREN of USEYI

Goodbye to a Dream

NORMALLY THE Mud camp was a modest, quiet place.

It sat in a small clearing in an otherwise unremarkable part of the jungle. In the back, near the tree line, was the long wooden sleep lodge, with bunked sleeping cots to fit dozens. In front of that, right at the camp's center, the Bowing ring stretched five strides across and was rounded by sandbags. A garden, chicken coop, and another, much smaller hut—a meeting space for the Mud Fam's leaders—completed the camp.

Normally the only sounds were the hush of the breeze through the branches, the yelps and giggles and thuds of girls training.

However, on the night of Swoo's first victory as a full Sis, the Mud camp was a party. A gaggle of Flagga boys was visiting with their drums and other instruments, leading the song and dance. Swoo, drunk off palm wine, was dancing so hard in the middle of the ring that she was covered in sweat. The Flagga boys stood in a circle around her, urging her on and nearly laughing themselves off their feet.

Sis Dirt, First of the Mud, sat at the high table. Beside her was Sis Webba, the Second of the Mud. These two eldest Mud sisters watched the festivities with amusement. So much of Dirt's life now was watching. She didn't mind it. Ever since the end of the last season, when she and Carra Carre had destroyed the Grand Temple in the chaos of their fight, she'd been banned from competing. Antie Yaya's decision. In a way, her life of watching was a return to how things had been before the Godskin powers changed everything.

"I must go, my Sis," Webba said.

Dirt nodded. It was late. And she knew that Webba's wrists sometimes pained her deep into the evening. Ever since her legs were destroyed by Carra Carre, Webba had moved herself around by rolling the large wheels on the side of her chair, a task that strained the arms. Dirt stood to help push Webba's rolling chair to the sleep hut.

"No," Webba said. "I must leave."

Dirt was confused. She went to stand in front of Webba to better understand her sister.

That was when Dirt saw it. It was easy to miss against Webba's dark skin, and hidden as it was beneath her hair, but it was unmistakably a Scar. A jagged curve following the arc of her ear, roiling deep inside with a black fire.

Dirt nearly choked. "When?" she asked.

Webba shrugged. "I see it today. Before Swoo's Bow."

Dirt sighed. "Look at us. Two oldold girls, eh? Time is cruel."

"Time is forever," Webba responded. "That is why I must go."

Dirt could see the somberness in her sister. "Antie Yaya will allow you to stay," she said reassuringly.

Webba looked up at Dirt with a smile unlike any she had ever given. "No, my Sis," she said. "In this world of Bowers and Godskins, I have no place. Na Fam does not need me. Look and see."

She nodded her head at the festivities, forcing Dirt to turn and look. There were the Flagga boys, teeth shining as they strummed kora and blew algaita and pounded talking drums. There was sweat-covered Swoo, feet flashing in the moonlight.

And there were fifty Bibi—last season's recruits—all laughing with the freedom of unburdened youth, swaying to the music and wind, chasing each other round the camp and through the trees with a reckless joy. Since childhood, Dirt had dreamed of building the Mud into a big fam, with her and Webba at the head. The day the recruits joined—six months ago now—that dream had been fulfilled.

"We are strongstrong now, my Sis," Webba said. "We have na thing we always want to have. But these Bibi do not know me. They know only you. Sis Dirt. Na Godskin."

Dirt turned back to Webba, shaking her head. "No, no . . ." She was surprised to find tears clouding her vision. She wiped them angrily. She refused to cry. Crying meant that it was really happening, that Webba was really leaving. "I need you."

"You will lead na Fam," Webba said. "And Sis Swoo will be your Second. Think how happy she will be. Let me leave for her, if not for myself."

Dirt swelled up to protest, only to see by Webba's amused expression that she was joking.

"That is not funny," Dirt said.

"I disagree."

Dirt couldn't think of any further argument. Webba was right. At some point, all of them were supposed to move on, go off to join the Mamas and Papas. Dirt had refused, and Antie Yaya had allowed it, but that didn't mean every girl sought the same life as Dirt. She had chosen her path. She had to let Webba choose hers.

"But tomorrow is Flagga Day," Dirt tried, weakly.

Webba bellowed laughter, rubbing her belly. "You want me to stay for na day with na Flagga boys and their mighty sticks, eh? You must truly despise me."

Dirt called a halt to the party and made the announcement to the Mud Fam and their guests. The reactions were more varied than she'd expected. Among the Flagga boys, there was jaw-dropping disbelief, followed immediately by them forming into a line to honor Webba. One by one they approached her and fell to a knee, thanking her for her career and for all the times she'd inspired them and any number of things. Dirt found it impossible to control her tears as she watched. It was exactly the respect Webba deserved.

The Bibi had a very different response. They mostly fell quiet and watched, polite enough to not interrupt the ceremony, but uncertain what else they should do. As always, Webba was right. It was Dirt they revered, not her. Webba's departure meant little to them.

It was not the same for Snore and Swoo. Snore immediately fled into the jungle and was gone for the entire night. Swoo was last in line behind the Flagga boys, and when they were finished, she knelt in front of Webba and simply laid her head in Webba's lap. After a long moment, she stood, gave Webba a long hug, then moved to stand beside Sis Dirt, her head bowed.

"We are na Mud sisters!" Swoo sang out, her voice cracked to the verge of breaking.

The song was picked up by the others..

We fight, oh yes, ooooooh!
We are na Mud sisters! (We are na Mud sisters!)
We never quit, nooooooo!

Webba had already packed her few things, so all she had to do was gather them before rolling herself off into the jungle toward Antie Yaya's. All the while the Mud Fam sang, ensuring that her departure was a melodic one. Even when she had disappeared into the dark jungle, the song continued.

As the Flagga boys left and the Bibi went to bed and Swoo went off to go exercise her frustrations away, Dirt stayed out, singing her sister off until her mouth and throat were too dry to make anything but the faintest noise.

Only then did she go to sleep. As her mind drifted, she hoped that she would at least continue to see Webba in her dreams, the one place where time held no power over Dirt and her sisters.

Flagga Day

TO REACH THE Rock Fam's territory, the Mud sisters crossed much of the South, passing from their familiar muddy jungles, across the soft beach sands, over to the glistening seaside cliffs that the Rock Fam called home.

Dirt had made the trip many times, as had Swoo, Snore, and some of the other girls. But never without Webba. Strangely, the sadness of the night before was gone. A night of sleep had reset Dirt's brain, so instead of knowing Webba was gone forever, she felt that Webba was simply out in the jungle collecting berries, or off to a nearby stream for a bath, or some other temporary departure. Dirt marched the path like it was any other day, her mind at ease.

For most of the Mud sisters, it was their first trip to the edges of the South, out from the sweltering density of the jungle and into the open air and its coastal breeze. They looked around in wonder, falling out of their marching formation as they chased after a scuttling crab or engaged in giggle-filled sand-kicking fights. The final leg of their journey took them from sea level up an ascent to the top of the cliffs, where the ground beneath them became cold, slick stone.

At the top of the climb was the South's biggest and most beautiful celebration: Flagga Day.

All the boys and girls of the region were along the edge of the cliff, some with feet hanging out over the water. Butterfly girls, the Daughters of Abidon, were in their finest dresses and jewelry, clad in high-heeled shoes despite the precarious rocks. Burly Pusher boys, the Sons of Eghodo, manned grills the length of felled palm trees, cooking fish and chicken and plantain over licking flames. Bowers, the Daughters of Oduma, held impromptu sparring matches, a rare opportunity to practice with girls from other Fam without the stress and stakes of competition.

But Flagga Day was, first and foremost, for the Flagga boys. The Sons of Ijiri. All year, they competed in Flagga, a game that Dirt had never been able to make sense of that involved sneaking into each other's hideouts and stealing their flags. Only on Flagga Day could they show their work, with each group of Flagga boys hoisting a stick a dozen strides high that bore each flag they'd managed to steal. This year, the Mud Flagga had done well, with six vibrantly painted cloth flags lined down from the top of their stick, each one rippling in the wind. Only the Creek Flagga had done better, their stick bearing an impressive fourteen flags.

Whether zero flags or a hundred, the Flagga boys were in a celebratory mood, drumming and dancing and biting into grilled meat with the reckless joy that only Flagga Day could bring.

Dirt led the Mud Fam up the cliff, where heads turned toward her, followed soon after by a roar of cheers.

"Sis Dirt!"

"Na Godskin!"

"Oos oos na Mud!"

After that, the Mud Fam dispersed. The younger girls rushed off to play with their friends from other Fam, showing off new techniques and trading gossip. Dirt and Swoo found a spot along the edge of the cliff, their feet dangling, the breeze pressing against their skin. Snore sat a few strides away, joining neither the older sisters nor the younger girls.

"Snore," Dirt nodded to an open spot beside her. "Come and sit."

But Snore only shook her head and looked away, staring out across the sea.

Dirt pursed her lips but said nothing more. Snore had not been the same since the Vine kidnapped her six months prior. Dirt had assumed the girl would be afraid for some time after—that was expected. But in the time that had passed, Snore had only gotten worse, each day retreating more and more into herself.

Something would have to be done, but Dirt had no idea what.

That was when a Butterfly girl walked over to them. She was propped up on heeled shoes, with her hair bound back in a ponytail and the dark skin of her cheeks painted with a muted, blushing red. Precious stones of every color wrapped around both wrists and ankles, glittered at her ears, were embedded in her hairband. Even Dirt—who had no eye for such things—could see the care and skill that had gone into crafting them.

She would recognize that work anywhere.

"How now, Mud Fam?" the Butterfly girl asked.

Though her back was to the girl, Snore immediately recognized the voice. Her eyes widened, her cheeks rose, she inhaled from nose and mouth, a full body gasp. She whipped her head around so fast that Dirt feared she may have hurt herself.

"BIBI NANA!" Snore howled.

Then the two girls collided, skinny arms crushing each other into an embrace that saw Nana giggling madly and Snore uncharacteristically solemn, eyes closed and pressed into Nana's shoulder. When Nana eventually pulled back, Snore refused to let go, keeping herself wrapped around Nana's waist.

"My sister," Dirt and Swoo said simultaneously.

Dirt gave Swoo an admiring nod. She knew the girl wanted to join the Bibi's embrace, but a Sis had to carry herself differently in public. Swoo nodded back, but then seemed embarrassed by the approval and looked to Nana.

There was much to discuss, and Nana told them all of it. In the six months since she'd left the Mud Fam to begin her life as a Butterfly, she had seen much of the South, made new friends, learned tough lessons, and crafted so much jewelry of such high quality that her work was already being sent to the Pusher boys to be traded to other parts of the Isle.

"My smartsmart sister," Swoo said with pride. "Of course your adorn is na best."

Nana grinned.

Dirt was about to add her own praise when a long, lone peal from an algaita split the air. All heads turned away from the water, back to where one of the Creek Flagga had climbed their flag-laden stick, holding himself high up its length with just one hand and his feet while holding a speaking cone in his other hand.

"Boys and girls of na South!" he exclaimed, earning a round of energetic whooping and jumping from his fellow Creek Flagga at the base of the stick. As this year's Flagga winners, they were able to lead the proceedings, showing off their trophies in the process. "Welcome to Flagga Day! We are na Creek boys. You know us, eh?"

He flashed a brilliant smile, and the crowd bathed him in adoration. Dirt had never had much patience for Flagga boys and their showmanship, but she supposed this was the one day she had to forgive them.

He raised a finger in the air, then a second, then a third, counting up to the beginning of their song.

> *Na Creek boys we dance! (Hey hey!)*
> *Na Creek boys we play! (Hey hey!)*
> *Na Creek boys we win and win every day!*

He repeated the song twice more, each time whipping the crowd up further and further until, by the end, nearly everyone was on their feet, singing and chanting the anthem of the Creek boys.

Once finished, he slid back down the stick and joined the other Creek boys in pulling it out of the shallow soil and walking over to the edge of the cliff. Up and down the cliff face, the Flagga boys of the South did the same, carrying their sticks over whether they held ten flags or none. They all lined up, sticks held out horizontally, flags dangling.

With a great collective heave, the Flagga Boys tossed their sticks out to sea to a great cheer from the audience. This was the send-off, the beginning of the end of Flagga Day. The sticks would drift for hours before disappearing over the horizon, and whichever group's stick was the last to vanish was said to have Mama Ijiri's favor for the next year of Flagga.

While the sticks made their way toward the edge of the sea, Dirt, Swoo, Nana, and Snore enjoyed each other like old times. They played the Gekko and the Guava, sparred lightly, giggled, and carried on like they were all back in the Mud camp's old, ramshackle sleep hut. The hours passed by too quickly, and soon the crowd was murmuring in anticipation, the last log a speck on the horizon.

"It is finished?" Snore asked, her voice filled with sorrow.

Nana, blessings upon her, immediately wrapped Snore in a hug. "It is finefine. I will come and visit soon, eh?"

Snore's response was drowned out by another peal from a Flagga boy's algaita, officially ending the day.

Yet no one moved.

Because there was still a speck on the horizon. Not a stick drifting away from shore, but a stick drifting *toward* it. As all the boys and girls of the South watched in confusion, the stick drew quickly closer, and soon revealed itself to be not a stick, but something different. A strange wooden device, growing larger by the second. It was narrow, shaped like a hammock strung between trees, but with tall wooden spires jutting up from its center and large triangular cloths that swelled with wind as it glided toward the shore.

They all watched in disbelief as the device crashed violently against the rocks at the base of the cliff, the wood making a horrendous rending sound and bursting in all directions. No one knew what to do, including Dirt. The strange thing fell into pieces from the impact and plunged into the sea, to be swallowed beneath dark waves.

It was only when the wood was fully submerged beneath the waves that anyone's eyes noticed the body remaining on the rocks.

No one spoke. No one even moved. Not just because there was a strange and unfamiliar body down on the rocks.

But because the body was big. A man.

An adult.

3

The Isle's First Man

OTHER THAN Antie Yaya, there were no adults on the Isle. There hadn't been since the days of the Mamas and Papas, when Mama Eghodo, Papa Oduma, Mama Ijiri, and Papa Abidon still cared for the children of the Isle. But they'd left long ago, so far back that none remembered, taking all the women and men with them. Since those days, every girl and boy left at seventeen to join them. Dirt herself was the first girl to ever stay as a woman.

Even Webba had left.

With the presence of the man's body on the rocks below, it was as if the world had changed from day to night. From calm and ease and safety to the unknown terrors of the dark. No one had yet figured out what the presence of an adult meant. But they all held their breaths, understanding that something deeply important had happened. Something that would change the Isle forever.

As stunned as Dirt was by the body, she could still see plainly the man was dying. He needed help.

I am brave. I am fat. I am Dirt.

A purifying steam scoured her, filling her from head and chest to each toe and finger. The world stood out with greater clarity than before. The clouds were wispy and white against the darkening sky, the sun an orange half disc sitting on the sea line, the thousands of boys and girls arrayed beside her on the stone cliffs, all looking down in the same direction.

Dirt leapt.

She plunged through wind, hair and clothes rippling from the air speeding around her. She still hadn't grown used to the power and all the ways it relieved her from the concerns of life. A year before, a jump like this would have ended her. Now, she landed on the rocks below with a concussive clap of sound and a splash of puddled water, her bones undamaged, not even a blemish on her skin.

Then there was an identical sound to her right. She turned, confused.

A behemoth of a girl stood beside her, her head wrapped all in vines but for two small spaces that revealed dark eyes beneath. The girl was over a head taller than Dirt and nearly twice as wide, her belly swelling out with good fat layered over firm muscle. The air shimmered around her, the same power the Gods had granted Dirt steaming from her hulking frame.

Carra Carre, First of the Vine Fam, the defending God Bow champion.

Dirt hadn't seen Carra Carre since their fight at the last God Bow—The Clash of the Godskins, fans had begun to call it. Their warring power had leveled the Grand Temple, scorching the sand of the arena floor and blasting away sections of seating. In the end, an uneasy peace had been reached, an acceptance that two girls so powerful could not fight unrestrained as they had. They had gone their separate ways with the understanding that there would be no more violence.

But that didn't mean Dirt had to like her.

"Sis Carra Carre," Dirt said, inclining her head as minimally as she could.

"Sis Dirt," Carra Carre replied, her own head dipping the same.

"I have no need of your assistance," Dirt said.

Carra Carre grunted. "I am not here to assist you."

"Good," Dirt said, and she turned away from her rival, approaching the man's body.

Much to Dirt's irritation, Carra Carre joined her.

The man was sprawled face up on the rocks, splashed in sea spray from the continued crashing of small waves. He wore strange clothes—a shirt of sorts but of a drab color, with little buttons all the way up the chest, where the collar folded against the neck. The shirt was tucked at the waist into pants that puffed around his thighs and slimmed down the calf, a design that looked almost like the pants of a Bower, but just wrong to Dirt's eyes.

Aside from his strange garb, Dirt was surprised at how tiny he was. He was larger than a Flagga boy, but no larger than most Pushers. Yet his face was old in the way that Antie Yaya's was, with a certain agedness to the skin, wrinkles and blemishes and splotches of inconsistent color. Dirt had always imagined that a man would be huge, the size of a hut or bigger. This man wasn't even as big as Dirt herself.

"Hello?" Dirt called. She knew that nothing could hurt her while she held the powers of her Godskin, but she still had to be cautious.

Carra Carre clearly didn't feel the same. She stepped forward and began to crouch near the body, but Dirt shot out a hand and grabbed her by the shoulder.

"Wait," she said. "You do not know if we can touch him."

Carra Carre tried to tug gently away from Dirt's grip, but Dirt held fast. Carra Carre shot to her feet and stared Dirt coldly in the eyes, flexing her shoulder muscles beneath Dirt's hand.

"Release me, Sis Dirt," she said, "and preserve yourself."

"You risk yourself by touching him," Dirt countered, keeping her hand in place. "We must send for Antie Yaya."

Carra Carre took a slight inhale, then threw a firm Slap into Dirt's shoulder. Were it a normal girl, the blow would have sent her crashing into the cliffs behind them, inducing an avalanche of falling stones. But Dirt was a Godskin, so the blow only made her stumble back slightly before she caught her balance and immediately took a Bowing stance, legs set and sturdy, arms up and ready.

Then the man groaned.

"Heeeeeelpp . . . ," he issued in a weak voice.

He released a string of deep, wet coughs, prompting Dirt and Carra Carre to both rush to his side. They gave each other a look, a silent agreement to put aside their mutual dislike in order to help this man. Together, they hoisted him up, one of them beneath each of his arms.

They timed their jump, crouching and leaping in unison with enough force to sail back up to the top of the cliffs. There, their two Fam were waiting, staring each other down with the same hostility their Firsts held for each other.

But between them was a woman, power and certainty radiating from her. She wore a blouse and wrapper of intricate red and gold floral design, with a matching gele. Coral beads sat on her wrists and dangled around her neck, drinking in and glowing with the dying sunlight.

"Thank you, my Godskins," Antie Yaya said. "I will take him from here."

Ever-Changing Winds

ANTIE YAYA had her Butterflies load the man into a cart and wheel him away. Just like that he was gone, and Flagga Day was finished, and the boys and girls of the South went back to their homes.

But news of a strange man appearing on the cliffs was the only thing anyone could talk about. All around the camp, the Bibi chattered like yelping monkeys. On the morning runs, they were so lost in gossip they veered off-route. During warm-ups, they congregated in groups to whisper instead of lifting heavy stones. By midday, they had done less than half of their usual work, and their appetite for discussion was still unsatisfied.

Swoo wasn't going to tolerate it anymore.

"Bibi up!" she barked, then released a shrill peal from the reed whistle she wore on a twine loop around her neck.

The Bibi were in the middle of lunch, and instead of rising to their feet, they glanced over at Swoo with confused looks.

"I. Say. UP!" she roared, and the Bibi bolted up so quickly that many of them lost their balance, falling into each other several times before stabilizing in ordered ranks, faces forward, posture alert.

"The rest of na day you will run!" she announced, pacing in front of the line of sisters. "And only run. Now go."

The sisters looked between each other uneasily.

"Run where?" Tiggi eventually asked. She was one of the former Butterfly girls who had joined the Mud after Dirt's win. A hard worker, but prone to overthinking and asking unnecessary questions.

Swoo looked them all up and down. "Anywhere out of my sight," she said with disgust.

". . . how long?" Tiggi asked.

Swoo's eyes flared with rage. "I say na whole day, you ramshackle goats, now GO!"

Snore went first, as she often did. Quiet, distant, and indifferent to Swoo's anger, she strolled toward the forest before breaking into a light jog and disappearing into the trees. Tiggi tried to follow next, but the other girls bumped past her, hastily trailing Snore into the jungle. Once they were gone, Swoo stood alone in the Mud camp, the sand of the ring between her toes, the breeze whispering against her skin.

Her next fight was just two days away. It was another important bout, one that would determine the tone of her Bowing season. With the Godskins disallowed from competing, she had a real chance to not only make the God Bow, but to win it, becoming the only Sis to ever do so in her first season. What better way to honor Webba's legacy? What better way to honor the Mud? That was all that mattered.

And yet . . .

The events of Flagga Day forced their way to the top of her attention time and again. Ever since Sis Dirt became a Godskin, something had changed in the South. Swoo wasn't the type to spend time dwelling on such things, but she noticed them, and it had become impossible for her to not worry that more changes were coming—worse changes.

"Sis Swoo is lazy today, eh?"

Sis Dirt's voice sailed over from the sleep lodge.

Swoo snapped back to attention, falling into a Bowing stance and facing off against an imaginary foe. "Never," she said.

Dirt lumbered over to stand beside the ring. Swoo could feel the First of the Mud's eyes on her, watching her technique with that blend of criticism and admiration that only an aged coach could possess. Swoo often found herself missing Webba, but there were rare occasions when Dirt seemed so much like Webba that the Mud Fam felt whole again, the one unchanged thing in the ever-changing winds of the South.

"If not lazy, then what is it?" Dirt asked. "A girl does not stare at na forest like that when all is wellwell."

"All that matters is na Bow," Swoo grunted, Riding forward and low, ever-sharpening the technique that had made her so success-ful. "All will be wellwell when I am na God Bow champion."

Dirt let the silence hang long enough that Swoo knew what she was doing—she was waiting for Swoo to reveal how she felt. And despite herself, Swoo did. She sighed in frustration and fell out of her Bowing stance, turning to her sister.

"I do not understand, Sis Dirt," she began. "One season ago, there is no Godskin. Sis Webba is whole. We are na small Fam, and there is only Antie Yaya. Now, there are two Godskins, Sis Webba is broken and gone, we are na big Fam, and there is na man in na South.

"I do not understand . . . ," she repeated, shaking her head.

Dirt nodded. "I forget that you are not there on na night na Vine attacks us."

Swoo had heard so many accounts of that night from Sis Webba, Sis Dirt, and Nana that she felt like she'd been there.

"And so?"

Dirt explained what Nana had told her, about Verdi's strange prophecy. "'Na Gods are returning.' Antie Yaya says na same. This man . . . perhaps na Gods send him."

"For what?" Swoo asked.

Then it was Dirt's turn to look uncertain. "I too do not know, my Second," she said. "But it is not for your mind to worry. You are na God Bower. Let your oldold Sis worry about such things."

Dirt wasn't the inspiring speaker that Webba was, but she was right. It wasn't Swoo's problem. She had a fight to focus on. "Thank you, my Sis," Swoo said.

Dirt nodded. "Where are na Bibi?"

"Running."

"How long?"

Swoo scratched her head, wincing. "I say na whole day," she said sheepishly. "I am irritated with them."

Dirt chuckled, a rare sound from the so-often-serious Godskin. "It is finefine," she said. "We do our best, eh?"

She said the last bit with a sudden somberness, and Swoo knew why. Dirt was doing her best to lead the Fam, but it didn't come naturally to her, and training so many young girls was a task, even for the best leader. Swoo was doing her part to help, but she knew she was inexperienced and impatient; the Bibi deserved better.

After a short silence, Swoo went back to her training and Dirt went to make herself tea. They weren't rivals like they used to be. In fact, they had formed a special relationship, one Swoo was beginning to cherish.

But neither of them was Webba, a fact that brought sadness to them both.

In the old days, the trek to the Grand Temple was like a small adventure, the five Mud girls on a jaunt through the jungle with Swoo leading the way. Now, Snore led the way, the little Bibi walking the well-worn jungle path from memory, and the small adventure had become a grand campaign, with the thudding footfalls of the fifty Mud sisters like the sound of a marching army.

As the competing Bower, Swoo was at the center of the formation. Even as her heart beat fearfully in her throat and her forearms trembled in nervous anticipation, she swelled with joy. Nothing made her happier than the prospect of an impending battle. Training was all about restraint. Care. Growth. In battle, none of those things mattered. All that mattered was who was superior, and Swoo knew that when she was able to perform her best, she was superior to any girl in the South. Every fight was a chance to prove it.

At the Grand Temple, they went through the Bowing ritual.

First, they ate. Because there were so many former Mosquito girls among the Bibi now, they were excellent cooks, knowledgeable in spices and fruit that were found well beyond the Mud camp. Then, they danced. Swoo in her Godskin, her sisters a single powerful voice, layered and harmonized far more than they'd ever been when they were five, their pounding feet rattling the arena sand.

Then it was time to fight.

Swoo strode into the ring first, as she always did. It was mental warfare, a subtle way of letting her opponent know that she was ahead of her, even before the fight began. Across from her stood Sis Ask of the Rock. Though she was Third of her Fam, she'd been a Sis for two full seasons already, fought in dozens of God Bows, and was a former God Bow tournament competitor—the highest level of Bowing. The water and oils drenching her skin lent her arms and legs a persisting glisten, and her torso was covered with a smear of stone dust. It was said she crushed the stone with her bare hands before rubbing it on herself.

The two Bowers stared each other down. Swoo searched her opponent's gaze for any hint of fear and found none. Then she stepped back and squatted, delivered the traditional Bowing salute, arms outstretched to her sides. It communicated that she came to the fight unarmed and of her own free will, prepared to accept any result: win or loss, safety or injury. She showed her open palms, then she clapped her hands together, sealing the contract of the fight. Ask returned the salute.

The timekeeper raised an arm, unstoppered the hourglass, then let the arm fall. "Bow begin!"

What ensued was one of the finest Bowing matches in years, even for a crowd that had seen the spectacle of two True Godskins. Despite the gap in experience, Swoo and Ask were near perfectly matched, and their identical Riding strategies resulted in the two battling like rams, slamming into each other over and over, the crowd cooing with each clash. Their Godskins were tattered, their lungs aflame. Knots bloomed on both of their skulls from accidental bumps of their heads. In the end, the fight was decided by a single moment. Swoo, exhausted, summoned her strength for a powerful Ride, but Ask dodged at the last second and shoved Swoo from behind. Despite every effort to slow, Swoo's momentum carried her out.

"Push!" the timekeeper called. "Sis Ask of na Rock is na winner!"

The Rock Farm rushed the ring, swarming their sister with hugs and praise, lifting her onto their shoulders.

Swoo looked to her Fam, all the young Bibi staring at her with open shock on their faces. None of them had ever seen her lose, she realized. They were still new—they did not know that losing was as much a part of Bower life as the morning runs or eating pounded yam. Dirt's face was grim but understanding. She knew why Swoo had lost, just as much as Swoo herself did. It was clear in the sheer quantity of Bibi and the shock on their faces.

Ask wasn't any better than Swoo. But she had dozens of girls her size and age to train with, so she could better prepare for a girl of Swoo's abilities. Swoo's only training partners were hapless Bibi and a True Godskin who could flip mountains. The Mud Fam was bigger than ever, but it was a camp designed to raise Bibi, not to train champions.

Swoo couldn't become a God Bow champion with this team. Not as it was.

But before Swoo could think of what to do to improve the Fam, her attention was drawn to the murmuring of the audience. All eyes, even those of her own Fam, were looking past her, over at the Grand Temple entrance. Swoo turned and found herself staring at the backs of the Rock sisters, who had ceased celebrating and were instead making way for an entering party. The only person who could make Bowers part like that was Antie Yaya, but she had no reason to be at the Grand Temple. And that didn't explain the restrained fear she saw on each of the Rock girls' faces.

Then the sisters right in front of Swoo parted and Antie Yaya strode between them. With her, drawing the eye of every girl and boy in the arena, was a man who Swoo immediately recognized.

5

Mister Odo

SWOO REMEMBERED how strange Antie Yaya used to be. She had seemed split between worlds, her eyes sliding all over, her demeanor almost like that of one who has had too much palm wine. Her face had been so severe that Nana and Snore used to tell Swoo of the nightmares they had about her.

Now, she was a woman in full control of herself and her surroundings. She was calm, softened. She spoke with power, authority, her voice carrying across the silence of the arena without a speaking cone.

"Children of the South," she said. "I would like to introduce you to someone." Despite her newfound normality, she still spoke in that strange way, unlike anyone else Swoo had ever heard. Even the Pusher boys who sometimes traveled in from other regions didn't sound like her.

Antie Yaya gestured to the man. He was still garbed in those odd clothes of his, the shirt with the collar and the Bower-like pants. Except now he wore other oddities—the pants were tucked into tall leather footwear that extended up to his calf, and he wore a puffy cap atop his head. A single gust of wind would send it flying, Swoo knew, yet he wore it without a care. Judging from the fuller flesh to his unstained cheeks, Antie Yaya must have given the man a meal and a bath.

Swoo was startled to find Dirt standing suddenly beside her. She'd positioned herself between the man and the Mud Bibi, and her gaze was focused, cautious.

"You may call him Mister Odo," Antie Yaya said. "He has come here from the land of the Mamas and Papas."

Stunned silence. Every mind in the arena grappled with what that revelation could mean, but they were all too taken aback to ask a question even of their neighbor beside them.

"Because Mister Odo is very impressed with you Bower girls, he wants to do a special God Bow. Not just for the South, but for the whole Isle. The two best girls from every region will come to compete. And all girls can compete. Godskins included."

Every tongue murmured the same names: *Sis Dirt. Sis Carra Carre.*

Swoo looked to Dirt, but the First of the Mud had not changed her expression at all. She was still watching intently, as if waiting for something more.

But the prospect of seeing the South's True Godskins once again meet in the ring was enough for the audience. Their murmur grew to a rumble, which grew to a cheer, part of the crowd chanting Dirt's name while a smaller part chanted Carra Carre's. Swoo could see Carra Carre's hulking form looming among the crowd on the far side of the arena. She had her arms crossed, taking in the announcement with the same quiet anticipation as Dirt.

"Hello, everyone," the man said, and Swoo immediately frowned, along with every other girl and boy in the arena.

He spoke like Antie Yaya. His voice was softer, his tone almost apologetic, but it was the same odd manner of speech.

"Thank you for . . . eh . . . welcoming me to your home," he said. "In addition to glory, the winner of this tournament will get to come with me back to the land of . . . the Mamas and Papas."

Swoo had to tighten her jaw to keep it from dropping.

No one had ever returned from the land of the Mamas and Papas. Going to them was a rite of passage undertaken alone, marking the end of one's life among their Fam.

He was offering them a chance to see beyond the realm of reality, into the realm of the Gods.

He was offering them a chance to see Webba again.

Finally, Dirt's face changed. Gone was the focused skepticism. Gone was the mistrust and inquiry. Instead, her features were flooded with relief. Tears began to form in the corners of her eyes, but Dirt looked directly up, masking her moment of vulnerability as the heavenly gaze of a quick, grateful prayer.

Once she saw that, Swoo had no doubt that Dirt would choose to compete.

"Those who wish to partake have two days to prepare themselves," Antie Yaya said. "Then, you will report to my compound and the Isle God Bow will begin."

Once finished, she left the arena, along with that Mister Odo.

There were no more matches that day, but everyone stayed in their spots, discussing in excitement. Swoo was grateful that her defeat was long forgotten.

But she had never been more uncertain about her future.

6

The Cats of the South

SNORE WAS sprawled out in the tree's branches, high above her training sisters. She didn't like this new big Fam. She missed NoBe Nana and Sis Webba, and she liked it when they could all eat together in the sleep hut. Now, there were so many sisters, and some of them were rude or dumb or boring.

But the one thing she enjoyed was that it was harder for Sis Dirt and Sis Swoo to keep track of her. She was often able to disappear during the day, exploring the jungle however she liked and returning for the evening training session, as if she'd been there all day.

The training was all a waste anyway. Snore knew that, but no one else seemed to. Sis Webba was the best Bower in the whole world, but Sis Carra Carre had hurt her so bad she never got to Bow again and now she was gone. Sis Dirt was a coach, but then she became a Bower, but then she became a True Godskin and

Antie Yaya said she couldn't Bow, but now Antie Yaya said she could.

Because Bowing was stupid.

It was just a game, but not even a fun, silly one. It was serious and painful and unfair. And, most of all, useless. Snore herself was almost five years old and was very strong, but that had not saved her when the Vine came. They'd picked her up as easily as if she were a mango.

"You too," Snore said to Nubbi. The jungle cat was curled against her in the branches, ears perked to listen. Snore petted her head. "I am sorry, Bibi Nubbi."

During their attack, the Vine Fam had put Nubbi in a small wooden cage. They took turns poking at her. First with their fingers, then when a few of them were bleeding from Nubbi's sharp baby teeth, with sticks. The big one, Sis Verdi, had been the meanest. She'd picked up the whole cage and tossed it around, and poor Nubbi had screamed and yelped, but all Snore could do was cry and call out for Sis Dirt and Sis Webba to save her.

"They cannot save you," Sis Verdi had said. She was so big and tall, but she had lowered herself to speak directly into Snore's face. "Na Gods have returned, little Mud child. Na Vine will unite na South, Carra Carre will be First of na First, and your big sisters will bend knee to na Vine, just like every other girl."

At the time, Snore had just thought Sis Verdi was a big, scary, crazy person. But now Mister Odo was here from the land of the Mamas and Papas. Maybe Sis Verdi was right. The Gods had returned and evil girls like Sis Verdi would be able to hurt whoever they wanted.

"Les us go," Snore said solemnly to Nubbi.

She slid easily down the tree, then stalked off into the jungle, away from the calls and grunts of her sisters training back at camp.

As she made her way deeper into the thicket, she thought about how she'd only been saved because of Sis Swoo. Sis Webba was broken. Sis Dirt had been ready to give up. Because they were both serious, boring sisters who only cared about rules and honor and all the other things about Bowing that Snore no longer liked.

Sis Swoo hadn't saved Snore with Bowing. She'd saved her with fire. And a handaxe. And a viciousness that Snore had never seen before, bashing and burning her way through the Vine camp until she was able to free Nubbi and Snore.

Snore's eyes had been opened that day.

Snore and Nubbi soon crossed an invisible threshold. The jungle seemed to darken. The pathways sealed up, so that every step was nearly swallowed in roots and vines. There were no birds here. No monkeys. No animal that valued its life would enter this space. It was silent, unmarred jungle.

One by one, spotted jungle cats slinked into view ahead of them, their paws silent on the damp ground, their eyes gleaming hungrily. Four in all, each three times Snore's size, each with a mouth full of sharp teeth and two puncturous fangs. One cat was slightly bigger than the others, and its left eye was closed from a gruesome wound. She raised her nose, sniffing to determine whether the intruders were friend or foe.

But Snore was impatient. She charged forward, barreling into the biggest cat's chest and wrapping her in a tight hug.

"WugWug," she said, rubbing her face in the fur of her chest.

The cat, WugWug, licked at Snore's hair and face until Snore released the embrace and rubbed heads with each of the other cats in turn. Nubbi trotted forward between the legs of the bigger cats, purring and brushing against them and yelping to declare her presence.

When the greetings were done, WugWug turned deeper into the jungle, waiting for the others to follow.

Snore nodded and followed after her. She was done learning Bowing, but she was still learning to fight.

And it was time to train.

New Directions

DIRT DID NOT sleep the night after Mister Odo's announcement.

The life of a Bower was always hard: muscles do not build easily; lessons are learned through error; broken toes and bent fingers; soreness and blood and tears. A girl did not come to be effective at breaking others' bodies without first breaking her own. It had always been this way.

It had not always been lonely, however.

When the new girls had joined, it had at first felt like fifty long-lost sisters had returned home. But Webba's departure had driven home a sad truth—these girls were strangers. Mud sisters in name but not in history. The Fam felt different, more like a team of Butterfly girls watching over recruits than a team of trained fighters.

Most importantly, they lacked Webba's smile. Her strength. Her optimism. Dirt missed her big sister the way she'd miss the wind or the trees, something so permanent and essential taken away.

Now there was a chance to fix it. At least for a little while.

Dirt ducked under the doorway of her room, emerging out into the orange haze of the late-day light. Swoo was leading the Bibi in drills. Not from beside the ring, as Dirt had led when she was training, but from within it, her skin slicked in sweat as she called out the techniques while demonstrating them.

"Again!" Swoo called, going smoothly through the sequence, from Slap to Ride to Trap to Bow.

Few of the Bibi had the balance to do the same. Most of them stumbled and stopped midway through, but several pushed on, only to topple into the girls beside them.

Only one girl managed to complete it: Tiggi, the former Mosquito girl.

Snore would have finished it as well, had she been there. But Snore had been leaving camp more and more often, disappearing all day only to sneak back in before nightfall, thinking none were the wiser. Dirt had noticed but hadn't yet decided what to do about it. If Snore no longer felt at home in the Mud camp, that wasn't something to punish her over. Especially since Dirt so often felt the same.

"Na Mud," Dirt called before Swoo could restart the training. "Breathe easy."

The girls all relaxed, many with sighs of relief and exhausted sprawls onto the floor. Swoo gave Dirt a curious look but didn't protest. There was a time when she would have been enraged at the interruption, but the girl had matured greatly.

Dirt waited for the girls to settle before she spoke. While waiting, she saw Snore sneak in from the tree line and sit at the back of the assembly, that cat of hers trailing her every step. She resolved to talk to the girl before she left.

When the activity was finished, Dirt cleared her throat.

"Tomorrow, I will go to Antie Yaya's," she said, and she was met with a wave of celebratory coos. "I will fight in na Isle God Bow. I will show na Isle who we are. And when I win . . . ," she trailed off.

What was Webba to them? All those young faces, staring up at Dirt with hope in their eyes. They admired her. They revered her. But they had only known Webba for a few months. In their minds, she was a broken old Sis, friend to the Godskin. Maybe a few had seen Webba's fight against Carra Carre. But they didn't know her. They couldn't understand what she meant to the Mud.

And what about the sisters who had come before? Before Webba. Before Sis Prom, who Dirt had watched leave all those years ago. Before Sis Okoa, the last Mud sister to win the God Bow. To all the sisters who had become forgotten memories, taken into Useyi's hands. Dirt knew nothing of them, just as the sisters to come would know nothing of Webba.

" . . . I will win," Dirt finished instead.

The Bibi were full of excitement, swarming Dirt with hugs and adoring words and plenty of "Oos Oos." Swoo watched from a distance, her arms crossed, her face impassive. Dirt let the Bibi enjoy the moment before telling them she had to rest.

As she returned to her room, she nodded for Swoo to follow.

"You understand, eh?" Dirt asked.

Swoo was leaned against the wall, head bowed in thought. "Of course," she said. Then she ran her hand through her hair in frustration. "Does this mean I am First?"

Dirt chuckled. Swoo could bear any news, as long as it led to her ambitions being fulfilled. "If you wish."

Swoo sighed. "Good. I do not like being na Second, Sis Dirt. How you do it for so long, I do not know."

Dirt shrugged. "It is easy to be Second when I do not fight. And I have Webba as my First."

Dirt knew she had not been a good First to Swoo. She helped Swoo train, of course, but the job of the First was to shoulder the burdens of victory and the Fam's survival, to cast a wide shadow that the Second could take refuge in until it was her turn to sit beneath the harsh light of competition. But Dirt had been barred from competing, so Swoo had to bear that burden herself while still maintaining her duties as Second. It was an uncomfortable position for them both—a Second who had to win and a First who couldn't.

"There are many worse Firsts than you, you oldold girl," Swoo said softly.

Dirt nodded, accepting the compliment.

They spent the rest of the evening planning out what the Fam would look like in Dirt's absence, just the two of them. Dirt made sure to let Swoo lead the thinking—Dirt had no idea how long she might be gone, and she wanted Swoo to feel comfortable leading the Fam however she thought best. With Dirt gone the Bibi would have one less pair of eyes on them, and both Dirt and Swoo agreed the Fam would need more structure to keep them active and safe.

"Snore should lead na Bibi," Swoo said.

"Should." Dirt replied. "But she cannot be trusted as she is."

Swoo grunted agreement. "That unruly duckling. How long will she be like this?"

"Time does not heal wounds," Dirt said. "Healers heal wounds."

Swoo sucked her teeth, staring at Dirt with a small smile. "You sound like Webba," she said.

"All the same," Dirt said quickly, uncomfortable with the praise. "Snore is not ready. You will need others who can guide na young ones."

Swoo nodded. "I will find a way," she said. "And what of you?"

Dirt raised an eyebrow, questioning.

"You will again have to fight that senseless swampdog Carra Carre," Swoo said. "Do you have na plan?"

Swoo was right. Even if all the Bowers of the Isle competed, it was inevitable that the True Godskins would be the final two. Memories of Dirt and Carra Carre's last fight came flooding back. Mostly memories of the anger. Of the violence. Never in her life had she wanted to hurt a girl so bad.

She didn't want to be that girl again.

"I will have na plan when I need it," she said.

Swoo snorted. "You have truly become Webba."

That night, Dirt again could not sleep. Despite the planning with Swoo, uncertainty still churned in her gut. Not just for how the Fam would fare in her absence, but how she would fare in the absence of the Fam. She would be walking into an entirely unpredictable situation, alone. And no matter how things went, the best possible end was that she won all her matches, only to face Carra Carre in the end.

The thought made her tremble.

And tremble.

And tremble.

No, that wasn't her body trembling.

It was the ground.

Dirt sprang to her feet and charged out of her room, out into the night-dark camp. Swoo emerged an instant later, shaking off the shackles of sleep as she peered around in confusion. The world was *shivering*. Trees vibrating with fear, the wooden planks of the sleep lodge rattling against each other like chattering teeth. The ground itself rolled in short, quivering waves, forcing Dirt to keep shifting her feet uneasily to find balance.

"What is this?" Swoo called.

Wailing came from the Bibi in the sleep lodge, and soon they were stampeding through their narrow door, a pushing panic of children scrambling for safety.

Then came an otherworldly groan. An ear-rending howl that approached partially from the East and partially from the bowels of the Isle itself.

I am brave. I am fat. I am Dirt.

Power filled her mind and muscles, burying her fears beneath it. Dirt didn't know what was happening, but if she needed to protect her sisters, she would be ready.

"Behind me!" Dirt called, and the Bibi immediately rushed into the ring, where Dirt and Swoo took up protective stances, circling slowly with the Bibi bunched behind them and watching the shadows of the forest for any unnatural movement.

But they found nothing. And less than a minute later, both the rumbling of the ground and its piercing peal had ceased. When it felt safe to do so, Dirt escorted the Bibi back into the sleep lodge, checking it first so they'd feel comfortable sleeping inside it again. Even then, many of the girls were so shaken by the event that they wouldn't go back to sleep until Swoo offered to let them sleep in her own hut.

Dirt knew she wouldn't be able to sleep anyway, so she stayed out in the ring to keep watch. Something in the South—in the whole Isle—had changed, and she had a troubled feeling that Mister Odo was somehow involved in it.

8

Bandits

THE CELEBRATION to see Dirt off was among the biggest the Mud Fam had ever seen. The Mud Flagga boys, intoxicated by both their second-place finish in the Flagga season and too many cups of palm wine, played music all night, and the Bibi put more energy into dancing than they had the whole day of training. Swoo spent most of the night sitting beside Dirt, a departure from how enthusiastically she used to lead the revelry. However, she got up once to show the young ones how dancing was meant to be done, resulting in a chaotic frenzy that was the highlight of the evening.

Yet even as each celebrant danced and sang and shoveled food into their mouths, the strangeness of the previous night lingered. Eyes frequently darted into the shadows of the tree line, ears cocked to listen for any screams beneath the music. Some of the Flagga boys asked if the True Godskins had fought again, tearing up the Isle while everyone slept. But most people only spoke about the night in small, whispering groups. There was a feeling that whatever had happened was beyond even the powerful magic of the Godskins, that it had to have been related to Mister Odo and the rumors of a prophecy about the Gods Themselves returning to the Isle.

The next morning, Dirt said a final goodbye to the Fam, bidding them health and strength in her absence. She embraced Swoo and patted the Bibi on their heads, then pulled Snore aside.

"Little Snore," she said. "How now?"

Snore's attention was past Dirt, *through* Dirt. She didn't respond. The jungle cat, Nubbi, was rolling on the ground, shredding a leaf with all four legs.

"I am going, Snore," Dirt said. "I need you to watch your big Sis, Swoo. You know she can be boring now that she is na Sis. Help her be sillysilly."

Again, Snore didn't respond. She was watching the jungle with a subtle desperation, as if she was supposed to meet someone there and Dirt was making her late.

Dirt sighed. She was no Webba, but she had to do her best.

"On that day, my sister, I fail you," Dirt said. "So I will not insult you with a promise that I will never fail you again. This I cannot promise." She knelt in front of the Bibi so that their eyes were aligned and put a hand on her shoulder. "But I can promise that I will always fight for you. Sometimes I will lose, yes. But I will fight. Na Mud will fight. Always. Know this."

Strangely, that seemed to get Snore's attention. She finally looked Dirt in the eyes, and the tears came soon after, sudden and strong, leaking down her chubby toddler cheeks.

"Sis Dirr," she groaned softly, crashing into Dirt with a hug and burying her face in Dirt's firm rolls of fat.

Dirt held Snore as long as she could, her fears over leaving the Fam renewed. In her seventeen years of life, it would be only her second time sleeping away from the Mud camp—the first being her time at Antie Yaya's. In a way, Snore was crying the tears that Dirt couldn't. The tears for a fearful future.

She passed Snore, who had fallen asleep, to Swoo, and with a final nod to her Second, turned and plunged into the jungle.

Dirt emerged from the tree line to the top slope of a hill, overlooking a great basin. At the center, sitting stoically in the soft green grass of a low plateau, was Antie Yaya's compound. Honeyed hues of the early evening light slathered its gray-brown limestone, each brick carved so smoothly it seemed the building had been sculpted more by the river than by human hands. Dozens of ornate columns were evenly spaced along its front face, supporting a single long hall that stretched fully across Dirt's vision.

This time of day, the compound was as active as it ever was. All along the narrow stone bridge that spanned from the hill to the building, Butterfly girls and Pusher boys traveled toward and away from the compound, transporting crates on wheeled hand wagons, hawking roasted plantains and other foods, carrying newly washed laundry to hang up on clotheslines overnight. As Dirt started down into the traffic, a lane opened for her, in part because of her status as a Bower, but more so because of her status as Dirt the Godskin. No matter how many times people had seen her, they still stopped to gawk or reach out reverently to deliver the faintest touch. Several Butterfly girls offered her free food and several Pusher boys offered arm wrestling matches, but she declined them both in favor of reaching Antie Yaya sooner.

Once she reached the stone stairs at the foot of the compound, Ebe was there to greet her.

"Na good day, Godskin Dirt," she said.

Dirt realized that she had not heard Ebe speak in years. The girl was a former Bower, a NoBe from the long-disbanded Bush Fam. Now, her body was a ghost of itself, all the good firm fat slackened into softness. She was Antie Yaya's chief assistant, but she never carried herself with the prestige such a position should have conferred her. Instead, she crept the halls of the compound, helping as needed, but otherwise remaining silent and out of sight.

"Na good day," Dirt responded. She was unsure what title Ebe deserved. "Where is Antie Yaya?"

Ebe nodded a long, slow nod. "Follow."

Dirt did just that, and Ebe took her down the same winding stone corridors Dirt had navigated months before. Then, she had been in a state of resigned misery, believing that her Scarring meant she would never see her sisters again. Now, Scar proudly displayed, she was there not to leave her sisters forever, but to reunite with the one sister who had left.

They soon arrived at a closed wooden door, on which Ebe knocked a pattern.

"Enter," Antie Yaya's voice called.

The room was designed for comfort, with a semicircle of tall wooden chairs, each thickly cushioned for both the rear and back. At the center of the chairs, a small round table held a steaming metal kettle and several ceramic cups, each hand-painted with colorful flowers. Dirt had spent the night among such resplendence the last time she was at Antie Yaya's, but it all still felt very strange to her. The floor was a perfectly good place to sit, and an undecorated cup held tea just as well as a painted one.

"Eh heh," Antie Yaya said with a look that took in all of Dirt at once. "The other Godskin has arrived."

Antie Yaya was in a pristine white lace dress with a matching gele. Beside her, Mister Odo was dressed as strangely as always, this time with a red-patterned vest of sorts over a beige puffy shirt that covered him to his wrists.

Beside Mister Odo was Carra Carre.

Even now she wore those foolish vines wrapped around her head, as if she had something to hide. Dirt had already seen her true face—during their fight, when the battle wore away her mask. She'd been surprised by how normal the girl looked. But for her massive size, Carra Carre was just a girl like any other.

A girl Dirt didn't enjoy being in the presence of.

"Hello, Antie," Dirt said, inclining her head respectfully. "Mister Odo," she added, unsure how much respect to grant him.

Dirt let the silence hang. She would not greet Carra Carre.

"I see you girls have much to discuss," Antie Yaya said, looking from one Godskin to the other with amusement tugging at her lips, "but we must be on our way if we wish to reach the Imperial Temple tonight."

Mister Odo started at that, his brows scrunching deeply. "But it is almost dark. There will be bandits on the road."

Dirt didn't know that word. *Bandit.*

"Bandits, eh?" Antie Yaya laughed, placing an affectionate hand on Mister Odo's shoulder. "There are no bandits on the Isle. And if there were"—she pointed two fingers in a V, splitting them toward Dirt and Carra Carre—"we are accompanied by two Godskins. You do not know what that means yet, but you will see."

Mister Odo's confusion remained, but instead of Antie Yaya, he turned it on Dirt. He beheld her for a long moment, and Dirt saw in him not just confusion, but a deep and bothered disbelief, like he was looking at something that wasn't supposed to be real.

9

Tiggi's Savior

THE MORNING AFTER Sis Dirt left the Mud camp was the worst day of Tiggi's life.

"Torture Tiggi!" the Bibi howled as they chased her through the dense jungle.

Tiggi ran as fast as her little legs could carry her, but her legs were indeed little, especially for a girl her size. She was seven years old, and big enough to be a NoBe, but she had short legs that just couldn't outpace the lengthier girls. Eventually, she knew, they would catch her. And when they did . . .

I am brave. I am fat. I am Tiggi.

She'd heard Sis Dirt say it to Sis Swoo once, and it had seemed to work then.

But it didn't work now.

Tiggi hadn't lived the life of a Bower for very long. In her previous life as a Butterfly girl, her days had been spent giggling with the other girls and trading supplies at the Grand Temple in exchange for all manner of Offer. Butterfly girls didn't have to brave, not in the same way as Bowers. And they didn't want to be fat at all. So even though Tiggi thought the words, she didn't believe them, and they did nothing to still her fear.

She tripped—she'd always had clumsy feet. Her fall was a hard one, missing the abundant jungle moss and instead landing painfully on the bulging root of a nyala tree.

Her pursuers burst into laughter.

"Tripping Tiggi!" one called, which spurred another wave.

Tiggi rolled over to her back to look up at Bubu and the others. They crowded around her, faces split with glee. They wouldn't hurt her physically. They were all at least a year younger than her and noticeably smaller—a true fight wasn't worth the risk. But they just enjoyed watching her discomfort.

She didn't know what she had done to draw their torment, but it had started almost immediately. The first week, there was a spirit of sisterhood, everyone joyous and welcoming. But then smaller sisterhoods began to form, clusters of four and five like honeycombs. In a blink, Tiggi found herself trapped alone outside every group. Where other girls' morning runs were filled with giggles and conversation, Tiggi's were silent. Where the other girls sparred playfully with each other, they were rough with Tiggi.

Sometimes she thought it was because she'd been a Butterfly girl—the rivalry between Bowers and Butterflies was well known. But she wasn't the only former Butterfly girl to have joined the Mud. She was just the only one they all seemed to hate.

"Get up, Tiggi," Bubu said, which the other girls immediately echoed.

Tiggi knew better than to take the words literally. Once she stood, they would only surround her so she couldn't leave, then make fun of her about something. How short her legs were or how clumsy her feet or how small her belly. Even though their bellies were just as small.

"I am fine," Tiggi said. "I like na ground." She even grabbed a handful of red dirt to prove how much she enjoyed it.

"Get up!" Bubu shouted, and the authority in her voice almost made Tiggi obey.

But she didn't. She stayed on the ground, keeping her back to the large tree root.

"Get up!" they cried.

"Get up!"

"Get up!"

Then a different voice, from behind. "Stan' up, Tiggi."

The faces of Bubu and her friends fell from glee to somber shame.

"Bibi Snore," Bubu said in a rattling voice.

Tiggi turned. Bibi Snore stood atop the large tree root, bathed from behind by golden sunlight, Nubbi beside her. The jungle cat was frozen in an aggressive posture, a cold, unsnarling set to its face as it eyed Bubu and her friends.

"Stan' up," Bibi Snore repeated, and Tiggi scrambled to her feet.

Bibi Snore was barely half the size of the other girls, but that didn't mean anything when it came to rank. She was one of the original sisters of Sis Dirt the Godskin. She had a year of Bower training already; had tamed a wild jungle beast; had fought and been kidnapped by the Vine, only to escape with the help of Sis Swoo. Everyone knew that Bibi Snore went off on her own to train, but who would dare say anything? Whatever Bibi Snore was working on was probably too advanced for any of them anyway—better for her to practice on her own.

"Wha's happening?" Bibi Snore asked.

Bubu immediately shook her head. "Nothing, Bibi Snore."

"Eh heh," was her only reply.

After a few seconds of uncomfortable silence, Bubu began to back away. Then she turned, tapped her friends, and ran back to camp.

Tiggi turned back to Bibi Snore, to thank her for her intervention, but the girl was already gone, her and Nubbi disappearing back into their jungle training grounds.

Tiggi breathed a heavy, grateful breath and brushed herself off, feeling around her face for any cuts or bruises.

But before she could complete her check, a thin but high-pitched sound split the air: Sis Swoo's whistle. Sis Swoo had said she would only blow the whistle for three reasons: 1. to tell them to hurry up during training, 2. to tell them to hurry back to camp after playtime, or 3. to warn them of an emergency.

This was the second reason, Tiggi knew. She broke off into a run back toward the Mud camp.

"Listen well, you skin-shedding rabbits!" Sis Swoo barked.

Tiggi was lined up among the other Bibi. Back straight. Eyes forward. This was how they'd been trained. The first week, Sis Swoo and Sis Dirt had walked through the rows and swatted any girl who was out of position or lazy in posture. The dumber girls took a few swats to learn; the smarter girls learned from watching the dumber ones get swatted.

But soon they all stood properly, and the result was a group of girls who looked ready to be Bowers, even though they were all still new.

"Sis Dirt has gone," Sis Swoo called, pacing back and forth in front of them. "So Sis Swoo is na First until she returns."

Sis Swoo went on to give a speech in the way that only she could—both demeaning and inspiring, brash and earnest. She spoke about the changes she intended to make, about the discipline that would be required for the Fam to become what she envisioned. She spent quite some time insulting the other Fam, but eventually returned to her main point.

"I will make this Fam na Fam of champions," she said with a passion that sent a tremor through Tiggi. "But as na First, I must have na Second."

Despite their attempts to remain stoic and disciplined, the Bibi couldn't help but buzz at that, glancing around at each other, whispering in excited confusion to the girls beside them.

"So we will have na Bowing tournament!" Sis Swoo declared, arms wide. "You Bibi will Bow each other here in na Mud camp. Na winner will become na NoBe and will be na Second of na Mud until Sis Dirt returns. Understand?"

"Yes, Sis Swoo!" they all shouted back, half of them giggling wildly, the other half with their eyes ablaze, ready to compete for the honor of leading the Fam beside Sis Swoo.

Tiggi was in the latter group. For months, she'd been the Fam's guilty goat, sought any time a girl wanted someone to make fun of. Nobody would dare treat her that way if she were Second. She'd joined the Mud not just to be a Bower, but to be the greatest Bower in the South, like Sis Dirt. Now she had even more motivation.

As Sis Swoo's declaration was still settling into all the girls, one of the Bibi broke rank, walking out from formation and into the jungle. A jungle cat trailed behind her. As she strode off, the other Bibi fell silent, their excitement melted away. All at once, they realized that none of them were going to win. Bibi Snore had a year more training than them, and she was wild and scary besides.

But that only made Tiggi more determined. As scary as Bibi Snore was, she was no True Godskin. She was just a girl. If Tiggi wanted to be like Sis Dirt, she had to be better than every girl—Bubu, Bibi Snore, all of them.

As the Bibi dispersed, breaking into their groups of friends to plan for the tournament, Tiggi remained in the ring. She flexed her toes in the sand, breathed in the drifting air, deciding right then and there that she had to win the tournament.

No matter what it took.

10

A Very Good Story

FOR THE FIRST time in years, Dirt was forced to carry supplies on a march through the jungle. It was no real burden—even without the power of the Godskin, the weight wasn't much. But that meager additional weight, combined with the heat of the jungle, meant she had soaked through her clothing miles back. She felt like a Bibi again, on a journey with a destination she couldn't know, all her importance stripped from her and only restored under the condition that she prove herself.

It was demeaning.

It was exhilarating.

In her youth, she would have been too terrified to undertake such a journey, away from her Fam, out in the insecurity of the larger world. She was not the girl she used to be, thankfully. Now, marching through the South's smothering jungles beside Antie Yaya, Ebe, Mister Odo, and Carra Carre, she didn't feel any fear whatsoever.

"Break," Antie Yaya said through panting breaths. She was breathing harder than any of them, and sweat poured down from her gele, carving creeks down her face. "I need a break."

Ebe found a bed of moss that was soft enough for Antie Yaya and paused their trek. Mister Odo and Ebe sat beside Antie Yaya, each of them drinking from a waterskin. Dirt remained standing, as did—much to Dirt's annoyance—Carra Carre.

After a long draught, Antie Yaya pulled the waterskin away from her face and released a loud exhale and an irritated sweep of her gaze from Dirt to Carra Carre.

"Being young should be illegal," she said.

It was uncomfortable watching Antie Yaya struggle. Dirt's earliest memories were of an Antie Yaya who didn't even seem part of this world. Now she was just a regular old lady, huffing and puffing from a short walk.

Dirt was even more uncomfortable watching it beside Carra Carre.

Up until then, there had been neither reason nor time for Dirt and Carra Carre to interact. Dirt had almost forgotten about the behemoth of a girl, despite her thudding footfalls.

"Tell us a story," Antie Yaya said to no one in particular.

Dirt frowned. She didn't know who Antie Yaya was speaking to, but she herself was no storyteller. Webba would have had a great many stories to tell, all of them memorable.

Just the thought of Webba made her heart ache.

"Eh . . . ," Carra Carre began. "Long ago, on na dark, dark night—"

"Not you, child," Antie Yaya interjected.

Dirt chuckled, reveling in Carra Carre's embarrassment.

"I mean you," Antie Yaya said, "Odo. Or Mister Odo or whatever your name is. Tell us."

All eyes turned to Mister Odo.

"Eh . . ." His eyes were wide and uncertain. "I'm afraid I don't know too many stories. . . . "

"On the contrary," Antie Yaya said, and there was a sudden coldness in her voice that took Dirt aback. "You know all the best ones. Tell us," she repeated more firmly.

Mister Odo swallowed and cast his eyes downward. "There once was a girl who did not like her skin," he said in a softer voice than before. Then he looked up at Dirt and Carra Carre. "She was about your age or even younger. Her skin was too dark, she believed. So she went and found bright mud and rubbed it all over herself, and she was no longer so dark. But she felt like her skin was still too loose. So she grabbed vines from the jungle and tied them tight all around herself to hold her skin close, and her skin was no longer so loose. But after hours in the sun, she now felt her skin was too dry. So she went to the creek and splashed herself with water until she was dripping. Her skin was now pale, tight, and moist, but she was not happy. Because the mud was heavy, the vines left her sore, and she had to spend all day wet.

"Only then did she realize that her skin was not the problem," Mister Odo said with a long inward sigh. "The problem was the world that told her not to love her skin. No mud, vines, or water could fix that. So rather than trying to change her skin, she decided to change the world."

He remained silent a moment, then brought his waterskin to his lips again and drank.

Mister Odo was a strange thing, Dirt decided then. It was not a very good story—there was no magic or Gods in it—but he seemed to be holding in tears, looking away from everyone and sniffling.

"Thank you," Antie Yaya said softly, and she pressed a hand against his shoulder. "It was a very good story."

Dirt disagreed, but she wasn't going to say as much. Until she noticed that Carra Carre also seemed unimpressed with the story.

"Na goodgood story," Dirt said. "Thank you, M—"

Before Dirt could finish, there was a rattling of the world, a vibration that started in the soles of her feet and spread up through her chest, until she had to force her jaw tight to keep her teeth from clattering against each other. Then there was a deep and horrifying sound, the groan of a great, dying beast, one whose mouth could swallow a mountain whole.

After nearly half a minute—what felt like half a year—it stopped.

Dirt had been afraid the first time the world groaned like that, especially with the Bibi around. But this time, she was better able to comport herself, which she was grateful for. Had she panicked in front of Carra Carre, she would never have forgiven herself.

Carra Carre, Ebe, and Antie Yaya all seemed to be equally unsurprised.

But Mister Odo's face was slack. His eyes were blank with terror. His mouth worked two or three times before it could find the right words.

"We . . . must go," he breathed.

Then he frantically gathered his belongings and continued eastward. Dirt looked at Ebe, who provided no expression in return, turning instead to help Antie Yaya to her feet, the two of them following after Mister Odo.

Dirt refused to consult Carra Carre. So she followed after the others further into the jungle, her mind on her sisters back at the

Mud camp, praying that they were safe and that they weren't as afraid of the earth's increasing rumbles as she was.

When they emerged from the trees, Dirt couldn't believe what she was seeing. Prior to that moment, the Grand Temple had been the biggest thing she'd ever seen. But the Grand Temple was only a Bibi compared to the structure before her now. This was a full Sis.

"What . . . what is this?" she asked, stunned.

"The Imperial Temple," Antie Yaya replied. "Impressive, is it not?"

Rather than weeping sand, the Imperial Temple was made of smooth red brick, even all around, as if Papa Oduma Himself had reached down and run his hands along its curves. It was high enough that Dirt had to look up to see the top, even from a distance, and it had to have been twice as wide as the Grand Temple. It sat atop an elevated expanse of sand, too low to be a hill, too gradual in elevation to be a plateau.

"This is where we will make fight?" Carra Carre asked.

"This is where you will make fight," Antie Yaya agreed. "Ebe will take you to your sleeping quarters. Odo and I have other matters to attend to."

Antie Yaya took Mister Odo's arm—though Dirt couldn't tell whether it was to guide him or to use him as her guide—and together they went around to the far side of the arena, presumably to an entrance Dirt couldn't see. Meanwhile, Ebe led them toward the main entrance and into the arena. Inside, it was nearly identical to the Grand Temple—an expansive arena floor with two seating areas for a band and for Bowers each, and rows of seats ringing up into the sky. But bigger, so much bigger.

And empty.

Even on days when there were no fights, the Grand Temple always had people around. This Imperial Temple, however, was lifeless.

"Who uses this place?" Dirt asked.

Ebe shook her head. "No Bowers fight here. Not until you."

Dirt wondered who would build a whole arena with no Bowers to fight in it.

But then she realized that she didn't know who had built the Grand Temple either. As much as she searched through her memory, she couldn't recall any stories about the Grand Temple's origins, whether the Gods had built it themselves or some cooperation of Bowers and Pusher boys had laid the bricks down atop each other.

It seemed like the sort of thing she would have heard about at some point.

"Na temple is na temple," Carra Carre grumbled suddenly. Unlike Dirt, she wasn't taking in the sight of the arena, instead folding her arms and staring straight at Ebe. "Where do we sleep?"

Rather than separate tents for each Fam, the Imperial Temple had rooms built into it. Ebe led them down torchlit corridors that reminded Dirt of the tight hallways of Antie Yaya's compound, up to a pair of large stone doors.

Dirt pushed on the doors, but they didn't yield. Yet when she pulled on the brass handles, it was the same result.

"These are no doors," Dirt said, backing away in confusion.

Carra Carre snorted and stepped forward, shouldering Dirt out of the way. She placed a hand on each of the handles, set her feet, and pulled.

It didn't budge.

She reversed her weight, pushing forward with all her might. Nothing.

It was Dirt's turn to snort. "Heavyheavy, eh?"

Carra Carre was quiet for a moment, then her skin began to steam, a shimmer of vapor radiating from her. She Slapped a hand forward, her palm pressing against the joint where the two doors met, now infused with the power of the Gods. At that, they groaned open.

"I see," Carra Carre said.

A door that only a True Godskin could open. Dirt could hear Snore and Nana coo at that.

Behind the door was a lavish room, rivaling those at Antie Yaya's compound, with table, chairs, and tea set atop a lush carpet, a porcelain tub in each of two corners, and two large, soft-looking beds. Carra Carre walked a full circuit around the room, stopping at each piece of furniture, reaching out a reverent hand to touch it, then staring for a few moments before moving on to the next one.

When she finished, she turned to Ebe. "I will sleep here?"

Dirt remembered her own disbelief at the level of comfort she'd enjoyed at Antie Yaya's. If she didn't hate Carra Carre, she might have found the moment endearing.

But her mind was elsewhere.

"Why are there two of everything?" she asked.

"Antie Yaya will send for you," Ebe said before bowing deeply and scurrying away.

"Mama Eghi's Teeth," Dirt swore to the walls of her new room. "No. I will not share na room with this one."

"Good," Carra Carre said. "Leave."

"It is you who will leave."

"Na Isle God Bow needs na winner. So I must stay."

"Worry not, I can win without you."

"Eh heh," Carra Carre agreed. "And only without me."

"How are na Vine recruits?" Dirt shot back.

They were interrupted by a low drumming, a rapid heartbeat of sound permeating the Imperial Temple walls. For a hair of a moment, Dirt's heart seized with terror—she thought it was the world shaking again, this time to bring the whole arena down on her head.

But it was actual drums, sounding from a distance.

Dirt immediately left the room to follow the sound, just as Carra Carre did the same. The two of them squeezed through the door and out into the hallway, where they could see Mister Odo down on the sand of the arena grounds, pounding on the talking drum slung across his waist. Antie Yaya was beside him, as were two others. They were both girls, both far larger than the adults, with protruding bellies of good fat and the wide, powerful bodies of Bowers.

Another two Bowers were walking toward them from the far end of the arena grounds, and a third pair emerged from a door far down the hallway from Dirt and Carra Carre, ducking their tall, powerful frames under the doorway and making their way down to the arena grounds.

Dirt took a deep, steadying breath, nervous despite herself.

I am brave. I am fat. I am Dirt.

It was time to meet the competition.

11

The Isle God Bow Prayer

ANTIE YAYA, Mister Odo, and the eight competitors sat in a circle. Mister Odo continued pounding his drum, but with less force, a heartbeat underscoring the face-off.

"There was a world before this one," Antie Yaya said, the opening words of the Prayer that had begun every God Bow tournament for as long as Dirt could remember, "where the Gods lived and loved and cried and celebrated. And fought. How they would fight. Oduma the Defender against Ijiri the Trickster. Abidon the Liberator against Eghodo the Lawbringer, Queen of the Gods. How the earth would shake beneath the nations. The bloodshed, the lives forgotten. What is left when the Gods wage war?"

The drumming stopped.

Mister Odo's cane hovered above the drum's surface, frozen. He was looking at Antie Yaya, his eyebrows squirming, his eyes glistening with tears. A very strange man.

Antie Yaya did not look at him. She continued on, but her speech felt different. More somber than usual, almost tinged with regret. Gradually, the somberness turned to sorrow, and the almost regret only grew, until by the end, Dirt felt like it wasn't a Prayer at all. The Prayer was supposed to be a celebration of a new God Bow tournament, but there was no celebration here. There was no chanting, no crowd of friendly and excited girls. Just a lone drum, with a drummer who was holding back tears for reasons Dirt could not understand.

"Daughters of Oduma, rise!" Antie Yaya concluded. "The North!"

Two of the girls stood, each wearing the usual Bower clothes, but with a twist. Their short shirts covered their bellies and arms and had a hood at the back, and their baggy pants were made of a thicker material, as if made for the cold.

"Sis Ahven of na Cave!" the first one proclaimed.

"Sis Bear of na Cave!" said the second, a mountain of a girl who rivaled Carra Carre in size.

Two from na same Fam? Dirt thought. In the South, it was incredibly rare for a Fam to have the two top Bowers. She hoped it meant the North was less competitive than the South.

"The East!" Antie Yaya called.

The East girls were the smallest overall, though each was still larger than Dirt. "Sis Boom of na Valley," cried one, her eyes already scanning around the circle to assess the competition.

"Sis Frog of na Spray," cried the other, who had a swagger about her that made Dirt think of Swoo.

"The South!"

Dirt and Carra Carre stood at the same time. Grudgingly, Dirt allowed Carra Carre, the reigning South God Bow champion, to speak first.

"Sis Carra Carre of na Vine!" Carra Carre said. She kept her eyes on Antie Yaya, as if none of the other girls were worth noticing. The most visually impressive Bower—with her massive size and face shrouded by vines—Carra Carre had an edge in this contest of unfamiliar foes. But not against Dirt. Dirt knew what Carra Carre was capable of, but she also knew how much of her was bluster. Maybe the First of the Vine could intimidate the others, but not her.

"Sis Dirt of na Mud!" Dirt called, and she could feel the unimpressed eyes on her. She knew she was the smallest and oldest of them, but she also knew something they didn't: she was a True Godskin. On their best days, none of them stood a chance against her. Carra Carre was her only competition.

"The West!"

"Sis Namaji of na Trunk," was issued in a calm voice from the face of the youngest Sis there, likely no older than Swoo.

"Sis Hammuh of na Reef," called a girl whose thick palms implied fearsome ability. Hands forged in the fires of competition.

"Oduma the Defender," Antie Yaya prayed, "He of the Untempered Heart, whose chest turns spear and arrow alike, whose Shield . . . eh . . . defends the Isle against Useyi and the Forgotten, who stood alone against the legion in the Ingue Pass." At the previous Prayer, Antie Yaya's closing had been delivered with a furious, fevered pitch. But this was calm, even hesitant. "Look upon Your daughters, Brave Oduma. See into their hearts. Pour unto them Your spirit. Choose, oh Oduma, Your Champion."

When it was finished, Dirt and Carra Carre returned to their chambers. They would have to share it for a week while they trained for the Isle God Bow. During training, Mister Odo would judge the talent of the competitors and rank them accordingly. Once the week was over and their rankings were complete, the tournament would begin, and each girl who lost would return home to her Fam.

"There will be other things, as well," Antie Yaya had added cryptically. "Differences in this God Bow . . ."

Dirt hoped against hope that Carra Carre would somehow lose early so that she could have the room to herself. And she knew Carra Carre hoped the same. But the odds of that were low—most likely, they would have to live together for the full month of the competition.

That first night, despite the comfort of her bed, Dirt didn't sleep. Not only because Carra Carre was on the other side of the room, her snores burrowing into Dirt's ears from a distance. And not only because she missed her sisters back at the Mud camp.

But because Mister Odo's face remained in her mind. That mix of surprise and fear and regret he showed when Antie Yaya talked about the Gods. Dirt thought about how both Verdi and Antie Yaya claimed the Gods had returned to the Isle. Mister Odo was from the land of the Mamas and Papas, where the Gods resided. If the Gods had returned to the Isle and if Mister Odo had walked among the Gods before . . .

Then why did their names make him so scared?

12

Sis Carra Carre vs. Sis Bear

7 Days until the Isle God Bow

DIRT'S TRAINING strategy was to simply think. She knew that Carra Carre would be her only test, and that the contest between them would be won by the smarter girl, not the stronger one. So while the seven other competitors were out on the arena floor, some of them jogging laps, some of them lifting stones or sparring with the other God Bower from their part of the Isle, Dirt sat in the shade of the arena wall, thinking.

Why did Carra Carre even want to win? Dirt had Webba waiting for her. Who did Carra Carre have? A previous sister of the Vine? Dirt worried that Carra Carre's participation in the tournament had something to do with Verdi's vision of Carra Carre as First of the First, serving the Gods as the leader of the Bowers. After thinking long on it, she realized it didn't matter: Dirt had to win.

Their previous fight had been won by the tiniest of advantages, and Dirt had often reflected that had she not had to fight the entire Vine Fam, she would have retained enough stamina to beat Carra Carre in the end. If she hoped to win this time, she had to conserve her energy better.

I am brave. I am fat. I am Dirt.

She slipped into her Godskin, her mind soothed by the power of the Gods flowing through her.

Then she released it.

Over and over, she entered and exited her Godskin, enjoying the fill of the power and growing more comfortable with the releasing of it. From afar, it looked like she was simply sitting, perhaps meditating. But each cycle took energy, and each time she reentered her Godskin, it was a bit more difficult as exhaustion gradually seeped into her muscles.

She decided that this was the best way to improve her chances against Carra Carre without revealing her true abilities. She could not know why the other girls were competing—maybe just the spirit of competition, maybe something more. But the Vine had been willing to attack the Mud at their camp to secure their chance at victory. Dirt couldn't risk any of these other girls being so desperate. The Mud Fam was much stronger now, but Swoo was still the only other full Sis. Who knew how many Sis the Reef or Cave Fam might boast?

Carra Carre thought differently.

She took the center of the Imperial Temple grounds, stomping around the sand as if she'd built the arena herself. She worked through some of the most difficult exercises Dirt had ever seen, putting herself through press ups, stomach crunches, and a half dozen other exercises at a grueling pace, back-to-back-to-back without pause. Even as the other girls did their own impressive workouts, they all kept an eye on Carra Carre.

Yet none of them seemed afraid. If anything, they all seemed amused.

Dirt watched with curiosity as Carra Carre noticed their responses and attacked her workouts with more fervor, clearly intending to intimidate her competition. It made no difference. None of them were bothered. Carra Carre hid it well, but Dirt could sense her growing frustration, until she suddenly halted her exercises altogether.

"You!" she called out to the two girls from the North, the sisters of the Cave. They were in the middle of a run, but they slowed at the force in Carra Carre's voice.

"Eh?" Sis Ahven, the smaller one, said. "What it is?"

"Not you," Carre Carre called back. Then her eyes slid to the bigger of the two, Sis Bear. "Come and make spar."

All activity in the arena ceased, Dirt's included.

They hadn't been given any rules about sparring. It was an essential part of Bower training, but it was something done between sisters, not against enemies. Sparring was a delicate clash of abilities and egos, and it could easily result in a real fight, even between longtime training partners.

Dirt looked up to where Antie Yaya and Mister Odo sat beside each other in the audience seats. They were watching the events but made no move to intervene. The spar was allowed.

Confusion furrowed Sis Bear's brow. "I am busy," she called back. "Go and spar your South sister."

"Busy?" Carra Carre called immediately. "Or breezy?"

There had likely never been a girl to equal Carra Carre in size and strength. But Sis Bear was as close as Dirt had ever seen. That much weight being tossed around could easily end in injury, even between friends. Sis Bear's reluctance was smart, not cowardly.

But no Sis would let her bravery be so publicly challenged.

Sis Bear shared a glance with Sis Ahven, who nodded gravely then turned loathing eyes on Carra Carre. "Teach her," she urged her sister.

As Sis Bear headed to the ring, Carra Carre prepared it for battle, rolling heavy stones out past the sandbags, smoothing the sand across the circle. The other competitors gave up any pretense of training, crowding around the ring with crossed arms and watchful eyes, relishing the free preview of what seemed to be the two biggest threats in the competition.

Dirt remained where she was. Nothing about this felt like a spar, and she didn't want to be close when the violence got out of hand.

The two girls exchanged salutes and Sis Ahven raised her arm, playing the role of timekeeper, even though there was no time to keep. Once the two combatants were in position, Sis Ahven dropped her arm in a swift downward cut.

"Bow," she called out, "begin!"

It was immediately clear to all those watching that Carra Carre was the superior Bower.

After brief Slapping, Sis Bear Rode in. It was a strange Ride, nothing like Swoo's or Wing's quick bursts of speed. Instead, Sis Bear Rode in like an ocean wave, measured but powerful, in a way where it wasn't quite clear what she was doing until she was already on you.

But Carra Carre responded to Sis Bear's Ride with equal force, meeting her in the center of the ring in a collision of bodies and immediately Trapping the Bower from the North. Sis Bear's eyes bulged once Carra Carre grabbed her. At her size, the poor girl must have been the strongest in the North. Likely she'd never been the weaker girl in a fight. But Carra Carre hauled her up and drove her into the ground as easily as she did every other girl, sand bursting all around them from the impact.

Sis Ahven stared on in disbelief, too stunned to keep score.

The beating continued from there. Carra Carre was Sis Bear's superior in nearly every aspect of Bowing, and anything Sis Bear attempted was painfully punished. Soon, Sis Bear's clothes were ripped in a half dozen places and she sported bruises across her back from repeated clashes with the sand.

Dirt watched with conflicted feelings. On the one hand, Carra Carre was a loathsome bully who enjoyed nothing but the domination of those weaker than her. On the other hand, the girl was a specimen of Bowing ability that any coach would drool at, and Dirt hated herself for taking some pride that Carra Carre was from the South.

After a few minutes, Sis Bear, climbing back to her feet from being brutally Bowed again, began to chuckle.

"Strong Bow, Sis Carra Carre of na South Vine," she said through heavy breaths. "Strongstrong. I cannot say I have met your equal."

Carra Carre, sporting only a few shallow scrapes and bruises, ignored the compliment, looking to the other sisters.

"Who else wishes to suffer?" she issued to the entire arena.

But Sis Bear raised a single finger, waving it back and forth. "I say you are strongstrong," she said. "I do not say we are finished."

Sis Bear took a deep breath and closed her eyes. It seemed like she was simply refocusing to continue the battle. But then her skin began steaming, the air around her rippling with waves of power. When she opened her eyes, they were filled with calm and clarity, wiped clean of any pain she might have felt before.

In all the South, there were only two True Godskins. Dirt and Carra Carre. Yet here was a third. Dirt didn't remember rising to her feet, but she found herself standing and staring in a mouth-agape disbelief that was mirrored in Carra Carre's face.

But unlike Dirt, Carra Carre was a seasoned competitor, and there is no room in a fight for surprise. She quickly gathered herself, and as Sis Bear flashed toward her with a speed only the power of the Gods could provide, she summoned her own power.

They met like two bolts of lighting, thunder clapping from the impact, a hot wind scouring the arena. They had their hands locked, each girl nearly horizontal as she pushed against the other with gritted teeth.

Then Antie Yaya's voice cut through the thrash of battle.

"Stop this at once!"

For a second, it seemed as if both girls would disobey, each refusing to be the first to yield. But a command from Antie Yaya was not to be ignored, and both girls managed to separate at the same time, ensuring neither felt the lesser.

"Chaaaiii," Antie Yaya cooed, her voice carrying from her spot in the stands down to the arena floor. She looked around with an amused twitch to her lips. "You Bowers lack subtlety. I did not believe I would have to outlaw sparring, but it appears I must. No more sparring before the tournament . . . lest you crash this whole place on my head."

Then she set out, tapping Mister Odo on the shoulder for him to follow.

But Mister Odo was still staring at Carra Carre and Sis Bear, and his eyes were full of wonder. It should have been harmless—the wonder of a person seeing a True Godskin for the first time. It didn't feel that way, though. There was a hunger to it, like a desperate jungle cat finding a piece of unguarded meat.

And Dirt didn't like it.

13

The NoBe Bow

EVER SINCE Sis Dirt's departure, Swoo's days had been spent train-ing. She'd realized that being both a coach and a champion-level fighter was impossible. Thankfully, with just two days until the first fight of the NoBe Bow, the younger sisters had fully taken over their own training. Swoo no longer had to tell them to go out for a run—she went for a run each morning and whoever wanted to follow was free to. When she lifted stones, they waited beside her, picking up the stones for their own lifts once she set them down.

The only thing she missed was sparring. But she had to make do, so she chopped down a palm tree and had the Bibi carve its trunk into the shape of a Bower with her arms out, as if it were mid-Slap. They propped it up near the ring, and Swoo spent hours each day practicing on it—Slapping against its out-stretched branches, ducking under them for Rides, Trapping its rough skin.

At night, Swoo went around and checked on the Bibi. They'd formed into small teams—Bibi Fam, they'd begun to call them—so she checked with each group to see how they were progressing and to give them a plan on how to continue improving. Then she'd lay down in Dirt's sleep hut and spend hours thinking about the future instead of sleeping. She mostly wondered if she was doing things right and if, with all the limitations on her training, she still had what it took to compete with the best Bowers in the South.

But she also wondered about Snore. The girl was growing increasingly distant, a trait made worse by how the other Bibi avoided her. Swoo couldn't tell if they avoided her out of respect or out of fear, but either way the result was an endless puzzle that kept Swoo up late.

Then the cycle repeated, days full of training and nights full of worry.

4 Days until the Isle God Bow

"Na good day, Sis Swoo," the Bibi chirped as they returned to camp, trotting in from the depths of the jungle. They were several minutes behind today—Swoo took that more as a sign that she was getting faster than that they were slowing down.

"Na good day," she replied absently as she went through her morning stretches.

Swoo was determined to spend the day improving her Riding. It had long been her strongest skill, but the fight against Sis Ask had shown that she had to elevate her Rides if she hoped to have the same success against Sis that she had enjoyed against NoBe. After stretches, she would go straight into forms, practicing her Rides for hours and hours, tweaking every little flaw until her technique was fluid, her speed was maximized, her balance was . . .

Swoo's attention drifted away from her exercises as she watched the Bibi. They were formed up into their Bibi Fam, four or five girls each stretching together in small circles. But two of the Bibi were alone. Snore, of course. And the former Mosquito girl, Tiggi.

She had promise, that one. A good mind for technique and a tall build that could support plenty of weight once she started eating properly.

"Come, Tiggi!" Swoo called, bending in half to touch her toes.

Tiggi rushed over, ever obedient. "Yes, Sis Swoo?"

"Why are you alone?"

"Because . . ." Tiggi hesitated long enough that Swoo unbent from her stretch to eye her.

"Because?"

Tiggi took a deep breath and spoke through her exhale. "Because na other Bibi do not like me."

Tiggi worked hard, was humble, didn't have any annoying habits other than her constant questions.

"Why not?" Swoo asked.

Tiggi shrugged and cast her eyes down in a way that reminded Swoo so much of Nana.

Swoo looked out at the other girls. They were laughing, playing, singing. All the things Bibi were supposed to do. She expected there would be some alliances and bullying—such was the way of young people trying to sort out where they belonged. But, as a whole, they did not seem a mean-spirited bunch.

Swoo sighed. She should have been focusing on her own training.

"Stay with me," she said, bending back down to touch her toes. "I will train with you."

The way Tiggi's eyes enlarged made Swoo know it was an offer she would soon regret. They spent the day side by side, and Swoo watched Tiggi's confidence grow as the other girls grew jealous of her new station. Swoo hated such Fam politics, but it seemed inevitable now that she was First. Anything she did affected the hierarchy of the family, for better or for worse—she may as well choose when to affect it for the better.

Tiggi's skills grew immensely. The girl's eye was attuned to details, not just of the physical aspects of being a Bower, but the mental as well. By the end of the day, she was far more certain in her movements.

But Swoo never found the time to work on her Rides, and by the day's end she felt even further behind in her preparations for her upcoming fight. Still, she spent the night awake in her sleep hut, worrying about Snore and Tiggi and all the other Bibi more than she was worried about herself.

She knew it was a matter of time before all that concern about things other than Bowing would cost her.

2 Days until the Isle God Bow

Swoo had never seen the Bibi so excited.

They streamed in from the edge of the jungle in their little Bibi Fam, dancing the clumsiest steps Swoo had ever seen. Were she still a NoBe, she would have shamed them for their abysmal skills, but since she was a Sis now—and the acting First, no less—she had to be gracious. She watched on with a vaguely approving expression on her face.

Until they started singing.

"Sola!"

"Tempo!"

"Wami!"

"Ngivi!"

Each Bibi sang her name and followed it up with a small movement that her Bibi Fam had worked out beforehand—one Fam had a cartwheel, another shook their shoulders expressively, another wiped imaginary sweat off their brows. Swoo tried to sit through it, but she soon found their grating, untrained voices unbearable.

"My strongstrong sisters," Swoo called, interrupting the festivities. The girls continued to silently stream into the center of the ring. "You all know why we are here. Today is na NoBe Bow. Fight your best. Make your sisters proud. Make na Mud proud."

Once the competition started, Swoo realized she'd made a great mistake. In pair after pair, fight after fight, the Bibi revealed themselves to be entirely unprepared for Bowing. Many of them didn't even know the rules. Of those who did, many more began crying the first time they were Bowed. Several girls forfeited their matches because they were too scared to fight. A few girls forfeited after making their friends Bow and feeling bad. It was a chaotic cluster of tears and feelings and hugs and very little actual Bowing.

Only a few of the girls actually demonstrated any ability. Bubu, one of the larger girls for her age, won via repeated Slapping, driving her scared opponent out of the ring. Another girl, Teeni, one of the smallest girls, tripped her opponent to the sand, then flexed her muscles menacingly at Swoo. Not much technique, but a very impressive display for a three-year-old new to Bowing life.

Two girls stood out as clear favorites, though.

The first was Tiggi. Swoo had matched her with a girl her size, another former Butterfly girl named Song. Song had plenty of determination, but very little sense or ability. She spent the whole match fighting for survival as Tiggi Bowed her over and over, scoring so many points that the match was out of reach in the first minute.

The other favorite was, of course, Snore. Swoo had matched Snore with a new Bibi, four-year-old Wami. She'd hoped just the prospect of a fight would relight Snore's flame for Bowing. And it did. Though not how Swoo expected.

Snore pressed forward the whole match, but instead of Slapping with her hands flat toward the ground, she Slapped with her fingers curled in like claws. She slashed at her foe half a dozen times, scratching Wami's hastily upheld forearms before dipping low and plowing through the girl. That should have been a Bow, but Snore then sat on top of Wami, continuing to slash down at her ferociously, the whole time making low growling and hissing sounds through bared teeth.

Swoo had to rush into the ring to pull Snore away, and even then Snore thrashed in her arms until Swoo shook her.

"Snore!" she shouted, and finally the girl seemed to come to her senses, looking up at Swoo as if seeing her for the first time. "What is wrong with you? Look what you have done."

Swoo swept an arm around the camp. Wami was still on the ground, crying. The other sisters wore expressions ranging from sadness to confusion to anger. Snore seemed to take it all in, but offered no reaction, taking her eyes from their gazes to Swoo.

"Nubbi, no," she said.

Only then did Swoo look over her shoulder and notice the jungle cat, Nubbi, creeping up behind her. She hadn't realized how big the cat had grown. It was nearly up to Swoo's knees and looked heavier than most of the younger Bibi. An animal that big could hurt someone. It was dangerous.

Swoo looked hard into Snore's eyes. "Who taught you this Slap?"

Snore just stared.

"Answer me! You sneakysneaky turtle . . ."

Strangely, Snore's eyes started to well up at that. She wrenched out of Swoo's grip, then turned away and charged on her little feet back into the jungle, Nubbi bounding after her.

With the matches finished, Swoo dismissed the other sisters to relax for the day and go about their usual tasks.

That night, Swoo felt worse than she'd felt in a long time. She'd always had two dreams: to become the First of a Fam and to become a South God Bow champion. Through a series of unlikely events, her first dream had come true. But now that she was First of a Fam, she realized how far beyond her the task was.

She was failing Snore. She was failing the whole Fam.

Most of all, she was failing herself. Because the next day would be her own fight, and she was becoming convinced, for the first time in her life, that she had no chance at winning.

14

Godskins

1 Day until the Isle God Bow

IT WASN'T JUST Sis Bear.

Each day of training, Dirt watched in disbelief as another competitor revealed herself to be a True Godskin. Sis Ahven, the other Cave sister, was first. She and Sis Bear spent the next day training in their Godskins, jogging laps that stirred the sand into cyclones and performing leaping squats that took them as high in the air as the Imperial Temple itself. Then it was the girls from the East, Sis Boom and Sis Frog. On the third day of training, they rolled boulders in through the arena entrance and spent the afternoon tossing them back and forth to each other. Last was Sis Hammuh of the Reef, who had a Riding technique that was so low and powerful that it pulverized the sand beneath her, creating a cloud of smoke through which she could emerge and grab opponents.

That was when Dirt understood that Carra Carre would not be her only competition.

Only one of the girls showed no powers: Sis Namaji of the Trunk, the other Bower from the West. She was the one who looked scarcely out of her years as a NoBe, and she proudly wore that confidence that only the young can have. So much so that as each of the other girls showed feats of divine power, Sis Namaji's face remained unimpressed. Unsurprised. Unlike the other girls, eager to display their strength to earn favorable seeding from Mister Odo, Sis Namaji spent her time either jogging lightly around the arena floor or sitting in the stands, her arms draped casually on the empty chairs beside her. She was undoubtedly going to receive the lowest seed of the tournament, but she didn't seem to mind.

Dirt's strategy at first had been to hide her Godskin powers to let them underestimate her. A low seed didn't matter if she was stronger than all of them. But once she learned that most of them were Godskins, she had to change her plans. She revealed her Godskin abilities but kept her Whip Slap for herself. It was the one advantage she held over the others, and if she could use it at the right time, it could make all the difference.

As the end of the week approached, there was still uncertainty over who would receive which rank. Dirt felt she had done enough to secure the sixth seed, above Sis Boom, whose Godskin powers had seemed least impressive, and Sis Namaji, who didn't seem to have any powers at all. But there was no such clarity at the top of the rankings. Carra Carre and Sis Bear were undoubtedly the most powerful of the competitors, yet every feat of speed or strength Carra Carre achieved, Sis Bear matched. The two had gone back and forth, sparring indirectly through deed since they were barred from any other sort, and as the sun rose on the final morning before the Isle God Bow, Dirt could sense Carra Carre's growing desperation to be the top seed.

"Na good day," Carra Carre said. She was seated on the edge of her bed, her hulking frame hunched forward in a rare moment of relaxation, her big, muscled belly hanging between her knees.

"Na good day," Dirt responded, rubbing her eyes and rolling out of bed herself.

They'd reached a peace, of sorts. Try as she might, when Dirt returned to her room after a day of hard training and saw Carra Carre on the other side, the exhaustion was too much to muster contempt. And she knew Carra Carre felt the same. So instead of acting like enemies, they had settled into simply acting like strangers.

"You ripe?" Carra Carre asked.

Dirt looked over at her strangely.

"Ripe . . . ," Dirt answered.

"You do not worry about your seed?"

Even considering their recent ceasefire, the two girls exchanged little more than morning and evening greetings. They never spoke with such sustained civility.

"I do not," Dirt answered, changing from her night shift into her training clothes. Antie Yaya had insisted on the night shift. Dirt hadn't been very interested at first, but she'd come to appreciate it— were she to face an attack in the middle of the night, the garment was light and flexible enough to not hinder her fighting.

"You are fine with seed six?" Carra Carre asked.

"Finefine," Dirt said. She slipped her shirt over her head and strode for the exit, eager to get in a workout before lunch.

But Carra Carre was standing there, blocking her way.

"Excuse me," Dirt said.

"You must be strong, Sis Dirt," the behemoth of a girl said.

"I am strongstrong. Or must I show you again?"

Carra Carre shook her head. "You see Mister Odo. You see na shaking earth. You see seven Godskins. Perhaps more. Do not be strong for me. Be strong for na war that comes."

Dirt had managed to avoid thinking about the strangeness of the last couple of weeks. In a day, she would be fighting again, not just as a girl but as a Godskin. There was too much at stake to be distracted.

"I do not know if I can win," Carra Carre said.

Dirt stared, stunned. Hidden within the vines that wrapped her head, Carra Carre's eyes were desperate with fear. It was such a pitiful expression that Dirt looked away, waiting a moment for Carra Carre to collect herself, but when she looked back, there was no change. Enemies were not meant to see each other so vulnerable. But Carra Carre was exposing herself willingly, offering Dirt her neck and trusting she wouldn't crush it.

"Of . . . of course you can," Dirt said. "There is no girl you cannot defeat." She winced inwardly as she said it.

Carra Carre continued on as if Dirt hadn't spoken.

"If I cannot win, I cannot meet na Gods. If I cannot meet na Gods, I cannot lead na Bowers. I must become stronger."

That is why she fights, Dirt realized.

Her voice was calm, but Dirt could feel the spiral of anxiety turning within her. The girl was on a mission to become the First of the First she believed she was destined to be. Now she was so close to that destiny being realized, yet the final hurdle—to win the Isle God Bow—was a daunting one.

She wasn't standing in Dirt's way to intimidate her. Or even stop her. She was there to make a request.

"What must you do," Dirt asked, "to become stronger?"

Only then did the fear in Carra Carre's eyes recede, dissolved by the same hungry glare with which the girl had built the most powerful Fam in the South.

"I need your help."

Outside the Imperial Temple, the breeze crept the sand along at a snail pace, grains rolling quietly beside Dirt's feet. This was the only place they could find that would be away from spectators' eyes while still allowing enough space for Bowing. All week, Carra Carre had been showing off her skills for Mister Odo, but this was about learning skills, not showing them, and learning was best done in private.

Carra Carre explained that, with every competitor being a Godskin, she no longer had a clear advantage. Dirt knew that their own fight was still fresh in the mind of the First of the Vine. It was a close fight, and it could just as easily have ended in Dirt's favor. Carra Carre needed to know that all the fights in the tournament wouldn't be so close.

"Your Slap," Carra Carre said. "Na one that shoots na wind. How?"

Dirt's Whip Slap hadn't even been her own invention. Webba had thought it up, straight from the cavernous halls of her own imagination. It had proven a useful technique against Carra Carre, allowing Dirt to fight from afar against an opponent who preferred to fight in close.

But it was a Slap—Dirt's best technique. And even then, it had taken Dirt days to learn. Carra Carre had just one day. She tried to explain to Carra Carre that there was not enough time to learn it before their fight, but Carra Carre insisted.

"What you can learn in three days, I can learn in one," she argued, head lifted with pride.

"Eh heh . . . ," Dirt said diplomatically. "I learn it because I am na Slapper. You are na Trapper. Na Whip Slap is not for you to learn."

Carra Carre was unconvinced. "Teach me. I will learn."

Dirt taught. She taught the positioning, the arm movement, the balance in weight. She taught Carra Carre the way Webba had taught her, through repetition. Yet the morning became afternoon and the afternoon became evening, with Carra Carre still failing to perform the technique.

"Mama Eghi's teeth!" Carra Carre swore on her final attempt, her hand slapping down on the air in front of her without the barreling wind that Dirt's Whip Slap released.

Dirt simply watched in silence, sat atop a slope of sand. She could see all the flaws in Carra Carre's technique, but she knew there was nothing that could fix them but time and repetition. She felt a small smugness that Carra Carre's overconfidence had resulted in failure.

In the end, with the day's light dying on the far side of the sky, they abandoned the Whip Slap and instead sparred as Godskins. They clashed again and again with the speed and power of the Gods, taking care to damage neither the arena nor each other. In a way, it felt like their first fight—Carra Carre's body was uniquely large, her fighting style uniquely vicious, her mind uniquely strategic.

At the same time, it felt as different from their first fight as the sea from the sky. They were sparring not to hurt each other, but to learn, and they soon established a comfortable rhythm. It had been so long since Dirt had enjoyed that sort of Bowing. Swoo was skilled but young—even in sparring, her competitive energy was unsuppressed. But Carra Carre moved with a veteran's grace, increasing and decreasing ferocity with deft control, always aware of Dirt's position and power.

Dirt hadn't enjoyed a spar so much since Webba, and when they were finished and plopped down on the sand recovering their breath, the sky overhead a dark blue sheet sprayed with dots of light, her mind and heart were focused on the sister who had left her.

"Why do you fight?" Carra Carre asked.

The question came suddenly, as so many of Carra Carre's comments seemed to come, as if she thought and thought and thought until the words burst out of her.

"For na Mud," Dirt replied.

"Na Mud is strongstrong now. Yet here you are."

Dirt took a deep breath. Why she had entered the tournament was none of Carra Carre's business. But in that moment she was missing Webba more than usual, and she couldn't help talking about her.

"I fight to win," Dirt said. "To go and see my Sis Webba."

Carra Carre was silent a moment before responding. "Your Webba is na strongstrong Bower. She is gone?"

Webba's departure had been a life-changing event for Dirt. It had overturned her entire world. She had assumed that everyone in the South—everyone in the whole Isle—knew about it. Yet even one of Webba's previous foes did not know, and how could she?

Dirt's world had changed, but the rest of the world hadn't noticed. Her vision watered, and a pain swelled in her chest that felt like it would kill her if she didn't find a way to let it out.

But, again, she didn't. She couldn't.

"So you are like me," Carra Carre said. "You too have reason to fear losing."

Dirt nodded. "In our fight, I see this. Your fear. Webba says this is why na Gods choose us. Because we are afraid, but we overcome."

Carra Carre grunted, then gained a thoughtful expression. "Verdi fears nothing."

"Webba is na same. Our madmad sisters."

Then Carra Carre made a strange sound, like a knife being raked over stone. Dirt was stunned to realize it was Carra Carre laughing. Or at least chuckling, a slight bounce of belly and throat. She didn't realize the girl was capable of such mirth.

"If it is our fear that gives us power," Carra Carre said with a deep breath, "then I will pray tonight for us to be afraid tomorrow. We will need it."

With that, they returned to the arena and retired to their beds. Neither spoke again, each too appreciative of the peace they'd reached to risk ruining it.

15

News from a Butterfly

1 Day until the Isle God Bow

TIGGI HAD NEVER felt so powerful.

Her first ever Bow had ended in victory, and against one of the bigger and stronger Bibi in Song. It hadn't gone exactly as intended—in the chaos of battle, she'd forgotten much of her training, and her fingers were sore from how desperately hard she was grabbing on to Song.

But she won, and that was all that mattered.

She was the first up this morning, and she left the Bibi sleep hut to find Sis Swoo out in the ring, doing her slow training. Tiggi watched for a while, trying and failing to mimic the moves. When Sis Swoo was finished, a light sheen of sweat on her skin, she went into her sleep hut without so much as looking in Tiggi's direction.

Tiggi knew she was just a lowly Bibi and that she didn't truly understand all the things happening in the Mud Fam, but she sensed there was something wrong with Sis Swoo. During the NoBe Bow, Sis Swoo had watched with a completely expressionless face—rare for the normally expressive Sis. Only Snore's wild attack had stirred her to action. Once the competition was over, Sis Swoo went back to her sleep hut.

Today was fight day for Sis Swoo. Maybe that was why she was being so reclusive?

"Na good day, Tiggi," a voice said.

A group of girls emerged from the Bibi sleep hut behind her, yawning and rubbing their eyes as they stepped into the day.

"Na good day," she said, a bit surprised to receive a greeting.

"What is it we must do?" one of the girls, Tempo, asked.

Tiggi tilted her head, confused.

"For Sis Swoo," Tempo added.

They were all staring at her. Tiggi was used to being stared at by the other Mud sisters, but this seemed different. They weren't staring at her because they felt she was strange or unwanted, but because they were looking to her for direction.

"We . . . eh . . . is na Mud Offer ready?"

Tempo motioned for two of the girls with her to go check. Then she looked back to Tiggi.

"Eh . . . do we have na food and na things for trade?"

More Bibi stumbled blearily out from the sleep hut, and Tempo immediately set them to work gathering the day's meals and everything else they would need to take to the Grand Temple. As they saw Tiggi, they each greeted her with a nod or a "na good day." Tiggi accepted each greeting with grace and confusion.

All because I win? she thought.

The sisters of the Mud scurried around the camp, following

her orders. Tiggi watched it all as if it were a dream, expecting any minute to wake up as the girl she'd been the day before.

That moment came soon after, as Bibi Snore suddenly walked out from the tree line into the camp. All the sisters froze, and Snore walked between and around them without a word, shuffling through the camp as if she didn't see them at all.

Then they all rushed to her, chirping like a squabble of rainbow birds, talking over each other as they asked Bibi Snore the same questions they'd been asking Tiggi just moments before.

"Bibi Snore, what must we do?"

"Bibi Snore, is na food finefine?"

"Where is na Mud Offer, Bibi Snore?"

Snore didn't respond to any of them. She cut straight through the camp and disappeared into the sleep hut.

When she was gone, the other Mud sisters blinked at each other for a while before going back to their preparations for the day. But the spell was broken. After that, they no longer asked Tiggi what to do, and Tiggi was reminded that there was only one way to keep the respect of the Fam.

Beat Snore.

"Bow . . . begin!"

The timekeeper unstoppered the hourglass and Sis Swoo leapt into action, forcing her opponent back to the edge of the ring with Slaps.

Tiggi would never grow comfortable watching Sis Swoo fight. On the one hand, she loved learning from her Sis's blend of skill and athleticism, the ferocity that she adopted the moment she stepped into the ring. On the other hand, every fight was so desperate, so high stakes. Even in her short time as a Bower, she had seen so many competitors fall from ruptured muscles or broken bones, faces full of agony as they writhed in the sand. It was impossible not to fear the worst when one's own sister took to battle.

Thankfully, the match ended quickly.

Unfortunately, not in Sis Swoo's favor. The temporary First of the Mud seemed afraid to use her Riding like she usually did, so the other girl, who was much bigger, scored an early Bow, then stalled for the victory.

"Na winner is Sis Hari of na Sand!"

Sis Swoo stormed out of the ring, ripping chunks of Mud Offer from her skin and tossing it across the sand. Tiggi didn't know enough to see any problem with it, but the way the crowd showered her with jeers indicated she was breaching tradition in some way. But Sis Swoo didn't seem to care.

"We leave!" she shouted as soon as she reached the rest of the Mud sisters, and she continued her stomping exit from the arena.

Tiggi was the first to follow behind her, with the other sisters trailing after them.

Silence reigned over their long trek home. Even the most energetic Bibi were afraid to utter a sound. Sis Swoo was a passionate girl, and it wasn't uncommon for her to fly into a fit of rage when training. But this was different. It wasn't just anger or frustration or anything of the sort.

It was pain. Sis Swoo walked with a slight forward hunch that Tiggi had never seen before, and sometimes she would stop at a tree or rock and survey it as if she had lost her way, and a pained grimace would sweep over her face. Tiggi had never seen Sis Swoo in pain before. None of them had.

When they reached camp, the silence remained. It was the quietest the Mud camp had ever been, each sister uncertain what would happen if she were the sole voice. Sis Swoo went immediately to her sleep hut—Sis Dirt's old hut—where she slammed the door behind her.

The rest of the Mud sisters sat in and around the ring. They were waiting for some direction, expecting Sis Swoo to come out and start barking orders, as she usually did. But minutes passed and Sis Swoo didn't come out. Then an hour. Then two.

Tiggi stood, feeling the weight of her sisters' eyes on her. She searched among them for Bibi Snore but soon realized she must have left the camp at some point, or perhaps she had not even returned with them. She'd hoped to ask Bibi Snore to ask Sis Swoo what they should all do, but that was not possible.

So Tiggi had to do it herself.

She crossed the camp, striding between her seated sisters, over to the sleep hut door. She raised her hand to knock, but she caught a glimpse of Sis Swoo between the wooden slats. She was seated on the ground, legs crossed, bent forward with her face in her hands. Her shoulders were bouncing strangely, and it wasn't until Tiggi pressed her ear to the door and heard the soft whimpers that she realized Sis Swoo was crying.

"Hello, Mud sisters?" a voice called.

Tiggi whipped around at the unfamiliar voice.

A girl stood on the edge of camp, just inside the tree line. She wore tight denim pants, with a flowing white blouse. Her hair was bound back from her heart-shaped face in a cute shoulder-length ponytail.

Pebble.

"Hello?" Pebble asked again. "Sis Swoo?"

Tiggi ran across the camp, glee on her face. "How now, Pebble!" she called.

Pebble stared at her blankly for a moment before recognition and joy slowly took her features. "Tiggi?"

Tiggi skipped right into Pebble's outstretched arms, embracing the older girl.

Last year, when she was still a Butterfly girl, Tiggi had been training to become a Bonemender. At the time, she'd thought she wanted to understand how the body worked and how to heal it, and Pebble had been one of her trainers. Tiggi was a good student, but after seeing Sis Dirt fight against Sis Carra Carre and the entire Vine, she realized that she wanted not to understand others' bodies, but to build up her own.

"How now?" Pebble laughed, smiling down into Tiggi's eyes. "So this is where you are, eh?"

Tiggi couldn't help but feel embarrassed. Like many girls, she had been so thrilled by Sis Dirt that she'd left without saying good-bye to everyone.

"I am sorry, Pebble," Tiggi said.

Pebble shook her head. "It is finefine. Seeing you lightens me." She looked up from Tiggi to survey the camp. "Where is Sis Swoo?"

"Sis Swoo is here . . ."

Tiggi turned over her shoulder to see Sis Swoo striding out of the sleep hut. Her face was dry, cheeks unmarred, eyes set in her usual stern determination. Tiggi questioned whether she'd seen the same girl crying just moments before.

"Pebble na Mos— Butterfly," Sis Swoo said carefully. "Today is na bad day made worse."

"Na good day, Honored Sis."

Sis Swoo waved away her greeting. "Why have you come?"

Pebble changed her voice into a startlingly perfect mimic of Sis Swoo's gruff and bothered tone. "Na good day, Pebble, my oldold friend." Tiggi giggled, until a look from Sis Swoo froze the sound in her throat. "It has been so long since you bring na recruits to—"

"*Why* have you come?" Swoo interrupted, glowering.

"I come with news," Pebble said, then fell silent, a small smile on her lips. She seemed to take immense joy from Sis Swoo's growing irritation.

"Your name suits you, Pebble," Sis Swoo said. "You are na pebble in my shoe."

Pebble only smiled more.

"What. News?" Sis Swoo asked through gritted teeth.

Pebble raised her chin, her face taking on a solemn joy befitting an official messenger from Antie Yaya.

"I bring news of Sis Dirt," she said.

16

Reunions

The Isle God Bow

FREE.

That was how Carra Carre felt after training with Dirt. Outside of battle, the girl had a presence about her. Calming. Sturdy. All the Sis who Carra Carre usually spent time with were Vine sisters, each of them carrying the intensity for which the Fam was known. Dirt was the opposite, though while she was less competitive, she was no less of a Bower.

Since arriving at the Imperial Temple, Carra Carre had felt the weight of the future on her shoulders. Verdi's visions were never wrong, and the arrival of Mister Odo had only made matters more urgent. Years of bearing the Fam's hopes as the First had turned into bearing the hopes of the entire Isle. Each day, the pressure grew and grew, and the only way she could get it out was to train harder, attempting to push her body beyond even the limits of the

Godskin. Yet despite how hard she worked, Sis Bear had been just as impressive, and the terror that Carra Carre wouldn't be able to achieve her destiny mounted. There were times she had looked out at the jungle and imagined plunging into it like diving into the river, letting it consume her and take her away forever.

Then she'd trained with Dirt, and for the first time in years, Bowing had been something fun rather than something burdensome. It was like being a Bibi again—training to learn, to grow, to help your sisters. Playful and challenging in equal parts. She'd gone into it desperate to learn something that would give her an edge in the Isle God Bow, but she'd come out of it realizing that the only edge she needed—the only edge she'd ever needed—was the love of Bowing. No technique would save her more than her passion, skill, and self-belief.

Carra Carre sat up in her bed, the morning shining hazy through the window to the room she shared with Dirt. She always woke up before Dirt and spent that time in silence, fortifying her mind for the day ahead.

And thinking about the Vine, missing her sisters. They would be training without her, competing without her, and she couldn't help but wonder how they were faring. Nuna would be acting First, preparing the younger girls while also preparing for her own fights, the first season in which she had a real chance to win the South God Bow. Then there was Murua, their newest and most promising Sis. Carra Carre wished she could be there to mentor her through the emotional turmoil of a girl's first season as a Sis, and to prepare her for what everyone knew would be the biggest fight of the year—Sis Murua versus Sis Swoo, the continuation of the rivalry between the Vine and the Mud.

But the only way Carra Carre would be home in time for such things was if she lost early. She would rather win and miss a hundred seasons of fights than lose and risk the fate of the Isle in the coming war.

She would rather die, if it meant her sisters could live on.

That was the duty of the First of the First.

There was a sound from Dirt's bed, that soft early morning groan that reminded Carra Carre how old Dirt was—a woman in a world of girls. The Mud girl rubbed her eyes, ran her hand through her ever-tussled hair, then looked over at Carra Carre. Every morning since they'd begun sharing a room, Dirt's eyes widened in alarm upon seeing Carra Carre, a quick second of fear and anger instilled in her from all her battles with vine-wrapped Vine sisters.

This morning, though, there was no such widening.

"Na good day, Sis," Dirt said.

"Na good day, Sis," Carra Carre responded.

"You ripe?"

"Riperipe."

"Last night I think," Dirt said, her eyes suddenly looking everywhere but at Carra Carre. "You will need help with your Godskin."

Behind her vine wrapping, Carra Carre smiled.

"As will you."

Only then did Dirt look at her. She nodded firmly, a gesture Carra Carre had come to understand was the equivalent of a hug from anyone else.

Carra Carre nodded back.

She rolled out of bed to her feet, only to hear a far-off sound, a whispered note of music.

"You hear that, eh?" she asked.

Dirt nodded, rolling out of bed herself, cocking her ear to listen.

Minutes passed, and the sound grew closer like the squawking of a flock of birds, approaching as a single mass then splitting into distinct voices all working together in a chorus.

Then, soon after, Carra Carre knew what she was hearing.

It was the stomping of hundreds of feet. The pounding of hundreds of fists against chests. The upraised voices of the most powerful Bowers in the land.

The hair on Carra Carre's skin rose; lightning split every bit of her flesh.

Na Vine!

Fight!

Crush!

Na enemy!

Dirt watched Carra Carre rush out of their room, charging for the walkway that overlooked the Imperial Temple ring. Dirt's ear had not yet deciphered the sound that had been approaching for moments, other than to catch the sound of girls singing. What they were singing, though, she could not tell.

But then the sound divided. Or rather branched in a half dozen directions, overlapping sheets of sound at varying volumes and pitches. One of those sheets held a familiar tune, a song she knew she was familiar with if she could just hear it better. If it could just come closer or—

Dirt crashed through the doors to the room, feet scrambling against the smooth brick floor of the Imperial Temple as she turned up the hallway and sprinted to the first overlook of the arena interior, the thousands of seats cascading from the sky down to the floor where the arena's eight arched entrances were issuing forth dozens of girls, entering from all directions. Their voices boomed from proud chests, each troop of girls singing a different song, dancing a different dance, the very overlap of sound Dirt had been hearing.

And within the cacophony was the song Dirt had recognized, the one that called her heart out of her chest—to swell, to leap, to burn as fiercely as the sun herself.

> *We are na Mud sisters! (We are na Mud sisters!)*
> *We fight, oh yes, ooooooh!*
> *We are na Mud sisters! (We are na Mud sisters!)*
> *We never quit, noooooo!*

Dirt watched her sisters stream into the Imperial Temple and had to immediately wipe the tears forming in her eyes. They were beautiful. Strong. Rather sloppy, if she were being honest with herself, but a dream nonetheless. The dream she'd always harbored in her heart—a Mud Fam as large and powerful as any other.

She would have given anything to have Webba beside her then, enjoying the same perfect moment.

All the Fam sang and danced their ways to the center of the arena, and stood at attention once they were finished, the sudden lack of sound a force in itself. Then Antie Yaya strolled onto the sand, a smile faint on her face. She raised a speaking cone to her lips.

"I thought you Godskins could use your sisters. What is Bowing Day without sisters to share it with?"

Everyone remained frozen where they were. The girls down on the sand looked up at their Godskins with adoration in their eyes.

And the Godskins leaning over the Imperial Temple mezzanine looked down with a mistrustful hesitation, as if what they were seeing were an illusion and moving would scatter it to the winds.

"Go on, greet each other!" Antie Yaya said.

Dirt entered her Godskin and leapt over the balcony, ignoring any concern about saving energy for the fight later that day. She landed in a cloud of sand, then immediately sprang forward, enveloping her sisters in an embrace.

They swarmed her, their multitude of tiny arms covering every inch of her flesh. She could feel Swoo's larger arms across her side and hear Swoo's voice beneath the sounds of reunion that filled the arena.

"Welcome home," Swoo said.

They didn't have much time before they had to prepare for the fights, but the time they had was spent catching up and cackling, playing rounds of the Gekko and the Guava with the younger girls, talking technique with Swoo. It felt as if a mountain had been lifted off her shoulders, and she could tell from the exhausted relief in Swoo's eyes that she felt the same. When the little ones had tired of standing still, Dirt released them to play in the arena, taking the time to give Swoo a tour.

"Chaaaiii, look at your life, my Sis," Swoo said.

They were strolling along the Imperial Temple's corridors, Swoo's eyes rummaging every surface, widening at the intricate wall carvings adorning the interior.

"This is not my life," Dirt replied. "It is only na moment."

"And so?" Swoo asked. "It is not na moment of Swoo's life. It is Sis Dirt's. Look where your legs bring you."

Swoo's face wore a warm pride. Even as tired as she was, even with what Dirt knew must have been overwhelming responsibilities with the Fam, Swoo bore no grudge. Dirt would've kissed her if it wouldn't have been so embarrassing for both of them.

"And what of you? How does it feel to be First of na Mud?"

For a moment, Swoo raised her head and chest, a confident grin emerging across her face. But then everything faltered, her cheeks melting down into a tight frown, her chest deflating, her eyes receding into fear and donning a glaze of moisture.

"It is not easy," Swoo said quietly.

Swoo explained everything that had happened, and Dirt was as regretful as she was stunned that so much could have occurred in a week. It reminded her that her time at the Imperial Temple was not for leisure; back at camp, her sisters needed her. The only way to justify putting them through so much was to win.

Especially Snore. That had been the most troubling part of Swoo's report. There was a time when Little Snore had treated Bowing like a game. Dirt could remember all the times she'd chided the girl to take training more seriously. Now she was supposedly attacking other girls for no reason? Her own sisters?

What is happening to na Mud?

"I do not know what to do," Swoo said.

After finishing a stroll of the building, they stopped on the balcony outside the competitors' rooms. Swoo was looking out over the arena grounds, where the younger girls of the various Fam were mingling with the invasive curiosity of children, pushing boundaries until older girls stepped in to swat civility back into them.

"With Snore?" Dirt asked.

"With any of it," she sighed. "I do not know if I must be Swoo na First, Swoo na big sister, or Swoo na God Bower. And so for now I fail at all of them."

Dirt thought back to last season, when Webba had gone down with injury and she'd been forced to lead the Fam. In truth, if it weren't for Swoo, the Fam would have fallen apart. Dirt alone was not enough to keep things together, and that had been with just five Mud sisters, not fifty. She could not imagine the strain Swoo was under.

But she knew that Swoo, of all people, could handle it.

"Fail if you must," Dirt said. "But do not lose hope, my Sis. At na end, hope can turn one thousand failures into success."

Swoo held Dirt's eye for a while, then grunted and turned away.

"When you win and go see Webba, please bring her back," she said. "I grow tired of your poor imitation."

But she seemed lightened, all the same.

Dirt was going to say more, but dozens of feet rattled up the hallway. Sis Ahven and Sis Bear led the way, and behind them, trailing like an infinite snake, were the Sisters of the Cave. Nearly a hundred of them were full Sis, large and mighty girls whose faces bore the confidence of those who have known battle and victory. They paid Dirt and Swoo no mind as they passed by, their eyes forward on the backs of their leaders, their steps unified in weight and precision, as polished a Fam as Dirt had ever seen.

There was a time not long ago when Dirt would have been intimidated by their might. It was just like the first time she saw the full Vine Fam flooding through the entrance of the Grand Temple. But now she knew they were all just girls. Each as full of fear as any other, each battling the whispers in her own mind.

Swoo didn't seem impressed either. She yawned as they streamed by, on and on, hundreds in total. And when they were finished, she called down to the Mud sisters to come up, then turned to Dirt the way she'd looked at Dirt so many times before— her eyes alight with competitive fire.

"Let us get your Godskin," she said, "and show these spineless crickets who we are."

17

The Isle God Bow

THE ARENA FLOOR had been transformed overnight. Where before it was all sand, interrupted only by the ring of canvas sandbags at the center, there was now far more. A lake of water sat on one side, several fallen trees on another. Large boulders were dotted all about, and there was even a pile of such boulders in one spot with a dark patch of garden beneath it.

Dirt stood in the arena with the seven other Godskins, taking in the wonder of their new battlefield. Each girl was clad in her Godskin. Sis Bear and Sis Ahven had strips of animal hide wrapped around their limbs and strange animal furs that Dirt had never seen before draped across their shoulders. Sis Boom was bound in a crisscross of flowers about her chest and forehead. Sis Frog with shins and forearms covered in short grass, a crown of pebbles atop her head. Sis Hammuh dusted in crystalline coral, and little Sis Namaji's skin painted with cracks like tree bark, her crown an elaborate creation of pine cones.

Behind each Godskin, her Fam sat. The largest was, of course, the Cave Fam, taking up two entire sections of seating in their black attire. Then the Reef and the Valley, with hundreds of sisters each, pink and peach in color. The Vine had never looked so modest with their two hundred green-clad sisters, and Dirt wondered how Carra Carre was faring, experiencing what it felt like to not be the most powerful Fam for likely the first time in her life.

The Spray, in pale blue, was roughly the size of the Mud, which left a large gap between them and the smallest Fam: the Trunk Fam of the West. With just ten girls, the Trunk were far from imposing, an impression heightened by their casual, slouched posture. They all seemed uninterested in the affair, and none of them more so than their First, Sis Namaji.

Mister Odo and Antie Yaya walked across the arena, arm in arm. Dirt did not understand their relationship—whether they were simply friends or something different—and it unsettled her that Mister Odo had appeared and been given so much power while explaining so little about who he was and what he wanted.

But he was in charge of the seeding. So Dirt suppressed her annoyance as he and Antie Yaya reached the center of the arena and he raised a speaking cone to his lips.

"Eh . . . na good day, Bowers," he said in that strange accent of his.

He lowered the cone and smiled around the arena but was met by a sturdy and disgusted silence.

"This mouthy rooster . . . ," Dirt heard Swoo mutter from the stands behind her.

Mister Odo cleared his throat and raised the cone again. "You have all worked hard this last week. Thank you for allowing me to watch you train, and I look forward to seeing you display your talents shortly. So, on that note ..."

He reached into a pocket in his pants and pulled out a flat square of some material, perhaps ... dried animal hide? But it was pale, like the inside meat of a tree. Mister Odo scanned it as if there was something on it, but even from a distance, Dirt could tell there were no drawings at all, just strange, orderly lines of scribbles.

He cleared his throat, eyes flowing down his scribbles. "I took the seeding for this competition very seriously, assessing your skills in consultation with Antie Yaya and Sis Ebe—eh ... former Sis Ebe, is that right? Anyhow, the top seeds will have the advantage of facing the lower seeds in the first round. So first will fight eighth, second will fight seventh, third will ... eh ... I imagine you all know how these things proceed. In that case, the seeding for the Isle God Bow will be as follows: eighth seed, Sis Namaji of the West Trunk!"

The Trunk scarcely responded to the announcement, and Sis Namaji showed no sign that she'd even heard him.

"Seventh, Sis Boom of the East Valley!"

Though her sisters cheered, Sis Boom frowned, clearly expecting to be seeded higher.

"Six, Sis Dirt of the South Mud!"

Cheers swelled up from behind Dirt, but she kept her gaze ahead. Six was exactly what she'd expected. Now, she was only worried about who her opponent would be.

"Fifth, Sis Frog of the East Spray! Fourth, Sis Ahven of the North Cave!"

Dirt watched as both girls immediately looked at each other across the arena grounds. This was the first confirmed fight, fourth seed against fifth, modestly sized Spray Fam against the behemoth that was the Cave Fam, gentle-looking Sis Frog against cold and intimidating Sis Ahven.

"Third seed . . ."

Dirt's breath held. As confident as she was in her abilities, the anticipation still got to her. The third seed would be her opponent, her first obstacle to seeing Webba. She had a sudden, terrifying thought that Carra Carre would be her opponent. There were only three girls left—Dirt certainly thought Carra Carre had done enough to be first or second seed, but did Mister Odo see it that way? What if this was how it would always be—Carra Carre always the giant standing between Dirt and her goals?

" . . . Sis Hammuh of the West Reef!"

Dirt immediately breathed out relief, a gesture that Sis Hammuh across the Imperial Temple saw. The Reef girl's face rose in surprise before falling into a dark, heavy glower, and Dirt immediately regretted her lack of tact. Sis Hammuh would see Dirt's relief as a sign that Dirt was underestimating her, and she would only be prepared to fight more viciously as a result.

"Second, Sis Carra Carre of the South Vine!"

Carra Carre's eyes narrowed as the Vine Fam roared behind her, and Dirt knew the girl was swallowing a pained pride.

Even before the final name was announced, the Cave Fam was rumbling in anticipation, whipping animal skins overhead, pounding their feet in a sound like approaching thunder.

"And first," Mister Odo finished, "Sis Bear of the Cave!"

Immediately, Sis Ahven's voice sang out, pure and powerful and vibrating with emotion. "Thiiiiiis is who we are!"

The response from her sisters was a quick, forceful blast.

Na Cave!

Thaaaaaat is who we are!

Na Cave!

Teeeeeell them who we are!

Na Cave!

Shoooooow them who we are!

Na Cave!

They sang so long and loud that Mister Odo gave up trying to give any sort of concluding speech. After a brief laugh and shake of his head, he stuffed the material he'd been reading from back into his pocket, then walked off the arena floor and into the stands, Antie Yaya on his arm.

Only when he was seated and all the Godskins had joined their Fam in the arena seats did the Cave gradually subside. In the newfound quiet, Ebe strode out onto the arena floor with a large hourglass in tow. She set it down and raised a speaking cone to her mouth.

"Na first Bow. Sis Hammuh of na West Reef and Sis Dirt of na South Mud!"

Dirt took a deep breath. Before her, Sis Hammuh's heaving chest glittered with dust from the iridescent coral of the Isle's western reefs, every pore seeming to shine. Around them both, the arena was a mishmash of environments—part desert, part jungle, with water and stones spread about. The ring itself was still sand, but all the changes to the surrounding arena made Dirt uneasy.

Sis Hammuh dropped into a low Bowing salute, which Dirt returned.

"Bow," Ebe shouted, "begin!"

I am brave. I am fat. I am Dirt.

The words came so easily, almost without thought. The power came with it, a coursing rush of clarity and strength pumping within her like a second bloodstream. Sis Hammuh's face took on a calm that Dirt knew only came with the power of the Godskin. She stayed where she was for a moment, cracking her neck from side to side, shaking out her arms and legs.

Then she attacked.

It was the same as when Carra Carre sparred with Sis Bear. No Slapping, just an instant rush of speed and power, an attempt to blast the opponent away with strength rather than technique. It made sense, in a way. Sis Hammuh was a large girl, bigger even than Webba. Doubtless, her physical prowess alone had earned her many victories. With the addition of being a Godskin, why would she assume any girl could withstand her?

But Dirt wasn't any girl. She wasn't a girl at all. She was a woman—one who had spent years out of shape, who even now was no physical specimen. All Dirt had was her knowledge. Her technique. And now, unlike in her fight against Carra Carre, she wasn't blinded by emotion.

So as Sis Hammuh sped toward her, the sand parting before the rush of her body, Dirt simply stepped aside. Sis Hammuh caught herself at the edge of the ring, turning immediately to face Dirt, her eyes narrowed. She was realizing, Dirt knew, that she had underestimated her opponent. A quick study. She would be more cautious now, which was just as Dirt had planned.

The fight was already over, only Sis Hammuh didn't know it.

Rather than Riding across the ring, Sis Hammuh kept her distance, falling into a more traditional Bowing stance and Slapping at the air as she waited for Dirt to move. Dirt responded in kind, feet sturdy and even-spaced, keeping to the edge of the ring. She began Slapping as well, pawing at the air with her eyes locked on Sis Hammuh, waiting for the girl to grow comfortable with the rhythm.

Then she saw it. The confident sheen in Sis Hammuh's eyes as the girl felt certain she'd discerned Dirt's timing. Just as her opponent took a step forward, Dirt unleashed na Spear, issuing three quick Whip Slaps in succession. Sis Hammuh, like nearly every girl in the Imperial Arena, had never seen it before. The bolts of air ripped toward her, each one punching her back, off balance, off her feet, out of the ring.

"Push!" Ebe called. "Na Winner is Sis Dirt of na South Mud!"

The Mud sisters exploded into a frenzy of cheers. Sis Hammuh remained just outside the ring, rubbing her chest in pained confusion. Dirt approached her and extended an arm.

"Strongstrong Bow, Sis Hammuh of na Reef," she said.

Sis Hammuh accepted Dirt's arm and gripped it warmly. "Strongstrong Bow, Sis Dirt of na Mud."

There was no anger in the girl. No haughty denial. Just a heavy sadness in the downturn of her brows and a disappointment emanating from her. Dirt remembered then that they were all Godskins—all powered by overcoming their fears and conquering Useyi's whispers in their mind. And they all had a reason to be fighting. For Dirt, it was to see Webba. For Carra Carre, it was to fulfill her destiny. Sis Hammuh must have had her own reason, and that had now come to an end.

Dirt nodded and was going to make small talk to get to know the girl better, but she was hit by a wave of Mud sisters. She'd expected it to be Swoo, but as she looked at all the faces swarming her, she realized it was just the Bibi, their chorus of giggles filling her ears. A brutal storm of hugs and kisses ensued, with each Bibi too excited to realize that Dirt was still in her Godskin, forcing them a moment later to spit Mud Offer out of their mouths.

Once Dirt managed to wrangle their joy and get them off her, the Bibi formed a singing honor guard, howling the Mud anthem as they escorted Dirt out of the ring and back into the stands. Dirt surveyed the arena, catching the eyes of her opponents. Most of the girls maintained a flat expression, betraying nothing. Sis Bear and Sis Ahven were in close conversation, clearly already planning for how to deal with Dirt's Spear. Carra Carre's face was hidden behind vines, but Dirt saw a small nod of her head and could feel the approval in her gaze.

Only one of the sisters responded unusually. Sis Namaji, the lowest seeded girl in the tournament, couldn't keep the smile off her face.

18

The Final Shaking

CARRA CARRE versus Sis Boom was a short-lived match. Carra Carre's aggression and skill was overwhelming, undeniable. Sis Boom did her best to survive, but after a few minutes, Carra Carre Bowed her so hard she crashed through a log sitting outside the ring. Dirt felt conflicted at the victory. She was happy for Carra Carre, all the more because she knew that Carra Carre wouldn't share her joy—only winning the entire tournament mattered to her.

Yet, she was also nervous. Regardless of how the other matches ended, Dirt and Carra Carre would face each other in the next round.

Those other matches came shortly later.

Sis Ahven and Sis Frog battled like eternal enemies, their conflicting styles resulting in a bruising match. Sis Ahven managed to win with a counter Bow, which brought the entire Cave Fam rushing down onto the arena floor in celebration.

Then it was time for the final fight of the day, the top seed versus the lowest seed, the North versus the West, Sis Bear versus Sis Namaji. In any other tournament, the match would have been a formality—the gap in skill was almost always impossible to overcome. But between Sis Bear's obvious prowess and Sis Namaji's unprecedented smugness, Dirt had never wanted to watch a one versus eight match so badly.

In the ring, the two girls could not have been more different. Sis Bear was intensity bound in flesh, releasing heavy breaths through her nostrils as she stared down into Sis Namaji's eyes. Sis Namaji, meanwhile, was as small and unbothered as ever. Were she not in full Godskin, Dirt would have thought she was about to take a nap rather than fight the most fearsome Bower in the whole Isle.

After a quick salute—Sis Bear's sealed with a thunderous clap, Sis Namaji's sealed with her palms flopping soundlessly together—Ebe called out.

"Bow begin!"

Sis Namaji didn't even raise her hands.

So Sis Bear didn't raise hers either. She walked toward the smaller girl, the calm of the Godskin entering her face. When they were a stride away, Sis Bear shoved forward with both arms.

Then something impossible happened.

Before Sis Bear's arms could push Sis Namaji out of the ring, there was a sound of cracking wood and a flurry of movement about the arena grounds. In an instant, one of the fallen tree trunks laying on the far side exploded into a shower of bark chips, sped through the air toward the ring, then reconvened one after the other in a stream, clattering into Sis Namaji's skin until every inch of her was covered in an armor of tree bark.

"What kind of thing is this?" Swoo uttered in awe beside Dirt.

Most of the arena was similarly awestruck, staring down at the ring with jaws slack. Yet the Trunk Fam, small but mighty, were a torrent of whoops and cheers, their voices echoing.

As Sis Bear shoved the newly armored Sis Namaji, Sis Namaji kept her ground. Sis Bear, however, bounced backward, reeling from some force Dirt couldn't make sense of. Sis Namaji kept up the pressure, walking toward Sis Bear, taking up more and more of the ring while forcing Sis Bear into an increasingly small space.

Sis Bear fought valiantly. Not just with power and aggression, but also with intelligence and adaptability, adjusting her strategy as necessary. Yet it made no difference. Sis Namaji had become invulnerable, and anything Sis Bear did seemed to weaken the moment she made contact with Sis Namaji's armor. Soon Sis Bear was doing all she could just to avoid Sis Namaji's counterattacks, the two of them zipping around the ring in a high-stakes game of chase.

Eventually, even with the power of the Godskin, Sis Bear began to tire. And Sis Namaji became a jungle cat, toying with her prey, showing the entire arena just how superior she was.

Dirt watched it all with a mixture of admiration and terror. This girl was stronger than any of them, and she knew it. Whether chosen by the Gods or the result of her own training, Sis Namaji had ascended to another level, above even that of a True Godskin. This was the new mountain to scale if she hoped to see Webba again. And what a mountain it was.

Dirt took a moment to survey the arena, and the faces of the other Godskin must have been similar to her own. Frustration.

Determination. Disbelief. Carra Carre's head was tilted in a casual confusion, like she'd come out in the morning only to find the sun was still down.

Sis Namaji continued her advance as the hourglass passed three-quarter sand, and as Sis Bear retreated, she tripped over herself, falling on her back to the sand.

"Bow Down," Sis Namaji said, and even the Trunk sisters fell silent at that.

Sis Bear rose to one knee but did not stand fully. She remained there, eyes on the ground.

"Ten ... nine ...," Ebe began counting.

"Bow. Down." Sis Namaji repeated.

The girls of the Cave Fam were in a state of distress. Several of them were weeping, faces buried in the shoulders of the sisters beside them.

"Five ... four ..."

Sis Bear was beaten. She knew it. Whether she rose or not made no difference in the outcome. But there was a threat veiled in Sis Namaji's casual tones, and it seemed clear that standing would lead to a physically destructive ending for her, whereas staying on the sand and Bowing Down would only be emotionally so.

So she did what any Bower would do.

Sis Bear rose to her feet, stamping her other foot on the sand and raising her gaze proudly. In response, the ground beneath her trembled from her power, the sand quaking, the whole arena seeming to shift.

No. It wasn't *seeming* to shift. It *was* shifting, and not from Sis Bear.

"Go down!" Dirt heard Mister Odo roar. "Go!"

Confusion reigned. All around the arena, girls were looking up and down, unsure of where to go or what to do. That was until Mister Odo sprinted down the stands, tugging Antie Yaya behind him. "Come down!" he shouted again.

Then the real shaking began. The Imperial Temple seemed afloat on a turbulent sea, a storm swelling and crashing in frightful jolts beneath their feet. Dirt spun to the Bibi, several of whom Swoo had already hefted onto her shoulders.

"Swoo, go!" she shouted, then turned to the fear-stuck Bibi. "On me!"

She entered into her Godskin just as the first several Bibi clambered onto her. Their weight negligible, she ensured they all had firm grips, then she ran down the stands and leapt over the rails onto the arena floor.

Then they all watched. Every Bower of the Isle huddled together in the center of the Imperial Temple, watching with unsettled stomachs as the highest seats of the arena swayed in a way none of them believed brick was meant to sway. Accompanying the movement were occasional belches from deep within the earth, as if the world's support beams were snapping beneath them.

But the ground did not collapse, and the shaking soon ended. When it finished, Dirt looked over the Bibi to make sure they were fine. Most of them were giggling, already forgetting the uncomfortable experience. Snore appeared wholly unaffected, staring blankly at the ground.

Dirt was going to approach Snore when she saw Mister Odo farther into the arena, gesturing frantically at Antie Yaya, whose face bore deep lines of concern. Dirt had never seen Antie Yaya concerned before. Not like that, with her brows bunched, her eyes in their corners, her thoughts loud enough to almost hear just from the look of her.

With the world stilled, the Fam began trickling back toward the stands, ready to resume the tournament, but Antie Yaya stopped them.

"The fighting is finished!" she called, and there was surprise on her face as she did so.

Every Bower froze. Traditionally, Antie Yaya oversaw the life of the Bowers, but she mostly distanced herself from the actual fighting. To stop a Bowing tournament before it had finished was a level of involvement that made every Bower in the arena bristle.

"Antie Yaya," Sis Bear began in a slow, respectful tone, "I can fight. Let us continue, eh?"

"I said it is finished!" Antie Yaya snapped. Then, at the mistrustful recoil of the Bowers, she took a deep, calming breath. "I apologize for the brusqueness. I know you all must want resolution. But we cannot get that now. Everyone go back to your rooms and prepare to return home in the morning."

Mister Odo whispered urgently in her ear, but she held up a hand. "The morning is fine," she mumbled, then raised her voice again to the Bowers. "Go! I will not repeat myself!"

Swoo led the Bibi back out to the arena's exterior, where they had set up a makeshift camp for the day. Meanwhile, Dirt returned to her room to pack her few belongings. She had very little to pack, just a couple training shirts and pants stuffed into a canvas bag.

Yet there was a knot of fear coiling her insides. It was the same knot that had arrived that day at the cliffs, the minute Mister Odo washed up against the rocks. It had only grown since then, and she'd been too distracted with the Fam and the Isle God Bow and Carra Carre and Sis Namaji to notice it. But the expression on Antie Yaya's face back in the arena confirmed what the knot in Dirt's gut already knew.

Something was wrong. Very wrong.

As she scooped up her bag and went out into the hallway, she stopped short at the sound of footsteps, immediately followed by Carra Carre entering through the doorway.

"Sis," Dirt said, nodding her head in greeting. Carra Carre seemed poised to respond when a cadre of Vine sisters came up behind her.

Verdi was at the head of them. The Second of the Vine used to be a large girl, thick and powerful. Ever since her fight with Dirt, though, her belly had softened and her formerly famous arms had thinned noticeably. Even her gait had changed, from a bold and boastful stride to a careful shuffle. Dirt knew she had done irreparable damage to the girl, and she felt not a drop of remorse over it. Verdi was a cruel and terrible person.

"Cee Cee, see who is here . . . ," Verdi said, her voice slower and thicker than before, but her violet eyes glittering with the same malevolence as always.

"Move from our path, S– Dirt," Carra Carre said.

Dirt immediately understood what was happening. Verdi hated Dirt, and Carra Carre was just being loyal to her longtime sister. She would have done the same for Webba. Understanding did nothing to dull the blow, though.

Dirt didn't respond, instead tightening her grip on her bag and her emotions and brushing past the Vine sisters. She wasn't interested in confronting Verdi, and there wasn't time for such things even if she was.

"You know you will lose, eh?" Verdi asked. "You know you will never again see Webba."

Dirt was already out in the hallway, but the sound of Webba's name froze her.

"I foresee this," Verdi added.

Verdi and her prophecies. The girl knew nothing. She was just saying whatever she could to provoke Dirt.

And it worked. "Did you foresee this?" Dirt asked, menacing toward Verdi with a dark glare on her face.

But then Carra Carre was there, all her mountainous mass blocking her sister from the repercussions of her words.

Dirt remained for a moment, searching Carra Carre's face for any sign of the familiarity and sisterhood they'd shared the last week. But Dirt found none of it. Just another angry Vine sister. So she turned on her heel and left, ignoring the taunts and chortles of the mass of Vine sisters behind her.

It was a short walk out to the surrounding arena grounds, where the Mud Fam had raised a large tent, though not so large that any more than a few of the sisters could stay inside at a time. As Dirt approached the camp, she was greeted with an equal combination of warm looks and confused, fearful stares, half the sisters thinking nothing beyond the glee of seeing their big Sis and the other half still dwelling on Antie Yaya's pronouncement.

She found Swoo inside the tent, seated alone atop a tree stump, deep in thought. She looked up through her eyebrows at Dirt as she arrived.

"Why did you bring your things?"

"We will not wait until morning," Dirt said.

Swoo frowned. "But Antie Yaya say—"

"I know what Antie Yaya say," Dirt interrupted, her frustration building. "But we will go tonight. Now. Something is not right here. When na tournament is ready, we can return."

This time, Swoo shook her head apologetically. "Na Bibi are hungry, so I send some to gather lunch. They will not return for hours."

Dirt issued a low growl. "Send Bibi to find them."

"I do not know where they are—I . . ." Swoo spread her palms wide. "Sis Dirt, what is wrong?"

Dirt couldn't say. She didn't know any more than anyone else, but she had a horrible feeling in her gut, and her mouth was filled with a nauseous watering. She needed to be away from the Imperial Temple, and she needed the other Mud sisters to be as well.

She sighed, trying to release some of her stress. "I do not know, my Sis."

So often, Dirt found herself missing Webba. But that moment was the first time she felt angry that Webba was gone. Of all the times for the Mud to lose their champion, this was the most unfair moment possible. The Mud Fam didn't need a Godskin. They didn't even need a leader. They all, Dirt included, needed a big sister, someone who could not only tell them everything was going to be okay, but believe it as well.

There was nothing to do but wait.

In the old days, it took an hour at most to gather food for the Fam. Now, with fifty mouths to feed, the Bibi were gone for hours. All the while, Dirt tried to distract herself through conversation with Swoo, but the fear in her gut remained, worsened. On several occasions, one of the Bibi would pop her head in to ask some question or another, and Dirt struggled to not jump at her sudden appearance.

By the time the foraging Bibi returned and the meal had been consumed, the sky was mostly purple, a fading burst of gold in the west the only light left.

"Up up, you lazy lizards," Swoo said. "We go home."

The Bibi were sitting in their little groups—Bibi Fam, Swoo had said—and they turned to Swoo in confusion.

"Sis Swoo, why?"

"We like na temple, Sis Swoo!"

"Sis Swoo, let us stay!"

"Enough!" Dirt boomed, and all the Bibi immediately fell silent.

They looked at her in a way they never had before, and it made her realize how little they knew her. In their minds, she was not the reliable old Dirt. She was Sis Dirt the Godskin, a once-in-a-generation might. They had not seen the Sis Dirt with Nana's head in her lap while she battled fever. They had not seen her struggle to sit up in the morning, her own weight and age keeping her down. They had missed most of the challenges of her life, coming only when she had reached a place of power and comfort.

As a result, the expressions on their faces held something Dirt had never before seen Mud sisters regard each other with: fear.

"I . . . ," Dirt stammered, unable to even imagine what words would be needed to erase their fear.

Before she could find such words, she was interrupted. Not by a sound, but by a sight.

Behind the mass of staring Mud sisters, out on the edge of the jungle, stood a creature tinged in a blue glow. At a distance, Dirt could not tell what she was seeing. But as it stalked toward them, she was able to make out some features. A jungle cat's head, but with a flowing cloud of hair from which two curved horns poked. A short, squat body above narrow legs that ended in hooves. A bulbous rear like a bee, complete with a stinger jutting out. One of its eyes was the attentive gold of a jungle cat's. The other was obscured in a pale blue flame that waved in the light wind.

The creature suddenly stopped its stride and issued an ear-rending howl that sounded like no beast Dirt had heard in all her life, guttural and high and pained. The Bibi slapped hands over their ears, and Swoo immediately fell into a Bowing stance, jaw tight with apprehension.

Dirt stared in confusion.

What is this? she thought.

She got her answer immediately, as a chorus of similar howls echoed out of the jungle, followed by dozens of blue-tinged creatures, each a mishmash of different animals and elements, striding out from the jungle like a tide approaching the shore. Some walked on two legs, some on four, some flew like birds or slithered like snakes, walked on their arms or rolled like boulders.

But Dirt knew there was no real difference between them. Because the terrible churning in her gut had ended. That would only happen for one reason. This was the danger she'd been fearing. It had finally arrived.

Then the monsters attacked.

19

The Monsters Attack

SWOO CHARGED.

She didn't know what the creatures were. She didn't know where they had come from or why they were attacking the Mud Fam. She had no idea what was happening. But anything that sought a fight with the Mud—girl or woman, natural or of the Gods—would get it.

As the gap between her and the monsters closed and she was able to make out their grotesque but almost transparent features, she had to swallow down a large knot of fear.

I am brave. I am fat. I am Swoo.

She ducked low into the most powerful Ride she had ever performed. These creatures were beasts, not Bowers. They might have the strength of wild animals, but they would not have years of honed technique, the unshakeable competitive desire, the experience of meeting an equal foe face-to-face with everything at stake.

She slammed into the torso of a two-legged beast, her shoulder driving into its gut, her arms coming around for a Trap and Bow that would break the thing's neck if Swoo so desired.

But she never got the chance.

The beast tossed her like a fruit gone bad. Swoo's world became an alternating blur of sand and sky as she tumbled through the air. It ended in a teeth-clattering crash and a pressure in her skull like someone had batted her with a palm trunk.

She couldn't tell how much time passed between her explosive landing and her painful sitting up. It could have been seconds. It could have been minutes. All she knew was that she was lying at the base of the Imperial Temple, back on the floor, feet up against the wall of the arena. She checked herself for any major injuries and was surprised to find nothing but a few damaged fingers on her left hand. They were likely broken, but if those fingers had somehow braced her impact enough to save her further injury, it was a small price to pay.

Swoo struggled to her feet, intent on getting back into the fight. When she surveyed the scene, though, she thought better of it.

Dirt was drowning beneath a sea of the monsters. They were attacking from every angle, leaping at her, slashing her with their claws, biting empty air where she had been standing moments before. Dirt was a one-woman army, as always. In between dodges of the monsters' attacks, she found room for her own offensive, flinging the creatures left and right.

Swoo realized with humiliating bitterness that she was of no value in this fight. Whatever the creatures were, they possessed divine power, like Dirt. Swoo was just a normal Sis—and not even an elite one, if she was honest with herself.

So she did the only thing she could: get the Bibi to safety. They were frozen, legs rooted and jaws agape as they watched Dirt fend off the swarming beasts.

"On me!" Swoo shouted, and she was glad to see her voice pierce their stupor. Tiggi was the first to turn, bless her. Swoo waved her over, and Tiggi was aware enough to tap the sisters beside her. All of them rushed together away from the battle.

But Snore remained, of course. She was transfixed, Swoo knew. No amount of screaming would reach her. And several foolish Bibi were lined up behind her, trying to prove their bravery in the stupidest way possible.

Swoo sprinted toward the growing cloud of sand that Dirt and the creatures had created from their brawl, a cloud that was drifting closer and closer to Snore and her followers. She reached Snore just in time to yank her back as a monster's body was flung past them.

"Run!" she screamed to the other Bibi. "Now!"

Finally, they heard her and turned toward the Imperial Temple, but it was too late; the battle had reached them. The monsters seemed to have realized that Dirt was the most troublesome, so they turned their attention to Swoo and the Bibi. From all angles they converged, a menagerie of dangers, teeth bared and claws outstretched.

Yet their physical ferocity wasn't mirrored in their eyes. As they descended upon her, Swoo saw that they each bore a pair of hazy blue clouds where their eyes should have been, no pupils, no whites. She realized with shame that those empty eyes would be the last thing she saw before they tore her apart.

Then her big Sis was there. Dirt grabbed one beast in a headlock and spun, hurling it back into the jungle. Then she was in another spot, yanking a beast by the leg from a midair leap and whipping it into the earth, its head issuing a hollow squelch from the impact. Then she was in another spot. And another. She was everywhere at once, defending Swoo and the Bibi with all the power a Godskin could muster.

As Dirt thinned the rush, Swoo sought an opening in the chaos. It soon came, and she pushed the Bibi toward it, rushing them toward the safety of the Imperial Temple.

But one of the Bibi fell behind. Swoo looked over her shoulder for the missing Bibi and there was Bubu, eyes wide and full of terror as she fled from a monster's outstretched paws. Dirt was speeding in to save the day, but even fueled by the power of the Gods she would not reach Bubu in time.

The monster's forearms closed around Bubu, a deathly embrace, and both beast and Bubu winked out of existence.

Swoo's heart pounded a sickly beat. Her mouth became a wet cave, dripping nauseously. It took all the resolve she possessed to not double over in a mess of vomit and tears.

Yet she didn't know why.

Her memory of the last few seconds was vague, a blank void where it should have held . . . what? The monsters were chasing, she was rushing the Bibi toward the Imperial Temple, and then . . .

She didn't have time to investigate. The monsters were coming and the Bibi needed her. She turned away from the scene and soldiered on until they were all safe beneath the arched arena entrance.

Distantly, Swoo heard the Bibi sobbing, and she knew they

were experiencing the same confusion she was, pain without the memory of what caused it. But the Bibi were safe; it was Dirt who was still in danger, her movements slowing in her continuing battle against the horde.

Eghodo . . . please.

Ijiri . . . please.

Abidon . . . please.

Oduma . . .

Swoo couldn't finish the prayers. But she prayed anyway, begging the Gods to be satisfied with taking Webba from her. Yet fearing that They were about to take Dirt, too.

She had to do something.

Swoo turned and sprinted down the Imperial Temple halls shouting so hard she could feel her throat tearing.

"HELP! COME AND HELP US!"

Each door she passed, she beat on, then moved to the next without stopping. Soon, Bowers were streaming out of their rooms and onto the mezzanine. The last door she arrived at opened just as she was about to knock.

And Carra Carre stood behind it.

Immediate rage swelled within Swoo at the sight of the Vine's champion. There was a time when she would have unleashed that rage on Carra Carre's skull, either barehanded or with whatever weapon she could find.

But she was a Sis now and acting First of the Mud. She could no longer be so irresponsible.

"Sis Dirt needs help," Swoo said instead. "Please."

To her surprise, Carra Carre's eyes grew wide. "Where?" she asked.

"Come!" Swoo turned to lead her and all the other Sis emerging from their rooms, but a voice stopped her.

"Na Great NoBe Swoo," Verdi said, slinking out from behind Carra Carre to fill the doorway beside her sister, "now na Not So Great Sis Swoo."

Swoo stared Verdi down, a hundred responses running through her mind. In the end, she chose the one that would get Dirt help the fastest.

"Your war has come, Verdi," she said, then she left, running back up the hall and urging all the Bowers of the Imperial Temple to follow.

She soon reached the main entrance, from which she saw Dirt in a fight for her life. She was no longer on the offensive. Instead, she was just fighting off the monsters' grabbing hands, Slapping any that came near, spinning in every direction to keep from being attacked from behind.

Carra Carre was the first into the fray, her skin steaming with the power of the Gods. She hauled a beast into the air and broke it in half like a dry branch, then tossed it aside and tore apart another. Her ferocity inspired the other Godskins, each of them blitzing into battle, wielding the power of the gods against their monstrous attackers.

Swoo had never seen anything like it. The Godskins, working together, dismantled the beasts—bashing them, breaking them, flinging them back deep into the jungle. In what seemed like no time at all, the only ones left were the eight Godskins themselves. They looked around at each other, coming down from the urgent heartpound of aggression, a subtle admiration and gratitude passing among them.

Then came the cheers.

All the other sisters—the Bowers from every Fam on the Isle, assembled for the first time in history—unleashed a blast of sound so fierce, Swoo felt her chest rumble. Whoops and hollers, pounding feet and clapping hands, from the windows high within the arena to crowds pooled at the arena's arched entrances, they roared. Not just for their own Sis, but for the Godskins as a whole, for their willingness to use their strength to protect those weaker.

Try as she might, Swoo could not feel the same joy as the others. For she realized fully in that moment that she was the weaker, and she would always be. Less than a year ago, there had been no Godskins. Sis Webba was the strongest Bower Swoo knew. It had been the struggle of her life to accept that Dirt was a Godskin, that Swoo herself would never be able to equal a girl chosen by the Gods. Now there were eight. Maybe more. And there were beasts as strong as those Godskins, against whom Swoo had failed.

The price of that failure was the tear-streaked faces of the Bibi who had looked to her for leadership, their arms wrapped around each other as they'd sobbed in terror and confusion.

"Don't rejoice too soon," came Antie Yaya's voice.

Antie Yaya slid through the Bowers, Mister Odo and Ebe in tow. When she made it far enough out of the Imperial Temple that she could be seen by everyone, she regarded them all with a sorrowful expression.

"Our thanks to the Godskins," she continued. "But more of these creatures will come. And more after that. This is only the beginning."

"But why?" someone asked. "What are they?"

Antie Yaya was about to answer, but Mister Odo put a hand

on her shoulder, pausing her. He stepped forward into the silence, raised his chin, and took a deep breath.

"I can tell you what they are," he said. "But first I must tell you who I am."

20

Mister Odo's Story

"MY NAME is not Mister Odo."

Every Bower in the Isle was silent. They'd all frozen where they were, whether seated with legs dangling from one of the openings high in the Imperial Temple or with crossed legs by one of its entrances. Dirt was out with the other Godskins in the sand surrounding the temple. She could see her sisters over by an arena entrance. Swoo was seated protectively among the Bibi, the muted fear in her face reflected in the younger ones.

Something had happened. Dirt didn't know what, but within her was a deep and discomforting sense of regret she couldn't understand, and she saw the same on the faces of her sisters. As far as she could tell, they had all made it out of the battle safe and uninjured. Yet it felt like something had been lost, and whatever it was, Dirt felt like it was her fault.

"And I am not from where you imagine me to be from," Mister

Odo continued. "The land I come from is not heavenly. It is not even so nice as the lives you all live here. It is full of war and death and cruelty. And I sought to end those things."

He swallowed, and Dirt realized that he was not comfortable like this, speaking to so many. It was a strange thing to notice, but it made Dirt feel sympathy for him in a way she never had before. He was still an odd old man, but he was human, just like anyone else.

"I believed that I could create a better world. One with no war, with no death, no cruel acts. Most importantly," he said, looking away, "a world where every child has a family that loves and cares for them."

His silence lasted long enough to draw Dirt out of her own mind. Both Mister Odo and Antie Yaya wore heavy expressions. Mister Odo seemed on the verge of tears.

He is crying?

"But my family wanted me stopped. At the time, I believed they were simply enjoying the cruelty. So I continued on my own and found an ancient magic that could help me create the world I desired. But my brothers and sisters discovered my plans and used the magic at the same time. The result is a world that no one wanted, a world that appears to achieve all that I desired, but that carries deep within it the horrible memories of the old world, readying to emerge. And they finally have."

Dirt didn't understand at all what he was talking about. His rambling, idealistic manner of speech reminded her of Verdi.

"So you bring those beasts, eh?" someone asked.

His face grew heavy.

"Yes. They are here because of me and my siblings. You know their names. Abidon. Ijiri. Eghodo. Oduma."

He is madmad, Dirt thought. He just claimed the Mamas and Papas to be his brothers and sisters. Next, maybe he would claim that he himself—

"And I am Useyi," he said.

Silence.

The God of Forgotten Memories was the most feared being in all the Isle. There was no worse fate than being forgotten, than being relegated to His hands. It was not a name used lightly, and it was unimaginable that anyone would claim the name for their own.

But it just couldn't be possible. Useyi was a God. This was just a man.

"What he says is true," Antie Yaya said. She slid her eyes across the assembly with a full understanding of the weight of what she was saying. "I have known Useyi since he was a boy. I have known all the children—the ones you call the Mamas and Papas—since they were young. This world is their doing, and the monsters we see today are the result of their error."

The silence yawned on, and Dirt knew that each girl was struggling to understand the implications of what Antie Yaya was saying. She *knows* the Gods? The Gods are just people? Were the other Gods across the water, where Mister Od—where Useyi had come from?

"The only way to stop the monsters is to close the Fault," Useyi said. "That is the wound at the heart of this world from which these creatures, these Remnants, flow. For that, I had hoped to find the strongest Bower to help me get there. But I was too slow."

"So instead, you must all return home," Antie Yaya said. "Go and protect your Fam. Useyi and I will decide who we need to help close the Fault, and we will come get you when the time is right."

Dirt didn't move, and she saw that no one else did either. They were still struggling to understand. For all of Dirt's life, she had looked forward to becoming a Sis. In her eyes, that was as big and as powerful as a girl could be, competing in the arena before thousands, being admired all across the South. Even in the last year, on the cusp of womanhood, that feeling hadn't changed. Being an adult felt smaller than being a champion.

Useyi's revelation had changed that. There was an entire world full of people fighting and suffering that she didn't know about. There was a wound in the world filled with creatures she'd never heard of. For the first time in a long time, Dirt felt small.

An inhuman roar from the jungle turned every head. There, another swarm of monsters stood. It was as if the jungle itself had turned against them, moving as a unit to wipe them out.

"Godskins, with me!" Antie Yaya shouted. "Everyone else, run! Go home! And prepare yourselves for the battles to come!"

21

Shapes in the Dark

TIGGI HAD NEVER been afraid of the jungle before.

The jungle was home. Filled with pretty colors and tasty fruit and lots of cute animals. In the daytime, it was their training grounds, with well-worn paths for their runs. Even at night, it held a special coziness, so big and quiet that it was easy to find solitude in, to take a few steps away and feel like you were in a new world, with crickets and your own thoughts the only sounds.

But now she knew better.

As she marched through the jungle she stayed tight beside her sisters, and they did the same to her. Every eye was focused on the dark spaces beyond the glow of Sis Swoo's torch, watchful. No one spoke; their ears were trained on the crunch of dried leaves beneath their feet, the innocent crackle of torch fire, and the occasional owl's hoot. The jungle was no longer a safe place. It was a den of twisted creatures, of beasts that could rival a Godskin in power.

Of the monsters who had taken … something …

Tiggi couldn't actually remember anything bad happening. One moment she'd been running for her life toward the Imperial Temple, and the next she was looking back at Sis Swoo and Sis Dirt and something felt wrong. There were tears in her eyes and a pain in her gut, and she didn't understand where either had come from.

Since then, Tiggi hadn't stop shivering, despite the stifling, humid heat of the night.

Sis Swoo suddenly stopped, causing wave after wave of Mud Bibi to bump into the girls ahead of them. There were whispers ahead, first Sis Swoo's voice, then another, deeper one. Through the harsh glow of the torch, Tiggi could only make out a large figure across from Swoo, but she couldn't tell who it was. Instead, she let her eyes drift back to the jungle, where in the twinkling dark she saw another shape—large and shadowed and still.

"Sis Swoo!" Tiggi shrieked. She scrambled backward, stumbling over the sisters beside her.

Then the panic started. Most of the Mud Sisters didn't even see what Tiggi had seen; they just saw her reaction and were so strained from the day that they immediately began screaming and scrambling and tugging in every direction, trying to flee while simultaneously too scared to leave the group.

"Stop!" Sis Swoo screamed, rushing over to the Bibi. "Stop, they are Bowers!"

Sis Swoo calmed them in small groups, laying her hands on shoulders, bringing her face in line with the Bibi, forcing their attention away from the shadowed form. Only then did Tiggi realize that there was far more than just the one shadow. There were dozens of varying sizes, but most held the firm, bulbous belly of a

Bower, not the grotesque form of the monsters from earlier. Her eyes adjusted until she was able to make out the pale-blue short shirts and pants of Creek sisters. She breathed a sigh of relief, as did her fellow Mud sisters. The Bibi all giggled quietly from embarrassment and relief.

Once order was restored, they continued their trek, but now the Creek's scouts had joined them, their torches pushing back against the stalking night. Yet while they were all trekking together, Sis Dirt was back at the Imperial Temple, fighting for the lives of every girl and boy on the Isle. Her absence was noticeable, and not just in the lack of her large physique at the lead of the Fam. It was in the slouched shoulders of each girl, in the deepening frown of Sis Swoo's face.

The column suddenly came to another halt. Sis Swoo walked up and down the ranks, holding the light so as to get a good look at each girl, her frown fixing itself further into her features.

Eventually, she stepped back, gave the Mud Bibi a final sweeping look, then spoke with a voice that was unable to hide its fear.

"Where is Bibi Snore?" she asked.

Snore never doubted this day would come. None of the other sisters seemed to accept it. Stupid. Even now that it was here, they wanted to hide at camp. "Defend" themselves.

But defending was for losers. The only way to end what was coming was to attack. To attack with endless ferocity until the enemy was gone forever. The other sisters didn't understand that. Not even Sis Swoo.

So once she had a chance, Snore broke off from the Mud Fam, striding into the jungle with only the stars to light her steps. Unlike the other girls, she didn't need a torch. The jungles of the Isle were her home. She refused to be afraid. Besides, there was no creature waiting in the dark that was more dangerous than Bibi Snore.

She soon found the path she was looking for. To any other eyes, it wasn't a path at all, just the scant air between two short shrubs. But Snore recognized it by more than her eyes. It was the smell of it, the *feel*. She recognized the passing of a jungle cat as surely as she knew her own hands.

After following the path for a while, she came to the top of a hill, overlooking a round area with thinned trees. It was an unremarkable clearing, but for the lone jungle cat sitting patiently at its center. Of course, most people would only see that one cat. But Snore knew them now, fully. She could see the three dozen cats: some perched in the branches above, their pale-yellow fur near invisible in the moonlight; some down on the jungle floor, melding into tree trunks and leaf piles, the lazy but alert languishing that only cats had mastered.

Snore looked down upon her new Cat Fam, then raised an arm in the air, fingers curled like claws. Her sisters each raised a paw, returning the salute.

"Is time," she said.

Jungle cats do not nod. They do not agree the way humans do. They simply take action. As one, they stood, padding down from trees, shaking off leaves, slinking out from their hiding spots. Whereas before they'd been nearly invisible, now even a stranger would have seen them. And that stranger would have understood that they weren't moving to play.

They were moving to war.

From Mud to Rock

"QUICKQUICK, you scampering frogs!" Swoo boomed. She was standing in the ring at the center of the Mud camp. The Bibi scrambled around her like an agitated anthill, sisters crisscrossing this way and that with loads in their arms. "I will not have na monsters eat me because of you lazy lot!"

Swoo had thought of it from every angle but came to the same conclusion every time: they had to evacuate the Mud camp. Mister Odo—or Useyi, a fact Swoo was still having trouble understanding—had made it clear that the monsters would not stop coming until the Isle itself was fixed. Maybe the Godskins could achieve that by working together. Maybe.

But that wasn't a risk Swoo could take. If those monsters got past the Godskins and found the Mud camp . . .

Swoo hadn't stopped thinking about Snore. She wanted to be upset with the girl for pulling her disappearing trick now, of all times. But she couldn't. Snore had been there the last time the Mud Fam was attacked. She had been the victim of it. Of course the girl would rather flee than risk being attacked again in her own home. At least then she'd had Sis Webba to protect her. Even a one-legged Sis Webba was a better protector than Swoo, yet Sis Webba had fallen all the same and Snore had been abducted by their enemies.

The Vine had only kept Snore chained. These monsters would do far worse.

Na Gods protect us, Swoo prayed, but she wasn't sure if her prayers even meant anything anymore. The Gods were just people, apparently. Just some boys and girls who had made a mistake and created a world that no one understood. What did it matter to pray to such people?

"Sis Swoo."

Swoo was pulled away from her thoughts to find a Bibi, Tempo, looking up at her with a question on her face and her arms full of squirming, squawking chickens.

"Should we bring na chickens?" she asked.

Only then did Swoo fully accept that they were leaving the Mud camp. Before responding, she looked about, taking in the bustle of the young Bibi, who were putting their panic into preparation. She took in the soft sand between her toes and the tall ring of trees around the camp. The scent of the Mud Offer, like brewed orange skins, and the distinct weight of the air, heavy and warm on the skin. Lastly, she took in the sleep lodge they'd only just built to house all their new Bibi and the old sleep hut that had become Sis Dirt's home, the place where Swoo had shared so many memories with Sis Webba and Sis Dirt, Nana, and Snore, curled up with each other every night during the best times and the worst.

She cursed the tears that began to build in her eyes. When had she become so weepy?

"Bring na chickens," she said. Then added a "thank you," just because it felt right.

Tempo returned to packing with the other Bibi, and in minutes everything of value in the camp was loaded into wooden wagons that had been hastily built from the disassembled wood of the sleep huts. The plan was to head for the Rock Fam territory along the coast. Not only was it the farthest point from where the monsters were, but the Rock camp was said to be the most hidden and well-protected. Swoo would need their help if she intended to keep the Bibi safe. She couldn't do it on her own.

She was grateful for how disciplined the little ones were on the trek. They had yet to sleep since the attack at the Imperial Temple, and it had been hours since their last meal. Yet not a one of them complained. On their own, they took turns letting some girls sleep in the wagons while others pulled, ensuring that everyone was able to take a short break. The strongest girls took extra shifts pulling, and the weakest thanked the others for allowing them to rest. Swoo almost couldn't believe these were the same girls who had spent the NoBe tournament making each other cry. Yet it seemed they took cooperation as seriously as they took competition.

Or maybe that shared feeling—that mysterious sense of loss—made them realize how much they needed to take care of each other.

As they transitioned from the swelter of the jungle to crisp coastal air, from uneven bulging roots beneath their feet to the sinking softness of beach sand, Swoo felt a swell of pride at all that her Mud sisters had accomplished. It was matched only by her fear that it would all be taken from them if the Godskins were overrun.

Stay strong, Sis Dirt, Swoo prayed. *For you and for all of us.*

Swoo and the Mud Bibi waited at the beach, the cliffs to their right. They could scarcely see the water in the dark of night, but they could hear its movement like great, deep breaths. Somewhere across the sea, Swoo realized, was where Useyi had come from. Not a divine land, but a place full of war and death and misery. Things he had brought with him that day he'd washed against the rocks below.

"Sis Swoo?" a voice asked. She looked down to find Tiggi beside her, also staring out toward the horizon, where the black of the sea met the black of the sky.

"Eh heh," Swoo replied.

"Will we be fine?" Tiggi asked.

Swoo resisted every urge. The urge to sigh. The urge to admit that she didn't know. The urge to tell the girl to take her stupid, scary questions and go sit with the other girls. The girl was afraid. Swoo thought of Sis Webba and Sis Dirt and all the times they'd comforted her when she was afraid.

She smiled down at the Bibi. "Finefine," she said.

Just then, there was the slightest rustling in the trees behind them, and Swoo spun, taking up a Bowing stance, preparing to give her life if it meant protecting the Bibi. But there were no monsters emerging from the bush. Instead, it was just other Bowers—blessed, normal Bowers—each of them in the gray half shirt and baggy pants of the Rock.

"Sis Swoo . . . ," one of the girls said. She was bigger than the others, with a great, muscled belly and a thick face. Her hair was in two braids tight to her head that curled like ram's horns. Sis Ask. She traced her gaze around the Mud sisters, a small smile on her face as she extended an open, beckoning hand.

"Welcome to na Rock."

Sis Ask led them up a rocky hill along the coast. Swoo had been to the area dozens of times, by herself, with Dirt, and even with some of the new Bibi. But Sis Ask led them across unfamiliar stones. These rocks were not quite so slick and sharp, but instead sturdier, rounder. Swoo couldn't tell at which point they'd crossed from the familiar rocks of the cliffs to this new space.

"Where is this?" Swoo asked.

Sis Ask smirked. "You think you know this Isle so well, eh? Today there is much you will learn."

They soon reached a jagged mound, three times the height of a Sis. On its face was an opening just large enough to walk into. Once they entered, it was completely black, even darker than the starlit night. Swoo couldn't see her own hand in front of her face, and she had to feel her feet forward to test the uneven ground before committing to any step.

"Bibi, take care," she called out, and was met with the unmistakable sound of children falling over each other.

A short while and several scraped knees later, the world came alive with light. Swoo squinted, raising her hand to shield her eyes from the sudden flare.

Before her was an entire world made of stone. Below her, in a yawning basin that must have been hundreds of strides in every direction, sat dozens of rounded stone homes. Each had a tall stick planted in front of it, with thin, colorful ribbons tied up its length. Swoo had never been inside a cave before, and she was surprised that it held a nice breeze, a light flow of pleasantly cool air.

As much time as Swoo had spent with the Rock girls, she hadn't given much thought to how they lived. She'd assumed they just slept on the rocks along the cliffs, waking up under the sun. There were only twenty or so of them; she'd never imagined they lived in such an enormous camp, far bigger than even the Vine's.

Sis Ask chuckled. "You do not expect this, eh?"

Swoo shook her head. "You senseless dogs live wellwell, eh?"

Sis Ask cackled at that, then continued forward, making her way down a long, even ramp that led them from the mouth of the cave down onto the central dirt path that cut through the array of stone homes. Given the late hour, Sis Ask seemed to be the only sister awake, but Swoo knew they had watchers patrolling the areas around the camp as well. Either way, as they passed by the rows of homes, Swoo kept expecting to see sisters inside, playing a game or singing or at least sleeping in clumps. Instead, most of the homes were completely empty, their large dark mouths seeming to yearn to be filled with life.

"Any house you see empty is for you and your sisters," Sis Ask said.

Swoo passed the information on, telling the Bibi to go get some rest. To Swoo's surprise, they didn't immediately run to claim a sleeping place. Instead, they formed into a line. Tiggi was at the front, and she approached Swoo with her sad, tired heart clear in her eyes.

"Na good night, Sis Swoo," she said, then surprised Swoo with a tight, warm hug. Swoo just managed to return it before Tiggi disconnected and went off to bed.

One by one, the Bibi gave Swoo a hug and bade her good

night before departing. When they were finished, Swoo watched in stunned silence as they retired to their new homes, groups of three and four settling in together.

"Goodgood girls, eh?" Sis Ask said.

Swoo grunted. "So it seems."

"Yet here you are."

Swoo had told Ebe to send a Butterfly girl to the Rock to let them know the Mud were coming to stay. It wasn't lost on her the direness of the request. A girl was not supposed to know the location of any camp but her own. Swoo would never forget how closely she'd had to follow behind the Vine to find their camp, and even then they had nearly lost her. Asking the location of another Fam was taken as a pledge of loyalty, a vow that the secrets divulged would never be used against them. Among Bowers, such cooperation was only expected under the most dire of circumstances.

"We must speak" was all Swoo said.

Sis Ask read the weight in Swoo's words. "I will not like this speaking of ours, eh?"

Swoo shook her head. "You will not."

When Swoo finished explaining, Sis Ask just stared.

Then she let out a peal of laughter, slapping her belly.

"I do not know you can tell such stories, Sis Swoo. You must teach Antie Yaya."

"I am no storyteller," Swoo shot back. "And what I say is no story, it is true."

Sis Ask sighed. "Sis Swoo . . ." She raised her arms in a shrug, seemingly at a loss for words. "How can this be true, eh? These Remnant monsters? Ten Godskins?"

"Eight."

"Eight, ten, one hundred. Can you hear your own words?"

Her face was an image of skepticism: eyebrow raised, mouth pursed with doubt.

Swoo took a deep breath. They were in Sis Ask's home, a squat stone structure that was significantly bigger than the others, with a more comfortably arrayed interior. Rather than a sleep mat, her bed was a rope hammock suspended from the ceiling. She had several wicker chairs around a wooden table, atop which sat a teapot and a bowl of mushrooms picked fresh from the deeper parts of the cave. The center of the floor was covered in a thick and colorfully dyed rug, which brought life to the whole room.

That sort of comfort changed a girl's mind, Swoo knew. It would make her resist any threat to that comfort, even words. Sis Ask wanted to spend her days training with her sisters, enjoying the cave's cool breeze; she wanted to spend her nights around a fire, dancing to drums. She didn't want to enter a war, to fight against hellish beasts who had no desire but death.

Swoo couldn't blame her. But she had to find a way to get her to see the truth. The survival of the Mud depended on it.

"My sister is out there," Swoo explained. "Snore."

Sis Ask scrunched her face. "Do I know her? The little one, eh?"

Swoo nodded. "I cannot leave her out there. They will not get her."

She didn't know what it was, but something about her—her face, her voice, her palpable exhaustion—must have gotten through to Sis Ask. The perpetual smirk on her face dissipated, replaced by a careful curiosity.

"You do not have to tell stories of monsters to get our help, Sis Swoo," she said. "Every Bower is our sister. We must find Snore."

Sis Ask woke up five of her sisters to accompany them on the search. None of them even asked why—they simply rolled out of their homes, alert and ready for the task. Swoo realized that no other Fam patrolled their camp the way the Rock did—they had girls who were more skilled at hiding and tracking than any other Bowers in the South. Swoo felt her confidence soar as she strode with them up to the Rock camp entrance at the mouth of the cave.

It was a short-lived confidence.

Upon reaching the cave mouth, the five other sisters froze, staring off into the dark of the night.

"What is—?" Swoo began, but a raised hand from one of the Rock girls silenced her. Without any communication at all, they each fell into a fighting stance, readying for battle. Swoo looked between them in confusion. She couldn't see anything that would warrant such alarm.

Sis Ask raised a finger to get Swoo's attention, then pointed toward the ground. At first, Swoo didn't see anything but the same rock that made up the rest of the camp. But then she noticed the tiniest of pebbles sitting in a groove along one rock. The pebble was shivering.

Over the next minute, the pebble's shivering grew more rapid, until Swoo could hear the source of the rumbling. Sandals on stone, dozens of feet all trudging up the mound in unison.

Swoo's first, terrifying thought was that it was the Remnants. That they had killed the Godskins and were now on to killing the rest of the Isle.

But then the owners of the footfalls came into view, and they were not monsters at all. They were just girls, Bowers, a few dozen clad in the yellow half shirts and baggy pants of the Sand Fam. At their flanks were the Rock sentries, and the girl at the head of the group was Sis Zuna, the Sand Fam's Third.

"Na good day, sisters of na Rock," she said, then added with a hint of confusion. "Na good day, Sis Swoo."

"Sis Zuna," Sis Ask said with a nod. Her eyes browsed the group. "Where is Sis Dream? Or Sis Hari?"

There was a sudden, momentary weakening of Sis Zuna's face, as if she were about to collapse into tears. But then her features firmed, resolute.

"They are taken," she said. "That is why we have come. We seek protection in na Rock camp."

Sis Ask frowned, then looked at Swoo, questioning. But Swoo shrugged—she knew no more than Sis Ask herself.

Sis Ask turned back to the Sand sisters, and for the first time since Swoo had arrived, she saw unease in her face. "Protection from who?" she asked.

"From na Vine," Sis Zuna said.

At first, Swoo didn't understand. Why, of all times, would the Vine be attacking the Sand now?

But it all made sense when Sis Zuna told her tale.

The Vine had descended from the jungle not like the victorious conquerors they usually believed themselves to be, but like wild animals fleeing from the skin-charring flames of a jungle fire. They had given no preamble, offered no explanation, simply unleashed violence on the Sand Fam, pummeling everything from Bibi to Sis. Sis Dream had ordered Sis Zuna to take the rest of the Fam and run, leaving just her and Sis Hari to fight off the entire Vine. Even before they had fully escaped the camp, Sis Zuna looked back and found her sisters being soundly beaten.

"But why?" Sis Ask questioned for what seemed like the tenth time. "Because Sis Dirt is not here to defeat them?"

"Because they are afraid," Sis Swoo said.

The two other girls looked at her, silent.

It was the only thing that made sense. Verdi and her insane prophecy. The war she had been praying for all year had finally come, and the only thing she could think to do was to fulfill what was foretold. Make Carra Carre the First of the First. While Swoo wanted to unite the Isle so they could protect each other from the Remnants, Verdi wanted to unite the Isle to rule it, to have them protect her from the Remnants.

When Swoo explained as much, Sis Ask quietly bit her lip for a while before letting loose a loud howl of pure frustration.

"Monsters and Verdi . . . ," she grumbled. "Chaaaiii!"

After that, Sis Ask devoted half of her Sis to fortifying the camp—rollable barricades, false entrances, secret exits. They needed to make sure that, when the Remnants inevitably came, the girls living inside the Rock camp would be able to hide.

While the Rock sisters fortified the camp, Swoo led a party out in search of Snore. Before, she had been afraid that Snore would end up in the hands of the Remnants. Now, she had to worry about the Vine getting her. Again. Snore hadn't been the same since that day. Swoo would never know what the Vine did to her, but she had done everything in her power to make them suffer for it. The thought of Snore back in the hands of the Vine brought sweat to Swoo's brow and a hot sickness to the back of her throat. She couldn't allow that to happen again.

She wouldn't.

They searched in a spiral, starting from the Rock camp and roaming outward in growing loops. There were moments of hope—small footprints in a soft patch of mud. But those always turned out to be the prints of jungle cats, not of a young Bibi or even the larger feet of her potential Sis captors. At the end of the first day, there was nothing new pointing them toward Snore.

The second day, Swoo was determined. She woke before the sun and was out at first light. They did not rest. They did not eat. Swoo kept them searching until the sun went down and even hours after, scouring the jungle by torchlight.

All to no avail.

"It is dark, Sis Swoo," said one of the Rock sisters. "We must go back, eh?"

In the old days, Swoo had hated Sis Dirt for how easily she accepted failure. For Swoo, failure was always unacceptable, always the result of weakness more than anything else. If success was not within a girl's power, the answer was not to give up. The answer was to gain more power. When the Vine had taken Snore, Swoo had found power in axe and flame. But now . . .

She returned to camp that night unable to speak around the lump in her throat. The Rock sisters were kind enough to give her the space she needed, and after checking in on the Bibi, she retired to her room to spend time alone, surrounded only by cold stone and regretful thoughts.

All her life, she had wanted to be the big sister. The one to lead the charge, the one the other girls could depend on. She had given everything to the life of the Bower—from long days to broken bones. Yet she would never be enough, she realized. No matter how hard she worked or how clever she became or how faithful she was, she would always come up short.

Dirt was the opposite. Whatever the challenge, she rose to it, no matter how unprepared she'd been. Dirt would have found Snore. Somehow, in some way, whether through her own power or that of the Gods. Sis Webba, too—she could have charmed the Vine into releasing her. Of all the Firsts of the Mud Fam, going back into time before memory, none had overseen such calamity in the Fam.

None except Swoo.

It was a feeling as dismal as anything she had ever known, and she was certain that, if no other good could be taken from the circumstance, at least she knew things could not possibly get worse.

And yet they did.

23

Five Must Go

DIRT LET LOOSE a long, shaking breath.

Her clothes were tattered. Her muscles aflame. Beside her, the other Godskins were the same. Together, they'd fought off wave after wave of the Remnants, and they wore the wounds to prove it. Here and there, flesh was streaked red with blood from where claws had blazed a trail through skin. Sis Frog had lost a tooth to a hammer-fisted monstrosity. Sis Avhen was limping badly until a concerned Sis Bear went to her aid.

Only Sis Namaji had left the battle unscathed. Early in the fight, she'd called the trees of the jungle to her, the trunks splitting themselves in the air and attaching to her skin, armor that had proven too tough for the Remnants to break through. She had single-handedly made a dent in the monsters' charge, taking on dozens of them at once.

Yet even Sis Namaji wore exhaustion on her face.

"You ripe?" a voice asked, and Dirt turned to see Carra Carre approaching, a cup of water in hand. Dirt took the cup and downed it in a single gulp, relishing the cool soothing of her parched throat before responding.

"There is no more ripe," she replied, her eyes on the tree line. It had been almost two days, with only an hour or so between attacks, and there was no sign of coming relief. Antie Yaya and Useyi were watching from the Imperial Temple, supposedly thinking up an escape plan. But before such a plan was produced, the monsters would come again. Again and again and again. "I grow tired, my Sis."

Dirt hadn't meant to say that. "My Sis" was a term of endearment reserved for close friends, those girls who had shared the battlefield of the Bowing arena together for years, grieved each other's losses and celebrated each other's victories. The slip of a tired tongue.

"I understand . . . ," Carra Carre replied.

"We cannot go on like this for long," Dirt quickly continued, glossing over the discomfort they clearly both felt. "Useyi has said they number like na stars. We will soon fail."

"We, yes," Carra Carre conceded. "But she?" She nodded her head over at Sis Namaji, who was tending to her fellow Sis from the East, Sis Hammuh. "She can fight forever, eh?"

"Even she must tire," Dirt said. "And when she tires . . ."

They shared a look, each unwilling to voice how helpless they felt.

Carra Carre looked away, thoughtful. "We must enter na Fault," she eventually said.

Dirt had come to the same conclusion. Useyi had told them where the beasts were coming from, and that he'd planned to have the winners of the tournament go in and end the horde. They couldn't survive many more attacks. They could either go immediately or wait until they had no more strength to go at all.

She nodded. "We must."

Dirt and Carra Carre found Antie Yaya standing beneath the Imperial Temple entrance. Her eyes were blank, staring into the distance. Her face was as slack and lifeless as Dirt had ever seen it. It was clear she had not been sleeping at all, and she suddenly looked much older.

"Is it time?" she asked.

Dirt remained silent, unsure of what she meant. Only then did Antie Yaya seem to notice her and Carra Carre, despite the fact that they loomed over her. Her eyes receded from the distance, shifting between their faces.

"Speak," she said.

"Antie Yaya," Dirt began, "na Godskins grow tired. It is not long until we can no longer fight."

"Sis Ahven already cannot," Carra Carre added. "Her leg is finished."

"I saw that. I . . . ," Antie Yaya's face faltered, twitching into somberness. "I am truly sorry, girls. I never imagined it would end this way."

"It need not," Carra Carre said, crossing her arms with all the endless appetite for a fight that Dirt had come to appreciate about her.

Antie Yaya raised an eyebrow.

"We will go into na Fault," Dirt explained. "Let na other Godskins stay. We will go and fight and use na magic to close this wound in na Isle."

Carra Carre added an emphatic nod.

But Antie Yaya didn't say anything. She just shook her head, and as she did, something cracked within her like the first break in a dam—just a single stream of water at first, then a flood. That ever serene and knowing mask collapsed, and what lay behind it was a woman consumed by fear, helpless to protect herself against beasts that children were fighting for her. Fighting and falling to injury and fatigue.

Dirt didn't want to watch. But she couldn't look away. Seeing complete defeat on Antie Yaya's face was like cold water poured on the nape, a frigid alarm of a feeling. Dirt hadn't realized Antie Yaya was capable of crying. There was no surer sign of how desperate their situation was.

Beyond desperate. Hopeless.

"Five must go," a voice said.

From behind Antie Yaya, emerging from the shadowed floor of the Imperial Temple, was Useyi. He, too, wore the scars of sleeplessness on his face, with deep, dark pockets beneath his eyes, his skin wan and sapped of life.

"Only five," he said.

"Why?" Dirt asked.

Useyi looked at her for a while in silence, his jaw tight with emotion. "That is my doing. I had hoped my siblings and I would fix it together."

When creating the new world, he had tried to ensure that any big decision required all of them to cooperate. It would be a way to keep them working as a team, rather than the fractured group they had long been.

"Your hope is failure," Dirt said coldly when Useyi was finished explaining. "A failure *we* must now suffer."

Did he expect her to pity him? He was not some foolish Flagga boy, fresh from Antie Yaya's cradle. He was a grown adult, he and all his siblings. It was their fault half the Godskins of the Isle were injured.

"I understand," Carra Carre said, prompting an incredulous glance from Dirt. "Sometimes to protect your Fam, you must hurt another."

Useyi had the sense to give Carra Carre a sheepish nod of thanks, but Dirt would extend him no such courtesy. Not until she knew her sisters and all the children of the Isle were safe.

"So we must find three others," Dirt noted.

"I will go," came Sis Bear's grumbly voice.

She and Sis Ahven approached from behind, the latter with an arm around the tall shoulders of her sister.

"I will not," Sis Ahven said with a self-deprecating raise of her eyebrows.

"When must we go?" Sis Bear asked.

"We need two others," Carra Carre said.

The only problem was that they couldn't get two others. When they returned to ask the other Godskins to join, none of them were interested.

"Go and do what, eh? I do not know this 'magic.'"

"Why five? Why not eighty-five?"

"I cannot fight one more, and you ask me to fight all of them?"

It was Sis Namaji who spoke what every girl was feeling.

"And when I am down in this Fault," she said, "who will protect na Trunk, eh?"

Dirt was having the same thought. If anything happened to her down in the Fault, the Mud would have no protection. But not the Mud. Swoo and the Bibi would be helpless, dreaming in sleep while unaware that death was rolling across the Isle toward them.

After Sis Namaji's words, they all went quiet. Half of them were trying to figure out reasons to go into the Fault, while the other half were trying to find the opportunity to leave.

It was Sis Frog who finally spoke.

"Where are they?" she asked.

"Who?" Sis Hammuh replied.

"Na Remnants."

Immediately, a growing terror seized Dirt, her heart beating in her throat. For the last two days, the creatures had come regularly. Once they defeated a wave of them, they had maybe an hour before another wave arrived.

But Dirt looked up at the sky and saw the sun approaching the horizon. It had been nearly four hours since the last attack. She wished she could believe that they had defeated all the creatures, but she knew better.

Something was wrong.

"How did na Remnants know to attack na arena?" Sis Ahven asked.

All eyes turned to Useyi, even Antie Yaya's. But he raised his arms, palms up and uncertain. "I don't know," he said. "I don't understand them any better than the rest of you. I just know that they are trying to restore the old world."

"How?" Dirt asked, nearly unable to get the words through her fear-tight throat.

"By making us forget what is new. They can sense anything of this new world. Once they find it, they wipe it from memory."

Dirt suddenly realized why there were no more monsters. Useyi was from the old world. Antie Yaya was from the old world. The only ones native to the new world were the children of the Isle.

Before, most of them had been assembled at the Imperial Temple. Now, the temple held just the ten Godskins. The rest of the children were . . .

"Na Mud," Dirt said, just as every other Godskin uttered her own Fam's name.

The jungle blurred by as Dirt ran. She was filled with the power of her Godskin, each footstep launching her a dozen strides forward. Her heart was trying to hammer free of her ribs, as much from the terror that seized her as from the exertion of her running. The last time the Mud camp had been attacked, Dirt had been too late, and the cost had been Snore's innocence and Webba's body. Dirt could not allow such a loss again.

"Sis Dirt, breathe easy, eh?" Carra Carre said beside her, calling loudly over the wind rushing across their ears. "You must save power to fight."

Dirt didn't respond. Carra Carre could not understand. The Vine had always been powerful. They had dozens of full Sis, even more NoBe. There would be girls at the Vine camp old enough and wise enough to get the young ones to safety.

At the Mud, there was only Swoo. A new Sis trying to bring some order to fifty crying and panicking Bibi as the Remnants began a massacre.

The thought only urged her on.

"Sis Dirt . . . ," Carra Carre warned.

Soon, Dirt had no choice but to slow. The jungle began thickening around them, choking tighter and tighter with an endless line of fat vines dangling heavy ahead. Dirt looked about in confusion.

"Where is this?"

"We are near na Vine," Carra Carre said, then she took a deep breath.

Dirt hadn't given any thought to what the Vine did after Swoo burned down their camp, but it made sense that they had relocated deeper into the Isle, where they were even harder to discover than before. Dirt had never been to this part of the Isle. She searched out a gap in the leaves and branches above, then used the stars to reorient herself.

"Then this is where we part," she said.

She extended an arm, but Carra Carre only stared at it for a moment before raising her gaze to Dirt's eyes.

"Come with me," Carra Carre said.

Dirt scoffed, turned in the direction of the Mud camp, and was ready to continue on her way, but Carra Carre grabbed her by the shoulder.

"If na Remnants attack na Mud," Carra Carre said, "they must pass na Vine first. If they are here, then it is here we can stop them. Together."

Dirt shrugged off Carra Carre's hand and continued toward the Mud camp. Months ago, they had been bitter enemies. Then, briefly, they had formed a friendship. But Carra Carre was not a sister of the Mud—Dirt owed her nothing, especially when the Mud camp could be being wiped out as they spoke.

Yet Carra Carre's words reverberated in Dirt's mind and brought her feet to a halt. She was right. If the Remnants were going from the Imperial Temple to attack the rest of the Isle, they would stop at the Vine first. Not only was it filled with the most people of any Bower camp, but it was directly on the path from the Imperial Temple to the rest of the South.

And when she thought of fighting the Remnants alone . . . her body was exhausted. Her mind as well. One slip of the foot, one missed evasion, and she would be dead. Gone. Forgotten. Dirt could still remember Swoo and Nana and Snore, but what if there were sisters she'd already forgotten? Had the Remnants already taken some?

The only thing worse than reaching her sisters too late would be to reach her sisters too late and be too weak to do anything.

Dirt turned back to Carra Carre.

"If na Remnants are here, we fight," she said. "If they are not"— Carra Carre's face clenched at that—"we go to na Mud. Quickquick."

She extended an arm, and Carra Carre took it.

"Quickquick," she agreed.

24

A Search for Sisters

IF A BATTLE was raging, it was the most silent battle ever known.

Carra Carre was just outside camp, ear against the wall of woven vines that surrounded the homes and training ground. There was a detachable piece of the wall not far from where they stood, but she was hesitant. She realized suddenly how foolish it was to bring Dirt to their new camp. If the Remnants weren't there and Verdi was . . .

Carra Carre pulled away from the wall and took a calming breath. At this time of day, hours before sundown, the camp should have been a frothing soup of noise and energy: Bibi chasing each other about, NoBe hasty to keep them in line, Sis ending the day with hard sparring. But there was none of that. Just silence.

In her mind, she saw bones and blood, the broken bodies of her sisters mangled and strewn in every direction as Remnants hovered over them, silence through violence. She checked her memory, running through the names of the girls of the Vine, senselessly trying to decipher whether she'd forgotten some. Of course, she couldn't think of any.

"What are you doing?" Dirt whispered.

"Nothing," Carra Carre replied. "Come."

She led Dirt over to the hidden entrance, reaching in between twisting vines to grab the small latch that unlocked a narrow section of the wall from the rest of it. She moved the detached section to the side, then took a deep breath.

Not just for yourself, but for your sisters, she thought, and power rushed into her, easing her anxieties, cleansing her mind.

Dirt raised an eyebrow but said nothing before diving into her own Godskin power.

With a final breath, Carra Carre charged into camp.

Gone was the powerful River coursing beneath it. Gone were the vines descending from high to low, connecting every girl to every other with a quick slide. Gone was The Climb, that singular rope dangling from the highest height above a plummet into the River's impatient waters.

The new Vine camp was a circular clearing of hastily built wooden huts. It held none of the splendor of their old home, instead doing just enough to house the Vine's two hundred girls. Carra Carre had built most of the homes herself, working late on that first night they'd settled there.

And it was empty. There was not a single girl in sight, no hens in the pen. Even the new dogs they'd begun training were gone. It was as if a cruel storm had swept through the camp, carrying every living thing into the jungle but leaving the buildings untouched.

"What is this?" Carra Carre muttered to herself. She ducked into a few huts, checked behind the garden and over by the clothesline, peered out into the trees to see if she could make out any movement in the darkening jungle.

Nothing.

The last time Carra Carre had returned home to such confusion was when Dirt's young sister, Swoo, had attacked the Vine. The stench of soot had hung in her nose for weeks, and she still couldn't start a fire without a pang of fear swelling up in her.

But at least then she had known her sisters were safe. She had known that the Fam had survived. Now, she couldn't even be sure of that. Her stomach felt like a wet shirt being wrung up tighter and tighter, and a nausea came with it.

"We will find them," Dirt said.

Carra Carre looked at her and was surprised to see how firm and resolute her face was.

"I still remember your sisters," Dirt continued. "As do you. They are somewhere. And we will find them, together."

Carra Carre didn't know what to say. She still felt sick with fear for what could have happened to her sisters. But Dirt's words had unwrung the tightness in her stomach, just a little.

"But that is for later," Dirt continued before Carra Carre could respond. "Now we must go to na Mud."

The Mud Camp was no different.

The big sleep hall was empty, and all the chickens were gone. Even the garden had been taken, with small divots of churned up red soil sitting where fruits and vegetables should have been.

Carra Carre watched in silence as Dirt roamed the camp, realizing that she must have looked the same back at the Vine camp. Eyebrows furrowed, lips pursed, eyes tinged with fear.

In the same way that the barren Vine camp had reminded Carra Carre of Swoo's attack, Carra Carre knew that the abandoned Mud camp must have reminded Dirt of the Vine's attack, when Webba had been injured. Carra Carre would never fully forgive herself for that. It was the most vicious thing she'd ever done, unfettered by the rules and rituals of Bowing. At the time, she'd believed it to be necessary. It had seemed the only way to guarantee the Vine's victory. And the Vine had indeed won.

But what had come of it? Verdi had been maimed and would never again hear fully. The recruits had been more inspired by Dirt fighting against all odds than they had been by the Vine's underhanded victory. Now that the Gods had returned, as Verdi predicted, the Vine was even less powerful than they had been before, less prepared to lead the Bowers of the Isle against the Remnants.

"I am sorry, Sis Dirt," Carra Carre said.

Dirt continued to investigate the camp, like a dog with a scent.

"I see no attack here," she said. "My sisters take everything and go. Much like your Vine sisters. So where is it they go?"

"I do not know," Carra Carre replied. "But we must look."

As far as she could tell, anywhere was just as likely as anywhere else. Whether they'd built a new camp or were hiding in the jungle or had traveled to the North, the only way to find their missing sisters was to get out and search. And time was running low.

"No . . . ," Dirt replied. "Swoo cannot go and not . . ."

Suddenly, Dirt froze, eyes on the narrow sleep hut. The last time Carra Carre had been at the Mud camp, that had been the only building there was. Dirt had tossed Verdi through it. Even though they'd built a much larger sleep hall for the recruits, they'd taken the time to rebuild the original hut, with all the same shoddiness it had held before destruction. The only difference was . . .

"Swoo's handaxe," Dirt said.

She walked over to the side of the structure and reached up to grab the handle lodged into its roof. Carra Carre had never seen the axe before, but she wasn't surprised to learn that a wild young girl like Swoo would have her own personal weapon.

"Why is it here?" Dirt mumbled. She kept a hand on the axe but didn't pull on it, instead looking between the axe and the rest of the empty camp.

"Take na axe and let us go, Sis Dirt," Carra Carre said. "Na daylight leaves us."

As she spoke, a ray of sun caught the axe blade. The sky was the turbulent orange-purple of sunset, and though Carra Carre couldn't see the sun from within the camp, she knew it was drifting toward the horizon, its lighting skimming just above the trees.

"Na West," Dirt mumbled. Then again, louder. "From na West."

She looked from the axe toward the distant horizon, her eyes following the sun's light. Then, with a satisfied nod, she yanked the axe out of the wood and slipped the handle into her waistband.

"I do not know where your sisters are," Dirt said. "But when we meet mine, we can search with more girls, eh?"

Carra Carre frowned. "Who says we will find yours first?"

"They are West," Dirt replied, trudging back into the trees, a confident hope in her stride. "With na Rock."

25

One Last Bow

THE FIRST Remnant struck before any of them were prepared. It was a monstrous beast, a crab with giant armored paws rather than claws and two narrow bird's legs. One of the Sand girls, oblivious to the approaching danger, was taken from behind and swallowed into its arms. Girl and Remnant instantly disappeared, and a moment later none could recall that the girl had ever existed.

But they all knew something horrible would happen if the Remnants caught them.

Swoo leapt into action, but she was wiser now and knew better than to attack the Remnants herself. Instead, she retreated toward the mouth of the Rock camp and yelled hard enough to fray her throat.

"INSIDE! NOW!"

She'd hoped to shock them into alertness, and for some she did—Sand and Rock girls heard her voice and immediately began running toward the cave entrance. But others remained enthralled, and a few even tried to fight, taking up Bowing stances and trusting their martial skills to protect them.

Swoo couldn't blame them, but they were fools all the same. As more Remnants charged down from the rocky hills north of the camp and snatched them up, they winked one by one out of existence, and one by one out of Swoo's memory, until she was left with just the memory of foolishness, with no girls to attribute it to.

Soon they were all running. Running and screaming, pleading as they were dragged into a Remnant's cold arms, crying out to their sisters before being yanked into nothingness. More Remnants poured down upon them, a mudslide of blue translucence. Swoo watched from just outside the camp, urging on the girls who rushed past her into the dark safety of the cave. Each time a Bower disappeared, so too did a Remnant. But for every Remnant that disappeared, three seemed to take its place, until Swoo realized that there were no more Bowers left. Everything coming toward her was a monster.

Only then did she step back into the shadow of the cave.

"Close it," she said, defeated.

From beside the entryway, a team of Rock sisters laid their weight into a giant boulder, shifting it in a slow roll. With each moment, the Remnants drew closer, and the boulder crept across the opening with all the urgency of clouds passing in front of the sun. Swoo stayed where she was, just inside the entrance. If the Remnants got in, she would be the first to die, to be forgotten. If that was how it had to happen, then so be it. She was the only one who had seen the Remnants beforehand and knew what they were capable of—it was her responsibility to protect the others.

The Remnant at the front of the horde had a bee head the size of a hippo's, and its body was like a crocodile's, long and scaled and swimming across the earth on stumpy legs. Its massive half-moon eyes were focused entirely on Swoo, and its mandibles were snapping feverishly in anticipation as it drew closer and closer and closer and—

That was when the boulder slammed home with a rumbling crash of stone against stone, sealing the opening to the Rock camp and eliminating the remaining light.

Swoo took a long, deep breath.

"Goodgood," she said, then turned to the Rock sisters. "Go and check na other defenses. We must—"

BOOOOOOM!

A drum of thunder pounded against the boulder beside Swoo. She turned in disbelief, frowning at the stone as if she must have misheard it.

BOOOOOOM!

It came again, a knock from a divine hand, smashing against the boulder with such force that Swoo felt it in her chest.

"Sis Swoo . . . ," one of the Rock sisters said, unable to keep the fear out of her voice.

BOOOOOOM!

The third knock was accompanied by a rumbling of the whole cave, with rocks and dust raining down from the ceiling atop their heads.

"Sis Swoo!" someone called again, urgent.

Of course stone would not be enough to stop them. These creatures had the strength of the Mamas and Papas, the same as Sis Dirt and the other Godskins. Dirt could easily fling a boulder out of her way or smash through it, if need be. Why would the Remnants be any different?

BOOOOOOOOOOOOM!

The fourth knock sent a blast of stone speeding into the cave. Swoo threw up her arms just in time to absorb a shower of sharp fragments, cutting her in half a dozen places and throwing her to the ground. By the time the dust settled and she uncovered her eyes, she was greeted by a beam of red sunset against her face, emerging from the large hole in the center of the boulder.

"Run!" Swoo screamed to the Rock sisters. "Go and warn na others!"

The Remnant's bee head poked into the hole, its mandibles snapping eagerly. As Swoo lay on the floor, looking up at a certain death, she realized what a coward she was being.

Pusher boys pushed goods. Butterfly girls traded. Flagga boys played.

And Bowers fought.

Bowers did not run. They did not hide. They did not set traps and barriers between themselves and their enemies. Whether victory was likely or just an ill-conceived dream, a Bower fought for herself, for her sisters, for her way of life.

I am brave. I am fat. I am Swoo.

As the bee-head Remnant squeezed more and more of its body into the hole, Swoo climbed back to her feet and steadied her mind. This, it seemed, would be the day she died. She would be grabbed in those pinching mandibles and vanished from the Isle, and the memory of her would vanish as well. Dirt, Snore, Nana, the Bibi— they would all forget her.

But just because she had to die, didn't mean she had to die quietly.

As the beast thrashed one way then the other, cracking the boulder on either side just enough to unwedge its thick, reptilian body, Swoo fell into a crouch and issued the Bowing salute. She spread her arms wide then clapped them together, sealing the contract. Once the Remnant freed itself, it stalked forward into the cave, a mere few feet away, its giant black eyes on Swoo.

One last Bow, Swoo thought.

Straight from her belly, she released the loudest shout she could manage, hoping that, wherever they were, her sisters heard and would remember this moment, if nothing else.

"For na MUD!" she roared.

Then she charged.

She wasn't stronger. She wasn't as durable. She had no claws or fangs or wings to help her. All she had was the same advantage she'd always had.

Speed.

Swoo bounced about the cramped interior of the Rock camp entrance, slipping left and right as the monster's mandibles snapped at her. Twice it cornered her, and each time she slipped just beneath its lunge, rolling painfully on the rocks and springing back to her feet in time to dodge the next attack.

All her life, she'd believed she was born for the battle of the Bowing ring. Sand and Slaps, the adoring crowd and the sharp-eyed timekeeper, glory dangling within her grasp, as long as she had the courage and skills to reach out and take it.

But she'd been wrong.

This was what she'd been born for. No sand or spectators. No chance at glory. Just survival. The dance of life and death. Her heart was beating in her throat with bone-deep fear, yet she'd never felt such a thrill before. She was grateful to have a fight like this before the end, so much so that she couldn't keep the smile from her face.

As she avoided the attacks of the monster in front of her, the other Remnants continued to break through the boulder piece by piece. But though the steady booms of their attacks rattled the Rock camp, they did not rattle Swoo's resolve. She kept her eyes on her opponent, ignoring the increasing number of cuts blooming red against her clothes, the haggard draw of each inhale, the fiery scream of every muscle.

As her body tired, the beast caught her with a headbutt, smashing her painfully against the cave wall. All the breath in her lungs rushed out, and the explosion of pressure behind her eyes made her wonder how they hadn't flown out of her skull. She crumpled to the ground, trying to keep up up and down down, orient everything to where it was supposed to be as she knew the bee's mandibles were descending toward her, ready to end it all.

A worthy end. She was at peace with it.

Yet as the seconds passed, the bee's jaws never clamped down. Instead, Swoo looked up to find the creature staring through the now large hole in the boulder. Only then did Swoo realize that the knocking of the other Remnants had stopped. It was quiet.

No. Not quiet.

There was no more pounding against the rock, but there was sound, just on the other side of the boulder. The sound of grunts and slapping flesh and heavy things hitting the ground with force.

Swoo only had a moment of confusion before Dirt's face appeared, illuminated by the day's dying light, a calm and terrifying fury etched into her face. Dirt's eyes swept the scene, immediately understanding. Then she stepped back and, with concussive force, shoulder charged through the boulder, sending the beast sprawling across the cave entrance.

Before the beast could recover, Dirt was upon it, hauling it up into the air by its back legs and smashing it into the ground in an explosion of blue shards that evaporated into smoke as soon as they touched a surface.

Dirt stared at where the Remnant had been a moment before and exhaled a forceful breath before turning to Swoo.

"You ripe, eh?"

Swoo stared back, speechless, then looked outside the cave. Carra Carre stood amidst a low haze of blue smoke, all that was left of the Remnant horde that had been beating at the entrance.

When she looked back to Dirt, she intended to simply say "thank you" and ask for a hand up. But suddenly Dirt and everything else became watery, and Swoo rubbed a forearm across her eyes.

"My Sis . . . ," Dirt said.

Those two words melted the last of Swoo's strength. The sobs that surged up from her chest were unlike anything she had felt since she was a Bibi. It was too much emotion, more than she could understand. She wasn't sure whether she was happy or scared or relieved or something else; the only thing that seemed to make sense in that moment was to cry so hard that there was nothing left of her but tears.

Then she felt Dirt kneeling in front of her and embracing her, their post-battle warmth melding together. Swoo let herself be supported by her sister's strength, be comforted by her sister's peace.

Somehow, it only made her cry more.

26

Sis Dirt's Return

TIGGI DIDN'T LIKE the Rock camp. It was too different from the Mud. Dark where the Mud camp was full of sunshine. Cool and dry where the Mud camp was hot and humid. The Rock sisters were friendly enough, but they liked to sing and dance loudly at all hours, and they played so much during training that Tiggi often felt she wasn't learning anything. Sometimes she wanted to tell them to stop being loud or to let her focus, but she was a guest, so she felt like she had to be even more polite than usual.

But then Sis Dirt arrived.

The stories reached them before Sis Dirt herself did. She had saved Swoo from Remnants. She'd saved *all* of them from Remnants, hundreds of them, by picking up a mountain and dropping it on the Remnants' heads. When Sis Dirt finally descended onto the main path at the center of the camp, she was met with a wave of cheers as every Mud, Rock, and Sand sister showed their appreciation for her valor. Tiggi stared with admiration at the God-skin, her big Sis, and a feeling of peace came over her.

That first night, there was a feast in Sis Dirt's honor. Tables were set out with platters covering every bit of them, filled with heaps of chicken and goat meat, steaming yams, and boiled mushrooms, as well as dishes with thick, red stew beside pots nearly overflowing with a special kind of rice the Rock made that was extra soft and orange and filled with flavor.

Sis Carra Carre was there, too, but everyone seemed uncomfortable with her presence, especially since she no longer wore her vine mask, revealing how strangely ordinary she looked. The Rock sisters, normally so friendly they were annoying, kept their distance, and the Sand Fam were even worse. They watched Carra Carre from across the festivities with hostility on their faces; Tiggi could almost hear the insults in their mouths.

She had never seen such open disrespect among Sis like that, even among bitter rivals. The Vine's attack on the Sand had created a hatred that years of competing could not.

"Tiggi, will you dance?" a voice said.

It was Tempo and the other girls, giggling from the flush of the celebration. Each girl held another girl's hand in a chain of merriment.

"Come and dance, Tiggi!" Sola said.

At one end of the chain, Ngivi slipped her free hand into Tiggi's, tugging. "Come and dance!" she said with a cackle.

"No no no, I am finefine," Tiggi protested. She had danced once, years ago, and the other Butterflies had claimed she danced like a "wounded frog," whatever that meant. Since then, she'd preferred to enjoy dancing by watching it rather than doing it.

Ngivi and the other girls continued to tug, forcing Tiggi to shake her arm in an embarrassing attempt to free herself.

"Breathe eaaaasy, Ngivi," Tempo said. She was the other end of the chain and used her free hand to pry Ngivi's grip off. "Bibi Tiggi must rest."

Tempo was the only one who had always treated her the same. When Tiggi was an outcast, Tempo treated her like a sister. Now that the other girls treated her like a leader, Tempo still treated her like a sister. Tiggi appreciated her consistency.

Between their desire for revelry and Tempo's interjection, the other girls were quick to rush the dance floor without Tiggi, and a cheer went up from the Rock and Sand girls who were already there. Together, the girls danced and sang and ate, and as the night tumbled on, every emotion seemed to heighten, both the good and the bad.

Until the bad spilled over.

"Speak it loudloud!" one of the Sand sisters shouted over the music. They were in the same distant huddle they'd been in all night, only now there seemed to be some disagreement among them, with one of the sisters frantically trying to quiet the others.

Then one of the sisters pushed past the pacifying one. Sis Zuna, if Tiggi remembered correctly. She was the largest of them, and the Sand Bibi had explained during training that Sis Zuna was First now that their real First was gone.

"Sis Swoo!" Sis Zuna called so loudly that the drumming faltered and stopped.

Silence.

Sis Swoo, who was seated at the high table with Sis Dirt, Sis Ask, and Sis Carra Carre, looked over with a face that seemed to know exactly what would happen next.

Sis Zuna stalked over to the high table, her Sand Sis following behind her. Every eye turned to watch, waiting. Tiggi's gut tightened with fear. There was a change in the air, as if before a fight. She hated that feeling.

"We honey our teeth all this night," Sis Zuna said, nose scrunched in equal disgust and rage, "but we can no longer be quiet. We will not sleep in na same camp as our enemy."

Sis Swoo barely reacted. Instead, her eyes shifted to Sis Dirt.

"What Verdi did to na Sand," Sis Dirt said, "is unforgivable. But that is not Carra Carr—"

"You *defend* her?" Sis Zuna asked, incredulous. "She breaks Sis Webba. She mashes na Mud Camp. And you defend her?"

Sis Carra Carre stood, an act that ignited the already tense air. The Sand Sis fell into Bowing stances, and the Rock sisters, who had been hiding amused smiles all through Sis Zuna's rage, immediately backed as far away from the high table as they could get, suddenly serious.

"I accept any punishment for my doing," the First of the Vine said. "But Verdi's doing is not my own," she added with such finality that Tiggi was surprised when Sis Zuna responded.

"Then *you* must punish her," she shot back. She looked up into Sis Carra Carre's gaze with no hesitation. Tiggi admired her bravery as much as she feared for her safety. "Your precious Verdi still keeps my First and Second. You will find and punish her, or we will punish you."

The Sand Sis all moved forward, forming a semicircle around the high table. And there everyone remained, waiting. A moment of uncertainty flashed in Sis Carra Carre's face, but it was immediately replaced by firm-jawed stolidity.

"I welcome your attempt," she said.

Before chaos could erupt, Sis Dirt and Sis Ask shot to their feet.

"Outside na camp!" Sis Ask pleaded, just as Sis Dirt said, "We need not fight!"

"Carra Carre did not attack na Sand," Sis Dirt continued. "But Verdi must be punished. I . . ." She swallowed. "I will find Verdi and punish her."

Sis Zuna, her eyes still on Sis Carra Carre, smiled a bitter but satisfied smile.

Sis Carra Carre looked at Sis Dirt, her face devoid of expression. After a few seconds, she moved, prompting fearful flinches from the Sand sisters. But Sis Carra Carre didn't attack. She calmly left the party, walking back in the direction of her stone hut.

The rest of the party quickly disassembled after that, as did Tiggi herself. Unlike the other girls, she had no one to share her hut with. So instead of gossiping about who would win in a rematch between Sis Dirt and Sis Carra Carre, as she knew the other Bibi were, Tiggi just sat in the quiet of the night, staring into the black. She'd thought Sis Dirt's return would mean everything would be happy again.

She should have known better.

27

Attack of the Remnants

"FIVE MUST GO . . . ,'" Swoo mumbled. "That spinning viper neck."

Dirt raised an eyebrow at the feebleness of the insult, but Swoo only shrugged.

"Viper neck or no," Dirt replied with a sigh, "that is what we face. Five sisters must go into na Fault, but we do not have enough Godskins. Until we have five . . ."

"We must wait to die?" Swoo asked.

Dirt didn't respond. She couldn't think of anything to say that would change the facts of their situation. It seemed unavoidable that their only option was to fight the Remnants until either the Remnants were no more or the Bowers were overrun. One of those seemed more likely than the other.

Their saving grace was that the Remnants would be attacking all the Fam, across all four parts of the Isle, rather than just the South. This meant there would be fewer Remnants and the waves of attacks would be much further apart, giving the defenders more time to recover.

"I will make sure we do not die," Dirt said. "Now or ever. Carra Carre as well."

Swoo squeezed her face in displeasure. "You trust that one?"

Dirt wanted to say that she did. Because that was the truth. In the time she'd spent with Carra Carre, she'd come to trust the girl as she would any of her Mud sisters. But she knew how Swoo felt, and she didn't feel right praising Carra Carre in Swoo's presence.

"What choice do we have? I cannot fight na Remnants alone. Not forever."

Swoo chewed unpleasantly on that reality. "And what of na Sand?" she eventually asked. "Carra Carre will allow you to feed Verdi to them?"

Dirt had told Sis Ask that the party was a bad idea. But Sis Ask, being a Rock sister, would never accept that there were problems a party couldn't solve. Now Dirt had an additional headache to deal with. Carra Carre didn't agree with what Verdi was doing, but that was her sister, and she still felt protective of her. Dirt wanted to believe that Carra Carre would understand, but she couldn't say for sure. And if it came to a fight between them . . .

"I do not know," Dirt admitted. "But I cannot go punish Verdi as na Remnants attack us. Take na Sand with you to find Snore. Keep them from na camp and they may calm."

Swoo wore a skeptical look, but she nodded.

"Do you . . . ," she added hesitantly. "Do you believe we will find Snore?"

Dirt no longer knew what she believed. But she knew what she hoped, and that was all she could offer.

"We must," she said. "We will."

Every day the Remnants attacked.

Dirt woke early each morning as the other girls were still sleeping, and together with Carra Carre, she went out on patrol around the Rock camp. Inevitably, the Remnants would come, dozens of them emerging from the jungle with weeping eyes and violent howls, storming toward Dirt and Cara Carre.

Sometimes the battle was quick. Sometimes the battle was long. Sometimes it ended with her clothes torn and chest heaving in exhaustion and sometimes it ended with her unblemished, looking out over a blue haze of defeated enemies with enough strength in her body for two more battles.

Yet every day Dirt survived, and every day she wondered whether she would survive the next one.

"Close, eh?" Carra Carre said with a chuckled breath.

The latest battle had been the most difficult. After six straight days of attacks, both girls were a hair slower than usual, and the Remnants had nearly taken advantage of it. Twice Carra Carre had saved Dirt from certain death, grabbing a Remnant that had come up behind and eliminating it before it could eliminate her.

"Too close," Dirt replied.

She looked down at her shaking hands. Between the fights and the continuing failed search for Snore, Dirt's nights were devoid of sleep. Additionally, the foods she was used to growing in the fertile mud from their camp did not grow so well in the sparse and dimly lit soil of the Rock camp. Between poor sleep and a poor diet, her body wasn't getting what it needed to keep up the fight.

Dirt released a long sigh. She needed rest.

Carra Carre's heavy hand settled on her shoulder. "You are fine-fine," she said. "Na Remnants will long remember how you punish them this day."

Perhaps. But Dirt knew the day was soon coming when she would make a mistake and the Remnants would win, and she would be forgotten like so many others.

Back at camp, Dirt did her best to busy herself so as not to dwell on her mistakes against the Remnants. First, she went to the Bibi, to look in on their training. She wasn't sure how much sense it made to keep them training. But in unstable times, routine provided comfort. They had been forced to abandon the camp—they didn't have to abandon the life of the Bower.

She wound down the central road of the Rock camp, past stone house after stone house, until she came upon the training grounds. The sand they used for their ring must have been imported from the nearby beaches. It was the same fine quality, and its pale yellow was stark and bright against the dark rock of the cave interior. It covered a wide patch, at the center of which was a circle of rocks to mark the ring.

At Dirt's appearance, a wave of cheers went up from the Bibi. They halted their training to rush over and swarm her with admiration in every form, from hugs and kisses to squeezing her muscles to just gazing adoringly. Though she knew the compliments of Bibi meant little, she couldn't help but feel good to have their praise after the tiring battles of the day.

"Na good evening, Bibi," she greeted them when they'd settled a bit.

"Na good evening, Sis Dirt," they cooed back.

Swoo was seated on the far side of the ring, but she immediately rose when Dirt arrived. Not out of respect, but out of what Dirt saw was urgency—and concern.

"Sis Dirt," was all she said.

They gave the Bibi drills to do, then went to a hut, away from the ears of the little ones. Swoo immediately set out a stool and retrieved a drum of Mud Offer.

"Sit, my Sis," she said.

Dirt was grateful for the relief. Once she sat, she felt even more the weariness of her bones.

"What is it?" Swoo asked. "You have pain in your eyes."

Dirt shook her head. "I am finefine. Only tired."

Swoo took Mud Offer into her palms and rubbed it into Dirt's skin. She paid special attention to her cuts and scrapes, and Dirt closed her eyes at the satisfying sting of the Mud Offer healing her wounds. Swoo worked her hands in silence for a long while before eventually speaking in a subdued voice.

"You are slowing, eh?" she asked.

Dirt had never been one to speak much. The mind was the proper place for words; the body was made for actions. However, with all the thoughts in her mind, there seemed no more room for words. They tumbled out of her, not just the ones from that day, but everything from Useyi's appearance to the Imperial Temple to training with Carra Carre to the attack by the Remnants to finding the Mud camp empty to learning what Verdi was doing to . . .

"I miss Webba," Dirt finally said. Swoo's massaging paused for a moment, as if she were going to say something, then continued.

"Na Remnants are divided," Swoo eventually said. "Some attack us. Some attack na North, na East, na West. I think all day about this, and I have na plan."

After a day full of fighting an endless foe, a plan was exactly the thing Dirt wanted to hear. "Go on," she said.

The plan was simple. If the Remnants were going toward the biggest pockets of people, then they just had to make sure they didn't keep too many people in the same place. That way, the Remnants would be more tempted to go after the other regions. Once the Remnants were redirected, Dirt and Carra Carre and three other sisters would be free to finally go into the Fault itself and close it.

Dirt grunted. "Carra Carre and I struggle to protect just na Rock camp. Now we must protect sisters all over?"

Swoo shook her head. "You will still protect na Rock camp. Come."

She led Dirt out of the stone home and onto the street. At this hour, the girls from each Fam were finishing up their training. Some of the Rock and Sand NoBe had ended early and were beginning dinner preparations. The camp was as active as ever, with the sounds and sweat of training here and there, pots of hot water beginning to boil, and the low chatter of Sis in conversation.

Swoo pointed far across the camp, over the many homes to the high rock wall at the back.

"What is behind it?" she asked.

Dirt raised an eyebrow. "You think na Godskin can see through rock?"

Swoo rolled her eyes. "More rock, Sis Dirt. Na Isle is just na big rock."

"And so?" Dirt wasn't understanding. She wasn't even sure there was anything to understand.

"So we move it," Swoo replied. "You and Carra Carre break na rock and move it and move it and move it. Make na new camp so we can take this one and make it two. Two *small* camps."

Dirt thought back to her arrival at the Rock camp, when she'd had to smash through a boulder to save Swoo from a Remnant. In her Godskin, the boulder had been no more an obstacle than a new sapling. With Carra Carre at her side, it wouldn't even take them a day to break down a league of rock.

Dirt regarded Swoo, grateful that she had been gifted with such a brilliant sister.

"Your mind will save us all," Dirt said.

Swoo looked uncharacteristically bashful, turning away with a small smile on her face.

Then there was a loud sound, a low *hrooooooo* that echoed off the walls, magnifying until Dirt could scarcely hear her own thoughts.

"What is that?" she asked as soon as it ended.

Swoo's smile had become a hesitant frown. "Na horn."

"What horn?"

"It is for emergencies."

Despite her exhaustion, Dirt immediately entered back into her Godskin. She carried Swoo in one arm and leapt toward the camp entrance, reaching it in a few mighty bounds. There, the Rock sisters on patrol all stood staring out of the entrance, unmoving. Only when Dirt and Swoo landed heavily behind them did they turn, their faces blank and helpless.

"What is it?" Dirt asked.

"Look . . ." The lead Rock sister pointed out toward the entrance.

Dirt strode past their gaping stares, prepared for a fight. Yet her preparation was unnecessary. There was no Remnant horde awaiting her.

Instead, it was a horde of Bowers. And Butterflies. And Flagga. And Pusher boys. They were in a desperate state, many of them leaning on others for support, their faces gaunt from hunger, with red-seeped bandages over wounds and splints holding in place broken bones.

Strangely, it was a Butterfly girl that led them. Thin and tall, but with a strength to her that spoke of a past spent training the body and mind for battle. Her hair was in the long, single ponytail it had always been in. She wore both her characteristic jewelry and hesitation, though underscored by the buoyant relief of seeing a lifelong friend who you'd feared you'd never see again.

"Sis Dirt . . . Sis Swoo," Nana said. "We need your help."

28

The Sneeze

SNORE SNIFFED the air. They were gone. She could finally move in.

The camp was spread across both banks of a narrow stream. The homes were made from sturdy wood, with vines strung up as clotheslines between homes on either bank and well-whittled chairs and tables placed throughout as small discussion areas.

Or at least that was what Snore imagined it should have looked like. Instead, the camp had been ransacked beyond recognition. The homes were blasted apart, the vines severed and pulled to the ground, the furniture smashed to pieces, most of which floated away on the current of the stream.

Snore didn't know what camp it was, but it didn't matter. She was only there for food.

"Go, Bibi Nubbi," she said.

Nubbi led the way into camp, with a dozen of the youngest jungle cats following behind her. Even at her young age, Nubbi was already showing signs of leadership. Snore was proud of her, as were the bigger jungle cats. They often even let her eat with them after a hunt, whereas they snarled at the other cubs.

Snore followed behind Nubbi into the camp, her eyes scanning for anything the jungle cats' noses missed. There wasn't much. She changed clothes into a fresh outfit she found and enjoyed a warm potato left in one of the homes, but the camp was otherwise empty, just like the last one. Snore didn't know what was happening to all the camps, but something powerful was destroying them.

For a moment, Snore wondered whether the Mud camp had suffered the same fate. But only a moment. She immediately pushed the thought out of her mind. She was no longer a Mud sister. The Mud had failed to protect her. They'd even failed to protect themselves. Now that the Remnants were here, the only ones she could trust were Nubbi's family members, the Cat Fam.

After scavenging for goods, Snore and the younger jungle cats took time to play in the stream. That was another advantage of being with the jungle cats instead of the Mud sisters—play. Everything was play. Hunting was play, eating was play, fighting was play. The only thing that wasn't play was grooming, but Snore didn't mind it. Most of the time, she'd just rest her head on their soft fur and go to sleep. When she awoke, she was picked clean of any bugs.

Nubbi had grown over the last month, so now she and Snore could play even better. Snore would pretend to be the cat, laying on her back with fingers and toes in the air like claws, clamping down on Nubbi's neck. And Nubbi would be the human, hopping about on her hind legs and pawing at the air like a Bower practicing Slapping. They played in the stream of the destroyed camp for hours, until the sun was well and truly set.

Only then did the older cats rise from their daytime slumber. They stretched and yawned, trotted out of the camp, and returned hours later with anteater meat. The first time Snore had eaten the raw meat, she'd gotten sick and had thrown up everything else she ate for three days. But she'd gotten used to it and had even come to enjoy the tough texture. She had to really tear it with her teeth to eat it, and she felt closer to her cat sisters when she did.

Bellies full, the cats returned to lounging as the night crept on. Jungle cats didn't tell stories or put on plays like Bowers did. That was one thing Snore missed about the Mud camp. But they did keep themselves entertained with The Sneeze, as Snore called it. The exact rules of the game weren't clear to her yet, but basically everyone took turns sneezing and sometimes someone sneezed twice and that was the best part because it meant The Sneeze started all over again.

On one round of The Sneeze, Nubbi sneezed so hard that a tiny squeal of gas escaped her. It was so unexpected that Nubbi herself jumped to her feet, startled. She sniffed the grass where she'd just been sitting, then pulled herself back in displeasure.

Snore cackled. Mostly at the fart, but really at the whole sequence of events.

That was when she heard the rustle in the trees.

Immediately, the older cats were on their feet, eyes reflecting the moonlight as they stared into the dark jungle. Then there was the sound—a dozen guttural howls, overlapping indistinctly. By the time Snore got to her feet, the Remnant was upon them.

It burst out of the jungle, sprinting on tall bird legs with an upper body and arms that were half bear and half beetle. Driller collided with the Remnant at top speed, her jaws around its thick throat, and the other cats were quick to follow. Like bees on an invader, they swarmed the creature, slashing and biting. The Remnant thrashed, flinging cats across the camp, but as soon as one cat was dislodged, two more took its place.

Snore watched it all with a growing ferocity in her gut. With each second that passed, her back curled more into a feral hunch, her lips peeled back to bare her teeth, her nose scrunched into a snarl. Then she was rushing across the camp and launching herself through the air, descending on a part of the monster's knee that none of the other cats were attacking. She tried to bite it, but it was like rock to the touch, so she just clamped the leg against her chest, hoping to at least tip it over.

Then suddenly, Nubbi was pulling at her, the cub's small teeth tugging delicately on her shorts. Snore blinked, looked down at Nubbi, then back up at the monster, only to find that it was gone. Her arms were wrapped around nothing but a blue mist.

"Wha . . . wha's this?" Snore asked.

The older cats had already left. She looked around and found them all huddled together across the camp. Snore and Nubbi jogged over to find the Cat Fam surrounding the bodies of Claw and Omen. Claw was still months away from being full grown but had the swagger of a cat twice her size. Omen was the Fam elder, past her prime but savvy and skillful.

And they were both dead, backs broken from being flung into trees.

Snore didn't like this. She didn't like it at all. As the Cat Fam all sat on their haunches in a silent vigil, Snore just stared at the bodies of her friends, her sisters. She'd seen it before. That was how Sis Webba had looked after the Vine attack, only this was permanent.

There was no jungle cat Bonemender to fix them, no splint and prayers that would realign their spines.

It had only been one Remnant. Snore had watched Sis Dirt fight off an army. The same Sis Dirt who had failed all those months ago to protect Snore from the Vine.

Snore loved living among the Cat Fam so much. She felt comfortable with them, happy, safe. But she was confused. She had come to them because she thought they could protect her and teach her how to protect herself, like big sisters were supposed to do. But she now saw that even they could be defeated. They hadn't failed to protect her this time, but what about next time? What if more Remnants came?

When it was time for sleep, Snore took Nubbi to a spot away from the others, in the shade of one of the camp's destroyed huts. Nubbi seemed confused, but she stayed. They curled up together, and as Nubbi drifted off to sleep, Snore couldn't stop thinking about her old Fam and how they were doing and whether they missed her as much as she missed them.

29

New Powers Revealed

THE CREEK SISTERS told the story of the day the Vine descended on them. As the second largest Fam in the South, the Creek Fam was best suited to fighting the Vine, especially with Carra Carre away. Their First was the formidable Wing, the best Rider in all the South and one of the most respected Bowers of her era.

Still, the Creek had fallen. The Vine had numbers, plus Verdi was a ruthless commander, launching an ambush that saw a half dozen Vine Sis pummel Wing before she knew what was happening. Wing still put up a legendary fight—rendering one Vine Sis unconscious and breaking another one's arms—but even a girl as talented as Wing had her limits.

After Verdi's attack sent the remaining Creek sisters fleeing across the South, the Remnants came upon them. With no Godskin to protect them, it was chaos. The Creek sisters fell by the second, trapped in a Remnant's grip and dissolved into mist, immediately forgotten. Girls ran with a friend's hand in their own only to stop and realize that they were running alone, with no memory of why or how that had happened. They would have been completely wiped out if it weren't for the arrival of the others—Pushers and Flagga and Butterflies. With that many people scattering in all directions, they were able to disorient the Remnants enough for many to escape, but it had still taken a surprise from some Pusher boys to manage it.

"He does what?" Swoo asked, incredulous.

Nana had brought a tower of a Pusher boy with her. Though he had a flat belly and very little meat on his bones, he was nearly as tall as Dirt, and his soft, boyish face only made his height more unnerving. On his shoulder was his Petti, a large brown-and-white-streaked hawk with the distinctly fierce eyes of a bird of prey.

"Show them, Ekko," she said.

Dirt looked from Nana to the Pusher boy and back. They were giving each other the strangest of looks, as if each found the other distracting but in a pleasant way. Dirt made a note to ask Nana about it later.

Ekko then crouched to the floor, mumbling to himself. His hawk hopped from his shoulder onto his head, where it too crouched, spreading its wings out wide to cover the sides of Ekko's neck.

But then the wings kept spreading.

Dirt watched in disbelief as the bird's feathers lengthened and melded into Ekko's skin. In no time, he seemed to be wearing a hawk-skin pelt over his shoulder and back, with the hawk's head stretched over his own so that his eyes were covered by the hawk's and his nose was covered by the hawk's beak.

For a moment, Dirt was swollen with the fear that Ekko had somehow been turned into a Remnant. She nearly used her Godskin to charge him. But she realized that he wasn't howling or attacking. He also kept his usual coloring and skin rather than turning into a hard blue crystal.

But not everyone was as level-headed as Dirt. Ekko's transformation caused several Rock and Sand sisters to leap into action, half of them speeding out the door of the cramped stone home and the other half barreling toward Ekko, their faces contorted with fear and rage in equal measure.

"Stop!" Dirt shouted, arms out to prevent the Bowers from leaping onto the poor Pusher boy. Thankfully, they heeded her call. "Look at him. He is no Remnant, my sisters."

The Bowers maintained their skepticism but stood down. The girls all looked at each other, as if trading reassurances that not attacking the boy was the right decision. It was Sis Ask who finally broke the tension, laughing loudly with her hand on her belly.

"Look at us play toughtough. If he is na Remnant, what can we do? We are no Godskins." She shrugged then extended a hand toward Ekko. "Welcome, Pusher boy."

After that day, Ekko helped Dirt and Carra Carre on patrols. He didn't have anywhere near the raw power of a Godskin, but his Petti powers granted him enhanced sight and smell that allowed them to be more prepared for Remnants when they arrived. Despite his boyish appearance, he also proved to be a capable patrol partner. He almost never spoke unless prompted, at which point he'd tell stories of his travels up and down the Isle. He was neither boastful nor shy, simply describing his adventures in a way that was naturally intriguing. For a boy so young—young to Dirt, at least—he had learned a lot, and he seemed to have become a respected leader among his squad of Pusher boys.

The only times he spoke unprompted were to ask about Nana.

"Godskin Sis Dirt?" he asked, even though she had told him the title of "Godskin" wasn't necessary. "You have known Nana long?"

They were trekking through the jungles on the outskirts of the Rock territory, awaiting the next Remnant wave. Up until then, Ekko had been intently eyeing the jungle and sniffing the air.

"I have," Dirt said. Pusher boys did not bother her the way Butterfly girls used to. And Ekko was better than most. But between him being a Pusher boy and him asking about Nana, her patience for him could be short. "And so?"

"Eh . . . does she like mango?"

Nana loved mango.

"She likes to sleep. And breathe."

"And mango?"

"I do not know," Dirt snapped. "Ask her yourself."

Carra Carre snorted.

As Dirt managed to keep such conversations short, Ekko countered by making them more frequent, approaching the subject in increasingly sly ways so that Dirt only realized what they were speaking about when it was too late.

"How is it to be First?" he asked once on the way back to camp. The blue haze of defeated Remnants still hung in the air. "It is not too much to remember?"

"Bowing is not in na memory, it is in na body," Dirt said, picking up the walking pace in hopes he would be too winded to talk.

"Not na Bow," Ekko said. "I mean you must lead so many girls. And they are all different. What if they like different food? Maybe

NoBe Swoo likes rice and Bibi Snore likes plantain and Nana likes . . ."

Dirt frowned. "Who told you these things? It is Swoo who likes plantain. Bibi Snore likes mudfish, of all things. And Nana . . ."

Dirt shot the boy a glare and broke into a jog.

When they returned to camp, they found a mass of at least thirty people jostling to get in, Pushers and Flagga and Butterflies among them. Swoo and her assistants were managing the intake, recording how many came in each group to ensure there was housing space for them. For several days, more and more children had shown up at the Rock camp, hoping for the protection they'd been hearing about. And each time, there was no choice but to let them in. Often, they already had friends there and simply joined them.

But other times, new homes had to be hastily erected to ensure that boys and girls from rival factions weren't forced to room together. Dirt hadn't even known there were factions among Butterflies, Flagga, and Pusher boys, but it seemed they were even more divided than Bowers.

The new homes required the enacting of Swoo's plan. Each day, after fighting, Dirt and Carra Carre tore chunks of stone out of the side of the cave and crushed them into smaller stones. Then Pusher boys would load the stones into small wagons and transport them to the cave entrance, where Swoo and her team had begun assembling walls and fake entrances to mislead the Remnants.

As efficient as the system was, it did nothing to address their biggest issue—exhaustion. What ease Ekko had brought to Dirt and Carra Carre was countered by the digging schedule. And so many new children were joining them each day that the camp was growing too quickly to split. Rather than the many small camps they'd hoped for, it was instead one giant, ever-growing camp, filling all available space.

Which only drew more and more Remnants.

"Ekko, behind you!" Dirt screamed.

The days of battle had taught them that hesitation was death, so Ekko dived forward immediately, covering his head with his hands as he fell face-first into the jungle floor. Dirt tried to launch herself at the Remnant that was attacking him, but the ground beneath her was soft and muddy. It shifted out of place and crumbled away, sending her tumbling backward down the side of the hill. She skidded to a halt and looked up to see the Remnant atop Ekko, its reptilian head and crustacean body crushing the poor boy into the floor. Two of its eight arms were descending toward him, moments away from hugging him into oblivion.

Dirt began to scream for Carra Carre's attention, but she saw that the girl was already fighting off three Remnants of her own. She couldn't help Ekko. And Dirt was too far.

It was the end for the poor boy.

In a final effort, Dirt reached out her arms and tried to pull the air itself toward her. She tugged on imaginary ropes, pulling into herself. It was a feat she'd never tried before, but she hoped there was enough power in her Godskin to do it.

There wasn't. The air remained unchanged.

However, both Ekko and Remnant suddenly slid down the hill toward Dirt, with enough force that the Remnant staggered away from the Pusher boy.

At first Dirt thought it was just a coincidence, that the floor beneath them had simply given out with benevolent timing. But then she saw the mud streaming from the earth into her arms in a slow, rust-colored coat. Dirt didn't understand what was happening, but she also didn't have time to question it. With the Remnant right in front of her, she grabbed hold of it, and all the mud on her arms rushed off her and onto the head of the Remnant.

Except it didn't cover the Remnant. Instead, it congealed into a human shape the size of a chicken, one with a round Bower belly and spherical fists. It rained its tiny fists down on the Remnant's head, pounding it like a talking drum. The strangeness of it was too much for Dirt to make sense of in the moment. She raised the Remnant in the air, spun, and slammed it into a tree, shattering it into a blue mist.

In the aftermath of battle, there was silence. Dirt was too stunned to speak, both from the sudden change in her powers and from the aftershock of nearly failing to save Ekko. Ekko hadn't yet risen from the ground—he was still on his back, staring up into the jungle canopy. Carra Carre slid into view atop the hill, glistening with sweat, her chest heaving from deep, steadying breaths.

None of them spoke until they were back at camp.

30

Friends

NANA WATCHED Dirt, Ekko, and Carra Carre return to camp with the slouch of defeat in their shoulders. It was a strange sight, one that confused Nana and so many of the other girls. They had fought back another wave of Remnants and yet there was no evidence of that in their expressions. Ekko seemed stunned, eyes wide and empty, staring at the ground ahead of him as if to ensure each step went as it was intended.

The trio came down the camp's central path, and Nana joined the throng coming out to meet them. It had become a daily occurrence and usually turned into an impromptu celebration, with food and music and dancing late into the night. This time, though, everyone was silent. The Rock girls brought out their drums but seemed to realize the mood didn't call for music, and the food was distributed in calm whispers. Dirt and Carra Carre went straight into the command house, where they and Sis Swoo and the other Sis spent much of their time.

But Ekko went straight to Nana.

He didn't seem to notice anyone else as he cut through the crowd, even his fellow Pusher boys. He did that sometimes—looked at her like there was nothing else that was of interest to him. Only when he finally reached her did she notice how desperate he looked, his eyebrows bunched and furrowed.

"Ek—" she began, but he cut her off with a hug that lifted her off the ground.

He smelled like sweat and soil. His cheek was smooth against hers. His arms were as firm as a Trap, and she was surprised that he was so strong, almost as strong as a Sis.

She realized that it was the first time they'd ever hugged.

"Nana . . . ," he said. "Do you like mango?"

"What?" she asked with a small chuckle.

"Is this how Pusher boys greet Bowers now?" said a voice from behind her.

Ekko's arms suddenly fell away, and Nana felt her feet touch back to the ground. She immediately knew who it was, not just by the voice but by Ekko's wide eyes and stiff posture. Only a Bower could rattle Ekko so.

"Sis Swoo," he said dipping his gaze toward the ground.

Swoo stood with an impatience that almost made Nana smile for how familiar it was.

"Go on, Pusher boy," she said. "I must talk with my sister."

Swoo had changed since Nana's days as a sister of the Mud. She was still relentless, still overconfident. But that relentlessness had been tempered by patience. The overconfidence by caution. She had always been a leader in action, but it was clear she had become a leader in attitude.

The change was even reflected in her room. The walls of Swoo's squat stone home were stuck all over with maps of the Isle. Swoo had always been a mapmaker, but only to satisfy her own curiosity. These maps were clearly made with precision, to be used for strategy and protection of the camp. She had one for the Rock camp, one for the area surrounding the Rock camp, one for the South, and one for the center of the Isle. They were fleshed out not just with landmarks but with notes about which places could make for good hiding or had plenty of wood and rocks for defensive fortifications.

"We search everywhere," Swoo said, "and do not find Snore."

The news of Snore's disappearance had ruined Nana's mood when she found out. It was hard to believe that Snore had somehow been kidnapped again, but even harder to accept, as Swoo believed, that Snore had left by choice. Snore was a loyal member of the Mud Fam—she would never want to leave her sisters. What good was waiting out there for her anyhow? The Isle was plagued with Remnants and with Verdi's army on the march, two things that would inevitably find her.

"We must continue to search," Nana said. "We will find her, eh?"

Swoo eyed Nana for a moment before responding. "Does Snore talk to you?"

"Eh?" Nana frowned. "How?"

Swoo sighed and looked away. "I am sorry. I am hoping that though Snore abandons na Mud, she does not abandon all her sisters."

Nana nodded but said nothing. She could only imagine how

Swoo must be feeling. She'd been the only one to go after Snore when the Vine had taken her. Whatever pain was still inside Snore from that day, Swoo had seen it up close, and she'd watched that pain bloom each day with no way to stop it. Now it had come to this.

"Can Sis Dirt help na search?" Nana asked.

Swoo shrugged, then turned to pore over the maps along the wall. "This is my fight, not Sis Dirt's. All day na poor woman fights na Remnants, those backbent baboons. She does enough."

"Maybe I can help her," Nana said.

Swoo turned over her shoulder and looked at Nana like she'd just asked to eat a basket of kola nut with no water to wash it down. "Na Butterfly make you madmad?"

"Not by fighting," Nana said with a roll of her eyes. "With armor."

She'd been thinking it over ever since the Remnants first attacked. They didn't take girls by hitting them. Or slashing them. Only by grabbing around a girl fully did their horrible magic work. If there was a way to make it more difficult for them to get a hold, it could save lives.

Nana raised her wrist, where a bracelet of pale blue river stones sat, cut into ovals, each laid in its own tin bed. "Grab me," she said.

Swoo stared with a bored expression before her hand shot out like a snake, latching on to Nana's wrist. Nana yanked her hand hard, and it slid out of Swoo's grip with such ease that the Mud sister's eyes widened. Then her brows scrunched in confusion.

"What trick is this?" Swoo asked.

Nana turned her wrist left and right, showing off the unblemished bracelet. "No trick," she said.

The stones were naturally prone to slipperiness, and she'd spent days polishing them as smooth as possible. With an additional layer of oil made from chicken fat, even an elite Bower would lose her grip.

"And your hand is soft," Nana explained. "It is good for grabbing. Na Remnants are hard. If they try this—*cham!*" she mimicked a Remnant pincer slipping right off.

Swoo's face softened in a way Nana had not seen since joining the Rock camp. She looked almost like she was going to smile.

But instead, she just said, "I have missed you, Bib—Butterfly Nana."

They began talking about times long gone, hard trainings and heavy meals and dances they rehearsed for weeks. There were so many memories that Nana realized they had never discussed before. The life of the Bower was about training for the future, not reminiscing on the past. But Nana wasn't a Bower anymore, and even though Swoo still was, Nana could see how much freer she felt talking with a Butterfly girl. There was no need to keep her face serious and hard, no need to be the strong and ambitious Bower that she'd always been. As sisters, Nana and Swoo had been close, but they had been kept distant from each other by the hierarchy of Bowing—Nana was a Bibi, Swoo was a NoBe.

Now they were just two girls who had shared so much of their lives together.

"So now a question," Swoo said with a coy smile. They had migrated to a corner of the room, where Swoo was seated with her back against the wall and Nana had her head in Swoo's lap. "Who is this Ekko?"

Nana felt her face warm. She just hoped Swoo didn't notice. "Eh . . . he is na friend."

Swoo snorted. "Indeed. And I am na goat's behind."

Nana giggled. "He is! What is it you want me to say?"

"I have many friends, former Bibi Nana," Swoo said, flicking Nana's nose. "I do not look at them as if—"

The door to the house creaked open, and in poked the head of a Mud Bibi. From the little Nana had seen, the new class of Mud Bibi were mostly rambunctious, if good-hearted, girls. This one was more soft-faced than the others, with a hesitant demeanor that Nana immediately felt sympathy for—she had worn the same hesitance so often in her Bowing days.

"What is it, Tiggi?" Swoo said, and she was back to her new self, stern and strong, the leader the Fam needed.

The Bibi, Tiggi, looked from Nana and Swoo and back seemingly a dozen times in the span of a few seconds of silence.

"Sis Dirt and Sis Carra Carre tell me to get you," Tiggi said.

Nana rolled off Swoo and watched her rise to her feet, slip her handaxe into her waistband, and head for the door.

"Make your armor, my sister," she said. "I will like to see it soon."

Then she was gone.

Nana took a long, deep breath and was ready to head back to her own house when she noticed that the Tiggi girl was still in the doorway, watching her.

"Tiggi, eh?" Nana said. "Na good meeting." She smiled.

But Tiggi didn't respond. She just stared, mouth opening and closing like a fish stuck on land. After a few moments, she disappeared, fleeing out into camp.

Nana laughed to herself. Bowers, she now realized, were very strange people.

The Sisters the Bibi Need

TIGGI HAD NEVER experienced that before, not even the first time she saw Sis Dirt. She'd met Sis Dirt on her first day at the Mud camp, along with fifty other girls. It had been formal, impersonal. Even then, she'd thought she was about as excited as she could ever be to meet a person.

She didn't expect meeting Nana to be so overwhelming.

Whereas Sis Dirt was a myth brought to life, Nana was a life turned to myth. Tiggi vaguely remembered seeing her dance into the arena with the Mud Fam and sit in the stands while the older Mud sisters fought, but most of what she knew about the girl was from stories. Nana was the quietest of the Mud five, the Bower turned Butterfly, soft and pretty and delicate and never suited to the life of the Bower.

All of that was true, and more. She was prettier than Tiggi expected. Pretty like a Butterfly, not a Bower. Tall, lean, with dark skin and big, honest eyes that seemed to drink in everything they landed on. On the one hand, with her willowy frame, she did indeed seem ill-suited to the grueling grind of Bower life. Yet there was a strength in her that was undeniable. She was soft-spoken, but not meek. Measured, but not afraid.

Nana knew what it was to be a Butterfly girl in a Fam of Bowers, and she was the former senior Bibi of the Mud Fam. She had already been everything Tiggi hoped to be, and she was just there, sitting on the floor of a stone house with her head in Sis Swoo's lap.

The moment was all Tiggi could think about for the rest of the day. As the other Bibi trained beside her, she thought about how Nana must have felt doing those same drills. As they paired off for sparring, she imagined Nana doing the same. As the other Bibi asked her questions about what the big sisters were doing and when they would be competing again and where Bibi Snore was, she answered as best she could, realizing that Nana must have answered similar questions for Bibi Snore.

Then it was dinner time, and they were all seated beside the ring around platters of steamed fungi, cuts of boiled black potatoes, a pot of root stew, and a half dozen other foods they had begun eating since joining the Rock camp. Though they often trained with the Bowers of the other Fam, dinner was still a separate affair, giving each Fam time to enjoy their sisters.

Except for the Mud. Sis Swoo and Sis Dirt took their dinner in the command house, planning each day's defense. So it was just the Bibi, with Tiggi in charge.

"Bibi Tiggi, will we all be forgotten?" Wami asked, and a sudden somberness fell over the sisters.

The way every sister looked at her made Tiggi realize that

though Wami had voiced it, they all had the same fear, simmering within them all day.

"Sis Dirt and Sis Carra Carre look weakweak, eh?"

"Not weakweak! Tiredtired!"

"Will na Remnants disappear us?"

Tiggi knew that the conversation would only end if she said something, but she didn't know what to say. She was just as concerned about Sis Dirt. But she didn't know any more than they did. Still, she had to say something.

"We will be okay," she said, though she knew she didn't sound very convincing.

The other Bibi glanced at her. Then they continued their worried chatter, unmoved by Tiggi's words. Tempo's eyes remained on Tiggi longer than most, but even she soon turned back to the other girls.

Some days, Tiggi was excited at the prospect of being the senior Bibi. Other days, she could think of nothing she wanted less. But she decided then that she would do her best to become the sister the Bibi needed. Now, at least, she had someone she could ask.

She just had to work up the courage to do it.

The Flaggas Lend a Hand

ANOTHER DAY, another fight.

Whatever power Dirt had discovered in their previous outing was growing. She was able to command the mud around them, pulling it up from the earth. From there, she tried to fashion it into an armor like Sis Namaji's, or at least pool it together to wash their enemies away, but every time she tried, the mud came together into a replica of a Bower, one that moved on its own. It was bigger than the last time, though, nearly as tall as Dirt's leg. It didn't last very long before it was trampled by Remnants, but it gave her confidence to see her newfound power improving.

The battle was fine until the mistake. This time, surprisingly, it was Carra Carre. She'd defeated nearly a dozen Remnants single-handedly, flinging them left and right, smashing them into mist. She fought so many that she lost track of those she had destroyed. There was one she had flung across the jungle, but it had survived. So as Carra Carre exhaled out of her Godskin in the aftermath, the Remnant charged her from behind, its hooves churning across the ground, its canine maw gaping wide.

Dirt screamed a warning and launched herself in that direction, but Ekko was there first, slamming into the beast and sending it off course. Carra Carre was able to easily dispatch it after that, but the shock on her face remained long after. Other than a quick and mumbled "thank you" to Ekko, the girl didn't speak at all on the way back to camp.

It wasn't until they were alone in the command house that she finally said something. She sat heavily onto a stone stool, elbows on her knees, head hanging.

"In all my years," she said, "and all my fights . . . I do not make a mistake like this."

The God Bow champion. The strongest girl in the world. Sis Carra Carre the Godskin, First of the Vine. Dirt had never imagined seeing the girl in such a state, and she wondered whether it was merely the mistake of the day that was weighing on her. That slouch in Carra Carre's shoulders reminded Dirt so much of herself after Webba left. Having sisters meant you never had to lift alone; there was always someone there to share the weight of life's burdens with.

Dirt had been reunited with the Mud Fam. The Rock sisters, the Sand, the Creek—they were all together in what had come to be known as the One Camp. Only Carra Carre was separated from her Fam. Though she treated everyone like they were her sisters, Dirt knew there was a difference between girls you were just beginning to trust and girls you could trust with your life without a second thought.

Dirt had been worried about herself slowing, but she hadn't considered that Carra Carre might be experiencing the same. Even with Ekko helping and the camp expanding, they were still each a mistake away from death.

"We need more help," Dirt admitted. The words were bitter in her mouth. "Ekko is not enough. If we can—"

"Na other regions . . . ," Carra Carre said, looking up at Dirt with tired eyes. "Na North, na East, na West . . . Do you think they still stand?"

Dirt sighed. It was a thought she'd been ignoring. As the waves of Remnants continued, she had to imagine the other Godskins were struggling just as much as they were. But then what did that mean for the North, where Sis Ahven was injured? Or the East, where Sis Boom was the only Godskin?

No, that couldn't be right. She thought all the regions had two Godskins . . .

"In na East . . . ," Dirt said, eyebrows creased. "There is only na one Godskin?

Carra Carre nodded. "Sis Boom."

But then she frowned and looked away, searching through her memory to confirm her words.

Before they could figure out what was wrong with their memory, there was a quick knock on the door and it opened. Swoo entered, and behind her came a half dozen Flagga boys. Their headbands were all different colors, implying that this was some alliance of Flagga.

"What is it?" Dirt asked.

Swoo had an uncharacteristic joyful bounce to her step, though her face was the same stern scowl it had been for weeks.

"It seems na Pusher boys are not na only ones with surprises," Swoo said.

Dirt looked between her and the Flagga in confusion until one of the boys stepped forward. He was Trip, one of the Mud Flagga who Dirt had long known.

"Godskin Dirt," he said with a bow of his head. "Na Mamas and Papas bless us."

Dirt managed not to scoff. Trip hadn't spent time with Useyi like Dirt and the other Bowers had. He didn't yet understand that the Mamas and Papas were in no position to bless anyone.

"How?" was all Dirt replied with.

The Flagga boys glanced at each other with excited grins.

"We can run," Trip said.

At Swoo's insistence, they all went outside to the main street. There, the Flagga boys lined up for a footrace.

"Ready!" Swoo called. "Go!"

The Flagga boys took off, pebbles spraying in every direction as they accelerated into sprinting. They were fast, but nothing unusual. Dirt glanced at Carra Carre, who returned her unimpressed look.

"Swoo, what are we watching?" Dirt asked.

Swoo only folded her arms and wore the hint of a smile. "Watch and see, my Sis."

The Flagga boys ran the entire length of the camp, then turned to run a path around the camp, all along the base of the cave. It was a few minutes before Dirt realized what was happening.

They weren't slowing down. True, they weren't running nearly as fast as a Godskin could move, but they were moving at top speed for hundreds of strides, then thousands, ten minutes then twenty then thirty. They completed several laps of the camp before returning, each of them with barely a hint of sweat, but with a joy gleaming in their faces that Dirt knew well—it was exactly how she felt the first time she used her Godskin powers.

"How . . . ?" Dirt asked.

Carra Carre grunted. "Na Gods are here," she said. "For all of us."

"They can only run," Swoo said. "They cannot fight, cannot change body like na Ekko boy. Just run and run and run."

"And so?" Dirt said. It was an impressive ability, but what they needed at that moment was a way to defeat the Remnants, not a way to deliver food.

"So they will mislead na Remnants," Carra Carre said, and Dirt immediately realized what Swoo and Carra Carre had both seen before her.

There would be no need to fight the Remnants directly, Swoo explained. The Flagga boys could run out in small groups and lure the Remnants away from the camp. When one group of Flagga got tired, they could lead the Remnants back to a central place, where another group could meet them and take over.

"How long can they run?" Dirt asked. "Na Remnants do not tire easily."

"I can run for two days," Trip said, chest puffed out.

"I can run for five!" said another Flagga boy.

"Ten!" chimed a third.

They were all lying, Dirt knew, boasting the way Flagga did. But even if they could only keep up their endurance for half a day, that would be enough. Dirt and four others could make it down into the Fault and put an end to the Remnants.

Dirt looked to Carra Carre. Gone was the glower from the

girl's face. Gone was the heavy-heartedness and defeat. There was confidence in her again, a thirst for conquest, the qualities that Dirt had come to rely on in their endless outings against the Remnants.

There was hope.

"Eh heh . . . ," Dirt said. "Let us see what na Flagga can do."

The Flagga practiced on their own for days, until Swoo eventually felt confident enough to test their abilities. But once the news traveled around the One Camp, Sis Zuna paid a visit to the command hut, a band of Sand Sis behind her.

"Na good day, my sisters," Zuna said, her eyes lanced on Carra Carre. "Exciting time, eh?"

Swoo spoke up first, putting herself between Zuna and Carra Carre. "Na good day, Sis Zuna. There is no need for violence this morning."

"Is there not?" Zuna asked, coming to a halt. Her Sis fanned out behind her. "Says who?"

There was silence, then, until Carra Carre pushed past Swoo to loom over Zuna. She didn't say anything, just stood there. To her credit, Zuna didn't back away. Her sisters even moved closer behind her, willing to share whatever fate Carra Carre decided to visit on them.

"Your Verdi still has my sisters," Zuna spat. "I do not care about na Flagga. I do not care about na Fault. I will see my sisters safe, or I will see that none of your sisters"—she looked past Carra Carre, her eyes stopping on Dirt, Swoo, and Sis Ask—"are safe."

Zuna left abruptly, leading her sisters back down to their homes in the camp. Dirt took a deep breath. Zuna was right, and any Bower would have done the same. If this Flagga plan worked, Verdi would have to be dealt with next. Otherwise, the sisters would lose trust in their leadership—and there was too much at stake for that.

Prey Becomes Hunter

SNORE COLLAPSED at the base of the tree, panting. Once again, she had narrowly avoided the Remnants. It was easy for the cats—for some reason, the Remnants never went after them. But for her, it was always a scary quest for a hiding spot until they gave up the search. This time, she'd scaled a tree and let its branches cover her as the Remnants passed by below.

The jungle cats slinked out of the shadows to join her. They each consoled her with a brush against her body or a lick of her mouth. Nubbi lay across her lap protectively. They knew how difficult it was for her to escape the Remnants, and they did their best to help, whether that meant scouting out hiding places ahead of her or fighting the Remnants off. But five more cats had died in the fights, so the big cats had decided it would be best to avoid the Remnants unless there was no other choice.

It was still midday. While most of the cats lay down for a nap,

Snore took the time to drink water and share some meat with Nubbi to replenish her strength. Not because she expected another Remnant attack, but because she wanted to play as soon as all the cats woke up. It had been long since they'd had a good tussle or enjoyed a few rounds of The Sneeze. She didn't like this new Cat Fam that didn't play so much. She wanted things to go back to the way they were.

For some reason, that made Snore think of her old Mud Fam, with the big, boring sisters and the days spent sweating from exercise instead of play. She wondered what they were doing, whether they were still alive or if the Remnants had gotten them. The Remnants were powerful and seemed to be everywhere. Sis Swoo and the Mud girls could not hide forever. Eventually, they would be found, and without Sis Dirt there to protect them . . .

A rustling in the trees. Snore froze, eyes peering into the jungle. On the edge of her vision, she saw all the jungle cats on their feet, creeping soundlessly into shadowed, defensive positions. The Remnants were on them again, Snore knew. She'd been worried about the Mud Sisters when she should have been worried about herself.

Only this time was different. The Remnants normally burst out of the jungle with ferocity. Even to the cats' amazing hearing, by the time a Remnant horde could be heard, it was already too close. But here, the sound was less aggressive, less a rush of Remnants and more the shifting of a slow-moving river. As the cats each took on the feral curl of combat, Snore listened with confusion as the sound grew closer.

And closer.

And closer.

Until she could see them. Not blue. Not hardened crystal. Not a mishmash of different animals. The sound was caused not by Remnants, but by girls and boys. Mostly Bowers. But not just any Bowers—the Vine.

The column of children was twenty paces away. Among them were dozens of Butterflies and Pusher boys and even Flagga, many of them with wrists tied in palm twine that extended to the person behind them so that they had to walk together in small trains. They all wore hopeless expressions as the Vine sisters walked beside them. The Vine girls walked with appropriate caution, each turning their vine-wrapped heads this way and that, peering into the jungle for any sign of danger. Several looked directly at Snore, but as still and camouflaged as she was, they saw nothing.

Even if Snore wanted to move, she couldn't have. Every inch of her was suddenly rooted to the ground. Except her chest. Her chest started bouncing with shallow breaths, and though she pressed her eyes shut, tears leaked free, cutting lines down her cheeks. She felt her face screwing up in fear and pain and a cramped loneliness that was identical to the one she felt that day when the Vine had taken her and locked her in a cage.

Nubbi's soft fur rubbed against her face, wicking away her tears, unrooting her limbs, deepening her breaths. As the train of Vine sisters and their captives passed by, Snore sniffed down her fear. The Vine had captured her before, but that was when she had been Bibi Snore of the Mud. Now she was Snore of the Cat Fam. She was stronger now, and smart, and she had a whole Fam of powerful cat sisters to protect her. She was safe.

No. More than safe.

Before, she was prey. Now, she could see them, but they couldn't see her. Now, she knew how easy it would be to jump out of the trees and scratch them across the eyes with her claws, bite down on them until her cat sisters finished the job.

The last one to pass was the leader, the big Sis with the sparkling purple eyes that Snore would never forget. She was the cruelest of them. The one who had told the Godskin to break Sis Webba. The one who had locked Snore in a cage, poked at her with a stick, left her to starve.

Snore smiled as she watched that last one pass by, unaware that Snore was watching. Before, Snore would have been too scared to do anything but hide. But now, she nodded to the big cats, and though they didn't understand Snore's mind, they could feel what she was feeling and knew what had to be done. Now, rather than trying to flee the Vine, she would follow them.

Now, she was the hunter.

34

The Vine Arrives

CARRA CARRE had never had any hope in the Flagga plan. Flagga boys were silly little things, as unreliable as a brittle palm on a windy day. Unlike Swoo, who seemed to enjoy them, and Dirt, who seemed to trust Swoo, Carra Carre had never suffered their presence before, and had no reason to expect anything but failure after failure from the troublesome boys.

Yet even she was impressed at how the test began.

Two groups of Flagga went together into the jungle, then split perfectly upon encountering a Remnant horde, leading the Remnants in opposite directions. They'd worked out a crude communication system, where one boy in each group would sling a black stone into the air, high enough that a third group of Flagga, waiting at the old Mud camp, would see it and know the plan was still working well. In all, the test would take a full day—the two groups would run for twelve hours before handing the Remnants off to the third group. Carra Carre and Dirt would oversee the handoff in case of disaster.

Three hours into the test, the first two stones soared into the air, tiny dots against the cloud-studded sky.

"Goodgood," Swoo grunted, her eyes tracking the rise and fall of the second stone. "You see, my Sis? Na Flagga can learn."

Dirt grunted, which was exactly how Carra Carre felt.

"We will see," Dirt responded.

In the hours before they had to go join the third Flagga group at the old Mud camp, Carra Carre and the other leaders ate and rested and discussed plans for the future. Swoo was already optimistic that the Flagga plan would work and wanted to discuss which five sisters would go into the Fault.

"Sisters?" the Pusher boy, Ekko, asked.

Swoo scoffed. "Yes, you overhopeful donkey."

Carra Carre could never like Swoo—the girl had burned down the only place Carra Carre had ever called home—but she'd come to enjoy the creativity of her insults. Each one was like a strange box that, when opened, revealed a rude gift.

"I can help!" Ekko protested. "Me, Sis Dirt, Sis Carra Carre, Sis Swoo, and one other."

"You are no Bower," Swoo countered with a dismissive yawn. "As much as you wish. You will stay. It will be me, Sis Dirt, Sis Carra Carre, Sis Ask, and Sis Zuna, if na Sand can remove their proud-proud heads from—"

"Ekko can come," Dirt interrupted.

Ekko let loose a small yelp of joy before swallowing it with a serious and confident cough.

Swoo scowled but kept quiet.

Carra Carre almost smiled. Dirt was no true warrior. She did not love battle the way Carra Carre or Swoo did. But that very reluctance was what earned her respect. The only thing more admirable than overcoming fear to fight a worthy battle was overcoming fear to fight a worthy battle when one didn't even want to fight.

There was a knock at the door, then a Rock Sis whose name Carra Carre had never learned popped her head into the command house. "Na third rocks are seen," she said.

Swoo nodded, bouncing her eyebrows triumphantly at Dirt.

The Flaggas had planned to send up rocks every three hours, which meant they would send three waves before meeting with the Flaggas at the Mud camp and passing the Remnants to them. The last rocks had gone up, which meant Sis Dirt and Carra Carre would have to prepare to leave soon.

They all left the command hut to go check on their respective Bibi, which left Carra Carre alone in her stone home, trying to avoid thinking about her Vine sisters. She failed, as she always did. She would give a finger to see her sisters for just a moment, a hand to see them for a day. She missed all of them, from the reckless Bibi to the overconfident NoBe to her proud and powerful Sis. To Verdi.

Verdi always floated to the top of her thoughts. Her exploits across the South were a burning mark of shame on the Vine Fam name. Yet the only thing Carra Carre wanted to do more than berate her was hug her. They were two stones on a balance beam—neither was ever meant to be without the other. Without Verdi, Carra Carre could never have built the Vine Fam into the power that it was. Without Carra Carre, Verdi . . .

Carra Carre sighed.

There was a muffled sound outside her door. Then another one, louder. Only on the third time was she able to make out the words.

"They are here!"

Carra Carre rushed out onto the main street, where Swoo, Dirt, and the other leaders immediately met her, all of them looking as one to the Rock Sis sprinting up the street, waving her hands in the air.

"They are here!"

When the girl reached them, she bent with hands on her knees, straining to catch her breath.

"Na Remnants?" Dirt asked.

The girl shook her head. When she righted herself, she looked directly at Carra Carre.

"Na Vine," she breathed out. "Na Vine is here."

Verdi looked the same as ever.

Somehow, that surprised Carra Carre. She'd thought her sister's tip into madness would have been accompanied by some physical change, yet there was no difference. Her beautiful, brilliant violet eyes shined out of her face just as they always had. Her body was still soft, as it had been ever since her fight with Sis Dirt. As were her once feared arms.

Behind Verdi was what appeared to be the remainder of the South. The entire Vine Fam was there, which made Carra Carre's heart light with joy. But so were hundreds of Butterflies and Pushers and Flagga. They were tied up, each boy or girl tethered to others in front and behind, their wrists bound. All the captive girls and boys of the South standing beneath the liquid sun, bare feet on prickly stone.

Carra Carre swept her eyes over the assembly, unable to keep the disappointment from her face.

"Are you not happy to see me, Cee Cee?" Verdi asked from behind her mask of vines.

It had been a long while since Carra Carre had spoken to another sister of the Vine. It was strange now, to hear a voice from behind the mask. The voice was obscured, with a faint hiss from where the air squeezed between the vines.

It had been even longer since she'd heard her nickname. Cee Cee. It was a reminder of who she was, a comforting transport out of the cold and dark cave to the sweltering and soaring heights of their old jungle camp. It was home.

"Verdi . . ." Carra Carre could do nothing but whisper.

"If you are here to join us," Dirt said, striding forward to draw Verdi's attention, "it will not be so easy. You have hurt many, Verdi."

"Join?" The incredulity was thick in Verdi's voice, though she kept her gaze on Carra Carre. "You see what I bring with me, and you think I come to join? Does na tree join na fruit? Does na sky join na sun? I come to make na offer to your hopeless and weary friends, Dirt."

"Na offer?"

Carra Carre's throat tightened at the sound of Sis Zuna's voice.

"Na *offer*?" Sis Zuna repeated, emerging from the camp entrance with a half dozen Sand Sis behind her. "If na offer is not my sisters and your cutoff hands, then you have come only to die, Verdi."

The murder in Sis Zuna's eyes was so fierce that Carra Carre almost stepped toward her, but for Dirt's pleading gaze stilling her.

"Ah," Verdi said. "You take orders from this one now . . ."

"I do not take orders. Sis Dirt is our ally."

"Sis Dirt?!" Verdi exclaimed. "So she is now your Sis, eh? And what of this one?" She tossed a lazy point toward Sis Swoo. "Na girl who burned our home? Is she now your bedmate, eh?"

"No more chatchat," Sis Zuna said. "Sisters!" she shouted, and the Sand sisters rushed forward.

But before the battle could begin, Verdi reached back and tugged on two ropes that were stretched out behind her. Sis Dream and Sis Hari, the First and Second of the Sand, stumbled forward, wrists bound.

Rarely had Carra Carre seen girls so badly beaten. Sis Hari had bruises all along her ribcage and lumps on her head that looked bad enough to warrant a Bonemender. But Sis Dream . . . the girl was barely recognizable. Her eyes were swollen too badly to see out of, and one of her cheeks was crushed in so badly that the whole side of her face looked immobilized.

Two Vine Sis, Evia and Murua, held daggers to their throats.

"Verdi . . . ," Carra Carre gasped.

"Why did you stop, Zuna?" Verdi asked sardonically. "Come and see na inside of your sisters if you so wish."

Sis Zuna's teeth ground loudly against each other, and for a moment Carra Carre was afraid that she would attack anyway—daggers be damned—and blood would flow.

But thankfully Sis Zuna restrained herself.

"You are foul, Verdi," Sis Zuna said instead, and there was seething rage in her voice. "Your time will come."

Carra Carre stared hard into Sis Evia and Sis Murua's eyes. She'd known them both for years. Evia was the Fam's Ninth, a skilled Slapper who had never had the endurance of the other Elite Bowers.

Murua was their newest Sis, a formidable NoBe who had always been hungry to learn, to grow.

They were kind girls. Patient with the Bibi, good listeners, calm sparring partners. Murua couldn't even break the necks of chickens for dinner, much less slash an innocent girl's throat. Both girls looked back at her with a mix of emotions: fear, confusion, defeat.

"My sisters," Carra Carre said. "Put down na daggers."

Before either girl could respond, Verdi interjected.

"Eh heh! Na First returns. What wisdom do you have for us, Cee Cee na Godskin?"

"Verdi, please—"

"Verdi, eh?" Verdi said, and her voice suddenly seemed different. A rising shout, vibrating with anger. "That is who I am to you? Dirt is 'Sis' but Verdi is just 'Verdi'? You stand here beside na girl who took my ear, eh? Who"—she turned her head to the left, slapping her right ear—"did this to me? You call her Sis, as if you know her your whole life, when I am here. Your true Sis!"

And suddenly Carra Carre could see clearly that it wasn't anger vibrating in Verdi's throat.

It was betrayal.

When Verdi spoke again, her voice was so small, so shattered. "Am I so bad?"

In the depth of her vine mask, those purple orbs welled with tears.

They were Bibi again, back in the days when Verdi was the bigger and Carra Carre was more than a decade away from becoming the Godskin. In those days, Verdi had been much more emotional. She'd cry when she won a Bow and rage when she lost, lifting heavy stones long past sunset as a form of self-punishment for defeat. They shared a hut, and Verdi would be up late, talking about her dreams, both her literal dreams and her dreams for the future.

That life changed often. One day, Verdi would want to be a God Bow champion. One day, she would only want to be a coach. Several times, she even discussed becoming a Butterfly girl, a Cooker, and selling her foods outside the Grand Temple. Once, after a particularly embarrassing loss in her second NoBe season, she'd even ranted that she'd disguise herself and become a Pusher boy, traveling the Isle and living stories instead of suffering defeat after defeat to girls she believed she was better than.

Despite all her varied dreams, one thing was consistent: Carra Carre. Whether God Bow champion or Bowing coach, Butterfly girl Cooker or Pusher boy traveler, Verdi never envisioned a life without Cee Cee at her side.

As much as Carra Carre had felt alone away from her Fam, she hadn't considered how lonely Verdi felt, how much Carra Carre's departure ruined every possible future Verdi could imagine. She had put her duty as a Godskin above her duty as a sister, and though it had seemed noble before, Carra Carre now felt nauseated at the thought.

Verdi was imperfect, yes. But being imperfect didn't mean she didn't deserve to be loved. A true sister loved you in spite of your imperfections. That was the meaning of Fam.

"I am sorry," Carra Carre said.

Verdi blinked. "What?"

But Carra Carre didn't get the chance to repeat herself. Because at that moment the jungle seemed to writhe like snakeskin. Leaves slid out of place and bushes elongated, everything distorting until Carra Carre realized it wasn't the jungle that was moving—it was beasts moving within the jungle.

But it wasn't Remnants.

It was jungle cats. Suddenly, her eyes could see them—dozens of cats slinking into view. The moment Carra Carre saw them for what they were, the cats pounced, speeding out of the trees and across the field of stones.

Running among them was a young girl—a Bibi by the look of her belly—who looked familiar to Carra Carre, though she couldn't tell why. She was bedecked in leaves that hid her, but her eyes burned bright with a violence that couldn't be shrouded by camouflage. Under any other circumstances, Carra Carre would have donned her Godskin and leapt to meet the cats, but she couldn't stop staring at the rage and pain and bloodthirst trapped within the little girl. It was leaking out in the form of tears that glittered at her eyes and drifted behind her as she sped forward, but that was only a drop of the flood within her, Carra Carre knew.

Carra Carre was so transfixed by the girl that she didn't react until the first cat sank its fangs into Verdi's calf. That spurred her into movement, but the second cat was already slamming claws-first into Verdi's belly. By the time Carra Carre reached her sister, the little girl was there, bearing down on Verdi with fingers and toes like claws, scratching for her eyes and throat as Verdi held her off with one forearm while her other forearm smashed down on the head of the cat attempting to disembowel her.

With a roar, Carra Carre flung one cat away, not caring whether it landed safely in the trees or was launched into the sun. Then she tossed the other cat, though beneath the emotionless void of the

Godskin, she felt a pang of terror as its face came away from Verdi soaked and dripping red.

Before she could do the same to the wild Bibi, she heard shouting from the trees.

"They are coming!" a Flagga boy shrieked, eyes wide in fear as he and two others sprinted toward the camp.

Only then did Carra Carre realize that the whole field of stones had turned into a battleground. Vine sisters were fighting off jungle cats. Pusher boys were mobbing their Vine captors. Flaggas were freeing each other from their restraints and freeing Butterfly girls in turn, who were launching stones at Vine sisters and jungle cats alike.

Dirt and Swoo were frozen solid, staring at the little Bibi with such devastation in their faces that Carra Carre realized she must have been their sister, the missing one.

Only Sis Ask seemed to have her wits about her.

"What?" she snapped at the trio of Flaggas.

"They . . . ," the lead boy began, panting.

Then three more Flaggas burst from the trees with the same terror on their faces, which delivered the message more fully than any words could have.

Ask's face sank into despair.

Of course. Before, Verdi's army had divided the children of the South. Now, they were all in one place.

"They do not follow us!" one of the Flaggas cried.

For weeks, the leaders of the One Fam had done everything they could to unite the South, to bring Bowers together with Butterflies and Flagga and Pusher boys so that all could be protected. And they'd almost succeeded. But at that moment, as Carra Carre surveyed the battlefield of children beating each other, binding each other back into restraints, getting torn apart by wild cats, she realized that she had been living a fool's dream. Peace and unity and love was a lie.

Verdi was right.

That was all Carra Carre could think before a crystalline blue body emerged from the trees.

35

The Battle for the One Camp

IT WAS THE biggest wave of Remnants Dirt had seen since the Imperial Temple. Then, there had been eight Godskins. Now, there were just two, plus a Pusher boy whose powers of detection were useless when the enemy was already at their door.

Dirt fought with a desperation she'd never felt before. Snore was home. The littlest Mud sister, the one most deserving of protection yet whom Dirt had repeatedly failed to protect. Snore had been lost for so long, and now she was home. They were all together again, and the feeling of her Fam whole and safe was like a weight removed from around Dirt's neck.

And here the Remnants had come to separate them.

She would not allow it.

All around her, children fled. She saw some of the Vine retreat back into the jungle in fragmented groups. The Butterflies, Flaggas, and Pusher boys who had been freed rushed toward the One Camp, and as they did, they had to push through a band of Bowers rushing out of the camp toward the battle. The result was a jam, blocking the camp from entrance or exit.

But Dirt walked straight toward the Remnants and was surprised to find Ekko suddenly at her side, his Petti's hawk wings merged into his shoulders, its beak and eyes settling over his face.

"How can I help?" the boy asked.

"Help na children," Dirt replied. "Get them into na camp."

Ekko nodded and was off, his hawkish voice piercing through the chaos to direct the clot at the entrance to the cave. Dirt turned her attention back to the Remnants and took a deep breath.

I am brave. I am fat. I am Dirt.

Even within her Godskin, she chanted her mantra, letting it fuel her. She flashed from one Remnant to the next, obliterating them with whatever was most efficient. An arm plunged through a chest. A slam against a tree. Head crushed between her palms or stomped beneath her feet. One Remnant's massive fangs used to sever the head of another. She quickly made her way to Snore, and any Remnant that neared her died. All she cared about was their destruction, about keeping them from tearing her Fam apart again, and soon the blue haze around her was as thick as the sweat rolling down her skin.

"Bibi Snore!" Dirt called, yanking the girl off Verdi and raising her up so that she could look her little sister in the eye.

"You are home," was all Dirt could think to say.

For a hair of a moment, she saw Snore's face screw up with anger and her hand raise up with fingers arched in like claws. Then the world flashed black, Dirt felt a knifing pain in her eyes, and she fell to a knee, hands instinctively rushing to her face to feel for injury.

It took several seconds before she could open her eyes again, and when she did, there was a Remnant upon her, its powerful bearlike arms nearly around her, its emotionless mantis head bearing down on her. Dirt managed to shoot her arms out fast enough to stop the beast before it grabbed her out of existence, but its weight and strength carried her to her back. As she struggled to wrestle it off her, she finally caught a glimpse of Snore.

The Bibi was soaring through the air, fingers ready for further violence. Her target was again Verdi, who was being helped to her feet by Carra Carre. As Snore's fingers approached Verdi's face, Carra Carre shot out a hand and caught her by the neck.

"No!" Dirt screamed. As much as Carra Carre had changed, Dirt didn't want to know what would happen if she had to choose between Verdi and Snore. "Carra Carre, wait!"

The First of the Vine managed to hear her through the rage of the fight and looked at Dirt just as a Remnant came up behind her.

It seemed to happen so slowly. Dirt's eyes widened. Carra Carre saw it, but it took her a second to understand. By the time she turned her gaze to follow Dirt's, the Remnant had wrapped its arms around Verdi. One of her legs had a large chunk bitten out of it, and she was bleeding from several punctures in her belly. But the moment the Remnant locked its grip on her, her face suddenly relaxed, as if she'd dipped into a warm pond. It was the most peaceful look Dirt had ever seen on the girl.

Then she was gone. The Remnant with her.

Carra Carre's grip on Snore released, but otherwise she didn't move at all. She seemed stuck in time at the moment just before the Remnant grabbed Verdi.

But Snore unleashed a scream that sounded more jungle cat

than human, a wild snarl that scraped its way out of her throat. She fell straight from Carra Carre's grip to her knees, not flinching at all as they smashed against the stone. Then she screamed again, a more human one, howling at the sky for a long and heartbroken note that frayed into hopeless sobs, her tiny body shaking.

Dirt needed to get to Snore, and not just because the Remnants were starting to shift in her direction. Mainly because the girl had broken again. Last time, Dirt hadn't been there to help put her back together, and it had set the girl on a path of reckless rage and loneliness, a path that could have seen her killed a dozen times. Dirt still barely forgave herself for letting Snore suffer once. She would never forgive herself if she let it happen again.

With a deep grunt and a mighty kick, she launched the Remnant off her and returned to her feet. She managed to catch two Remnants before they reached Snore's hunched, weeping form and bashed them together. Though the Remnants' numbers were thinning, Snore and Carra Carre were defenseless. So Dirt hovered around them, fighting off any that came near. She was both confused by and grateful for the help of the ten or so surviving jungle cats, who swarmed each Remnant despite the dozen or more of their Fam that lay dead across the rocks.

But she had been fighting long, and she soon started to make mistakes, slipping here and there, missing what should have been an easy death blow. On top of that, more cats fell, their fresh corpses a reminder of how dangerous the foe before her was. She needed more help, but Carra Carre was still frozen. There was no help coming.

Which meant she needed an escape. She would have to carry Snore and Carra Carre with her, but that would be easy enough with her remaining energy. Far easier than fighting off the remaining Remnants, at least. But where would she go? The minute she left, the Remnants would have no reason to go after her. They would just go into the camp, and the children of the South would be defenseless. It would be a massacre.

A Remnant's pincer as large as Dirt's belly shot toward her. She just barely slipped away, and rather than clamping down on her body, it pinched her side, biting deep into her skin and tearing away a thick strip. Another Remnant crashed into her headfirst, with such force that her vision flashed and she felt her legs turn liquid for a moment before she regained her footing.

"Sis Dirt!" a voice called from behind.

Dirt risked a glance in its direction, where Ekko stood in front of a wide open One Camp entrance. The lanky bird boy wore a triumphant grin as he beckoned Dirt over. Behind him, Swoo led a group of Bowers in bracing their bodies against a giant boulder, readying to push it across the opening.

"Sis Dirt, come!"

Dirt had to risk it all. She summoned the last of her energy to plunge her hands into the ground, splitting stone until she could feel the soft mud underneath. She yanked up as much as she could manage, cracking the ground in every direction and sending the Remnants staggering. Then she let the power of the Godskin do its work as the mud congealed into a Bower, one that immediately began swinging its mud arms at the Remnants. As exhausted as Dirt was, it didn't seem to be doing any damage, but it didn't have to.

It just had to keep them busy long enough.

Dirt hauled Snore and Carra Carre onto her shoulders and charged for the camp. Ekko was still there, smiling, waving her forward. Swoo and her patrol squad began their shove, the boulder crawling into place.

That was when the last Remnant appeared. Dirt didn't know where it came from, but it hadn't been one of the ones she was fighting. It came from ahead of Dirt rather than behind, leaping off the top of the rock formation at the entrance to the camp.

Even if Dirt had had enough energy to stop it, she wouldn't have known how. Rather than jumping toward her, it simply plummeted straight down, its four antelope legs dangling from a body that was scaled like a fish, but bloated and spiky. She realized too late that it wasn't going after her at all. Rather, its target was Ekko.

The boy had the senses of a hawk, but even a hawk lets its guard down when it thinks it is safe.

The Remnant fell upon him with terrifying impact. Its legs clamped onto him, pressing him from four points. He didn't even have time to stop smiling before he was gone, the Remnant with him.

Dirt continued forward, passing beneath the protective shade of the One Camp entrance as the boulder slid into place behind her. She collapsed, exhausted, the power of the Godskin falling away from her.

As she sat in the ensuing silence, she felt a terrible weight suddenly sit inside her. It was like some creature was gnawing on her spirit. Or like she had just lost something that was important to her.

Something she knew she would never see again.

36

Bibi Snore's
Return

NO ONE KNEW how many the Remnants had taken. Swoo and
her patrols went around and asked, but no one could name anyone
they had lost. Despite the pain and loss that many girls and boys
were feeling, it seemed that the One Camp had only added to its
numbers.

Yet what appeared to be a seamless reunion brought Nana
no joy.

A part of her was elated to see Snore safe and back with the
Fam. That first day, she had wrapped her arms around her former younger Mud sister with the tightest hug she could manage,
smoothing her hair and kissing it, overwhelmed by the moment
when the four of them—Dirt, Swoo, Snore, and herself—shared a
group embrace.

But that good feeling could not overcome the emptiness inside
of her, like a scoop of her had been hollowed out in her sleep.

During the day, she tried to ignore it by staying busy with making armor, but in the quiet of night, it consumed her. She cried for hours without knowing why, holding the center of her chest as if it would fall away if she removed her hand. She hoped that no one else could hear her, lest they check on her, ask questions, force her to make sense of her nonsensical grief.

Then, on the second night of her sobbing, the door to her stone home scraped open. She wiped hastily at her eyes and lay down facing the wall, as if she'd been sleeping.

"Who is it?" she asked.

When there was no answer, she half-turned to look over her shoulder.

Snore stood in the doorway, a silhouette against the dim moonlight that crept in through the cave's ceiling. As small and round as she was, she was unmistakable.

Nana sniffed and sat up, propping her back against the wall.

"Na good night, my sister," she said. As a Butterfly, she wasn't supposed to talk to Bowers that way anymore, but she didn't know how else to address Snore.

Snore didn't respond. She walked across the room and lay down next to Nana on her sleep mat, cuddling up beside her.

"Snore?" Nana said, confused. "What is it?"

Moonlit tears sat at the edge of Snore's eyes, welled but not falling.

"You feel na same, eh?" Nana asked. Snore looked down, burying her face in Nana's shoulder. "Like na thing is gone, but you do not know what it is. I know." Nana felt a sudden wave of relief wash over her. She'd thought she was the only one bearing this confusing pain. She thought there was something wrong with her that she couldn't fully enjoy their victory over the Remnants. But if Snore felt it too, that meant that Nana wasn't weird. And that she wasn't alone.

"Why do we feel this way? Why is it only we who feel like this?" She rubbed the back of Snore's neck. In their Bibi days, it was the fastest way to get Snore to sleep.

This time, though, it didn't work. Snore's body soon began to shake with sobs, and they both stayed awake throughout the night, sharing their grief as they had shared so much of their lives together.

Snore returned every night, and they healed each other in the unspoken way that sisters can, by closing physical space in order to create emotional space. Nana knew that the feeling would not go away soon—she was still sad from Webba's leaving months before—but she knew that, with Snore's help, she would continue to get better.

But deep within her, Nana knew the Remnants were some-how responsible for their pain. The Remnants and Useyi and all the strangeness of the last couple of months. Just as the power of the Gods had come to the world, so had this new, empty type of pain.

So Nana increased her efforts to defeat the Remnants once and for all. Each day, she woke as early as possible and immediately set to work on her jewelry armor. With help from some of the Sand Bowers and Flagga boys, she'd already gathered all the stones she needed. Now, she shaped and polished them, taking her cloth from a shallow bath of water and rubbing it endlessly over each stone, wearing away the thinnest of layers until it was exactly as she needed. In a way, the repetitive physical work reminded her of her Bowing days, when she'd Slapped for hours or lifted heavy stones all afternoon. The tiring of her muscles was similar, and she sometimes took breaks to shake out the knots in her hands and forearms. But the level of focus was even more similar, and she enjoyed the familiar feeling of blocking out everything in the world except the task at hand.

Soon her house was full of smoothed stones of varying size and color. Lavender stones as small as a fingernail, rust-colored stones as big as a Bower's belly, and everything in between. Only when looking at them together did she realize how little thought she'd put into it all. It was as if a spirit had guided her, told her the ingredients without telling her the dish to be made.

Whatever had guided her, the recipe was almost ready. The next step was to acquire leather to hold the stones and strap them to the body. With small jewelry, she preferred to use metal, but it would be impossible to shape such a large amount of metal in any reasonable amount of time, so she had to seek out the best source of leather she could find.

"How now, Mud sisters?" Nana greeted.

The Mud Bibi halted their training to stare at her, mouths agape. It was still strange that they reacted that way to her. She understood why Sis Dirt had that effect on them—she was large, Scarred, the Godskin. But Nana was just a Bibi turned Butterfly. She wasn't anyone special.

"I need your help," she said.

Flaggas were great at fetching stones, but leather came from animals, and animals meant food. Only Bowers had the steady supply of animal flesh Nana would need.

"Na good day, Butterfly Nana," one of the Mud girls eventually responded. "What is it you need?"

It was Tiggi, the one Nana had met before. Nana knew there were no NoBe or even Senior Bibi among the new Mud sisters, but Tiggi seemed to be emerging as a leader. The girl moved with a certain fearlessness—there was no small amount of Swoo in her.

"You are wellwell, eh?" Nana asked.

Tiggi nodded and drummed on her belly.

Nana laughed. It was such a Bower thing to do that she hadn't seen in a long time.

"I have need of skins," she said.

As expected, the Mud had plenty. Tiggi led Nana to the garbage heap, where skin from the previous night's pigs was laid out in cut strips among a week's worth of banana peels, onion skins, and all sorts of discarded foods.

"They are here," Tiggi said. "We can bring them to your home, Butterfly Nana."

Nana nodded. It wasn't enough, but she expected the other Fam would have skins as well. Then she just had to dry it and prepare it and the leather would be ready.

"Thank you, Tiggi," Nana said, then turned to be on her way.

"Butterfly Nana," Tiggi said, "why do you leave na Mud Fam?"

The abrupt change in tone brought Nana to a halt. She turned back to Tiggi and tilted her head curiously.

"Why do you ask?"

Tiggi shrugged, shy again after her moment of boldness.

Nana smiled. It was a question she herself had asked so many times, especially in those first days as a new Butterfly. It had not been easy to join a new group of girls, make new friends, live a new life. But even her worst days as a Butterfly had felt right, and she'd soon earned respect not for what she could do—as Bowers showed respect—but for who she was.

Tiggi, Nana realized, must have been asking herself the same question in reverse. Why did she leave the life of the Butterfly? Nana could never know what was in the girl's mind, but it seemed like a good choice.

Ultimately, the biggest difference between Bowers and Butterflies was not how they lived, but what they wanted out of that life. Butterflies wanted, above all else, to stand out. They wanted to be unique and to be noticed for that uniqueness. That was why they wore the high shoes and face paints and flirted with boys.

Bowers wanted to fit in. The fighting was secondary. Deep down, what Bowers truly wanted was to be like those around them, one part of a whole. That was why they all wore uniforms, danced together, trained and ate and slept together.

One life was about learning to express yourself, and the other was about learning to share yourself with others. Nana was where she needed to be, and as she looked at Tiggi, she could tell that Tiggi, more than anything, wanted what the life of the Bower offered.

"I leave na Mud Fam," she explained, "because my heart tells me. Nothing else."

Tiggi simply stared at her, so Nana reached out and rested a hand on her shoulder, then turned and left the Mud Bibi. Nana had faith that Tiggi would find her way, just as she herself had. When the heart spoke, it spoke loudly.

Nana spent the rest of the day visiting the other Bowers and taking whatever leftover skins they had. By the end, she had not only plenty of strips of discarded skin, but she had some skins that had already been dried, salted, and even tanned. In less than two days, the armor would be ready.

Then she could finally do something to fix the emptiness in her chest.

37

Nana's Armor

IT HAD BEEN two days since the Remnant attack.

Dirt spent the first day recovering. The fight had been desperate, brutal. By far the most difficult fight she'd ever had, and her muscles and bones wore the strains of battle. Still, with how many Remnants had come after them, she was in disbelief that not a single boy or girl had fallen.

At least that was how she remembered it.

Yet she had a feeling inside that was hard to ignore. A feeling of defeat. A feeling of loss. No matter how fine the camp seemed, a bone-gnawing paranoia persisted that there were things Dirt had simply forgotten. People the Remnants had taken. Dirt didn't see that same paranoia in anyone else, though. As she walked the camp that first day, all she saw were smiles, music, dancing, the revelry of another day survived. She began to think that she was the only one concerned about what the Remnants might have done.

Until she met with the other leaders.

"Na empty-head jackal Remnants," Swoo spat. "They take our brothers and sisters. I know this."

Ask nodded. "Sis Swoo speaks true. Something is wrong."

While before, Zuna and Carra Carre could not be in the same room together, the tensions seemed to have vanished. Zuna was leaned back casually in her chair, balancing on its two rear legs, her feet up on the map table.

"I know I have more sisters before," she said. "I cannot say who is gone, but . . ." She shrugged as if it wasn't a big deal, but her brows were bunched in confusion.

Carra Carre didn't speak. She stood in a shadowed corner of the room, her heavy arms folded protectively across her chest. She seemed more affected by the recent attack than anyone, and she hadn't said anything since it happened, her expression alternating between unfocused confusion and an inward-facing anger. Dirt had no doubt that Carra Carre, too, was battling with the fear of what may have been lost to the Remnants.

Which left one question lingering in the room.

"And when na Remnants come for us, eh?" Swoo asked, biting her lip with an unsettled frown. "Who in this room will we forget by our next meeting? Who is in this room before and not now?"

A cloud of silence descended.

As Dirt looked around, she realized that this time was different from the others. Whether they were willing to admit it or not, they had never truly believed they could lose to the Remnants. They had two Godskins and had taken protective measures on top of that, turning the One Camp into the most fortified spot in the South.

Yet it hadn't been enough. Nothing they did would be enough. And that dreaded feeling they all had—that corrosive fear that their lives were gradually being stolen from them—would only grow.

"We must go into na Fault," Dirt said solemnly. "It is so."

No one agreed at first. They shifted uncomfortably, eyes sliding from one girl to the next, pursing their lips thoughtfully. But they all soon realized that there was no other option. The Remnants weren't just twisted beasts; they were time itself. And time always won in the end. It turned the day to night, turned seeds into trees, girls into women. Eventually—inevitably—it turned every living person into a memory, and then even that memory was turned into something forgotten.

They couldn't ignore the Remnants. They had to confront them directly, no different from time.

"It is," Carra Carre was the first to say.

"It is," said Sis Swoo of the Mud.

"It is," said Sis Ask of the Rock.

"It is," said Sis Zuna of the Sand.

"It is," said Sis Splash of the Creek.

For the first time in memory, the Bowers of the South were united.

"Now who of us will go?" Swoo asked.

They debated that night and into the morning about who would be the five to go.

Dirt and Carra Carre were obvious, and Swoo demanded to go as well. At first the others were all competing to see who would go, but eventually Ask stepped down from contention.

"I am First of na Rock," she said with a sigh. "I will stay with na Rock."

So it was decided: Dirt, Carra Carre, Swoo, Zuna, and Splash.

Until the Remnants came again.

They came with no warning, bearing down on the patrol team suddenly. They managed to get through the camp entrance and charge down the interior ramp before Dirt and Carra Carre were alerted.

The two Godskins successfully dispatched the beasts. But none of the patrol team was around afterward, and no one could remember who had been assigned patrol that day. It was enough to rattle the resolve of most of the girls and boys of the One Camp. Even the leaders.

"I cannot go," Splash said, her eyes centered on the map table to avoid looking at the others. "I am no Godskin. What can I do to na Remnants?"

Zuna looked filled with shame as she explained her resignation. "If na few Remnants can do this to us . . . how can I fight them in their home? I am sorry . . ."

From five, they were down to three.

"I wish I can say I will go," Ask said apologetically, "but I see now how na One Camp needs me. While you Godskins are in na Fault, I must be here."

Dirt couldn't blame any of them. There was nothing they could do against the Remnants except risk their lives. Would she have left her own sisters behind to fight a foe she couldn't beat?

But that still left them in a bind. Useyi had insisted that they could only use the magic of the Fault with five children. They only had three.

"What of Sis Hari?" Dirt asked.

Zuna shook her head. "She says she will not. None of na Sand Sis will come."

"Na stinking cowards," Swoo spat, staring hard at each of the other leaders, daring them to challenge her. Not a one of them did.

"Not cowards," Dirt countered. "All girls must choose, and they choose what they believe is best." She swept her eyes around the room. "You all can stay. We will find two others."

Easier said than done.

None of the Sis were willing to go. Each of them refused to risk dying down in the Fault when they could instead die protecting their Fam. For some reason, the Pusher boys had been especially shaken since the Remnant attack days before. They were too afraid to leave camp at all, much less venture to the center of the Isle. The Flaggas were the same.

It was beginning to look like they wouldn't have enough girls to even go into the Fault.

"I never think I will see Bowers so afraid," Swoo said.

It was well into the night. Swoo had just come to visit after overseeing the change in patrols, whereas Dirt had been sitting in her stone home for hours, thinking.

"There is no shame in fearing na Fault," Dirt said.

"There is no shame in urinating on oneself, yet I sit here with drydry pants."

"Swoo . . . ," Dirt scolded. "Breathe easy, eh? Na Bowers, cowards or no, are not our enemies. We must plan for na Fault. If three is all we have, then we must plan for three."

Swoo sucked her teeth and rolled her eyes but had nothing to say.

"Are you not afraid?" Dirt asked her. "You have no Godskin. You do not worry about na Fault?"

"Of course I worry," Swoo replied, her voice softer than usual. "I worry for you. I worry that overlarge coconut Carra Carre will fail us. I worry I will slow you."

"And if you do?"

"Eh?" Swoo asked, confused.

"Slow us."

"Then I will move faster."

"You will go. Return to na camp. Promise me."

Swoo snorted, dismissing the thought with a wave. "No."

"Promise. If I tell you to go, you must go. We do not know what we must face in na Fault."

"It does not matter what we must face. 'We never quit, noooooo,'" Swoo sang.

Dirt began to smile, but every muscle in her face froze before she finished the expression.

The Mud Anthem. "We need only two," Dirt realized.

Right then, seeming to emerge straight out of Dirt's thoughts, Nana poked her head in. She looked back and forth between Swoo and Dirt before delivering her announcement.

"Na armor is ready," she said.

Armor was something from the stories, from the days of the Mamas and Papas and their battles against Useyi and the Forgotten. Papa Oduma wore a shirt of armor made of hundreds of coral stones, each the length of a finger and linked side by side in long columns like the walls of a wood hut. He wore a coral skirt around his waist as well, and it was said that the armor could deflect any weapon.

Dirt had never considered whether Nana really listened when Webba and Antie Yaya told stories, but the way the armor was an almost perfect replica of Papa Oduma's spoke clearly enough. Dirt looked down at herself, amazed by the stones glinting all along her skin. These coral stones were more round than long, but the way they were strung together by leather, with scarcely a gap in between, made Dirt feel like Papa Oduma himself.

It wasn't just the design that was impressive. Dirt felt a familiar power emanating from it, the same as when she used her own power. This, in more ways than one, felt like a true "Godskin."

"Chaaaiii, Nana . . . ," Dirt said, raising her arms and turning in a slow circle. "You are truly na wowwow girl."

Nana, standing across the room, smiled sheepishly and crossed her arms behind her back. She wore face paints now, and her shoes even had a bit of a heel on them, but she was still the same Nana.

"Thank you, Sis Dirt."

"How did you do this, eh?"

Nana shrugged. "At first I get na stones. Then na leather. Then . . ." She looked away, her brows scrunched in focus and memory. "I feel quiet in my head, and . . . it is easy. I just make it."

Dirt wasn't sure she understood at first, but then it dawned on her. It was the same as the Flagga boys' enhanced endurance. She looked upon Nana with a warm smile. "Na power of na Gods has indeed come back to na Isle."

Nana had made armor for Swoo and Carra Carre as well. Rather than coral, Carra Carre's was made from a deep green stone, while Swoo's was a rich red. They spent the afternoon wearing the armor, testing it against rocks and knives, adjusting the size and tightness as necessary. When Carra Carre first put on the armor, she shared a knowing look with Dirt, then gave Nana a nod of respect.

For Swoo, it was a very different experience. Once the armor was cinched in place, her body immediately stiffened, and her eyes widened. Then the tears began to fall, sliding unchecked down her cheeks and dripping free to the floor. Swoo's mouth worked, but no words came out, and it was several seconds before she gave up the attempt, rushed across the room, and lifted Nana into a crushing hug.

"This is how it feels, eh?" she said as she placed Nana back down. Nana was all giggles, her face flushed. Swoo turned to Dirt and took a long, deep breath, a slow blink. "This is na power of na Godskin?"

Dirt remembered that day so long ago when she had discovered her powers in the Grand Temple. Dirt couldn't remember who she'd fought that day, but she remembered Swoo's response that night. She'd cried then as well, though not from the beauty of the moment but from drunken jealousy that it was Dirt favored by the Gods rather than herself.

How far my Swoo has come, Dirt thought as she looked at her sister. Finally, in a way, she had gotten a taste of the power she'd so desired.

There were limits, Nana explained. Swoo would only have the protection of a Godskin, but she wouldn't have the speed and strength of Dirt or Carra Carre. Still, the armor would allow Swoo to go into the Fault with less fear of the Remnants, and to defend herself long enough for Dirt and Carra Carre to rescue her, if necessary.

"We are in your debt, Nana," Dirt said. "Yet I have one more favor to ask."

Nana tilted her head, curious. "You want me to join you in na Fault," she said.

"We want you to come with—" Dirt began. "Eh? How do you know?"

Nana shrugged and gave a self-satisfied smile. "I hear you invite all na Sis and NoBe, and none say yes. So who else? And if I come, I can fix na armor."

Dirt hadn't doubted that Nana would join them. Not really. Some Bowers prided themselves on their bravery, but they weren't truly so. They only appeared brave because they were too foolish to feel fear when they ought to. Bravery wasn't something fearless people understood—it was only found in those who were afraid but overcame.

Nana was the bravest girl Dirt knew.

"So we have four," Swoo said, hope in her voice. "Better than three."

Nana cleared her throat, drawing the other girls' eyes back to her.

"Actually . . . ," she said, her smile growing.

38

The Five

IN LESS THAN a day, final preparations were completed. The One Camp had enough food and water to last a week, and every girl and boy knew their role in case of a Remnant attack. As soon as the five left, the boulder would be rolled behind them, sealing the entrance. They had two additional boulders behind that one, ready to roll in place if the Remnants began to breach the first. They also had a plan to retreat to the new interior chambers, one that would require everyone's effort to pull off.

On the morning of departure, Swoo was the first one up, as usual. She started her morning with a jog around the camp, taking in the scent of the cold stone, the sight of the pockmarked spread of the squat homes and the dividing center path, the feel of the damp cave air against her skin.

She would miss the One Camp. Not as much as she missed the Mud camp, but the place had come to feel like home in its own way.

When she'd left the Mud camp, she'd made sure to prepare herself for the possibility that she would never live there again. She did the same with the One Camp as she finished her run, committing as much to memory as she could.

Then she packed her things into a canvas bag and was on her way to the camp entrance, taking a final walk up the long ramp.

Carra Carre was the first to join her. Unlike Swoo, she was already wearing her armor, torso and thighs shielded by green stones, a few of them as big as a Bibi.

"Na good day," Swoo said. She would never like Carra Carre, but they were companions for the time being and would soon battle side by side. Greeting her was the minimum respect owed.

"Na good day," Carra Carre grunted back.

Swoo had always called the Vine cowardly for hiding their faces the way they did, but now that she'd spent weeks being able to see Carra Carre's face, she wished the girl would cover it back up. Something about seeing her every expression was even worse than seeing none. Before, Carra Carre had been a faceless giant. Now, she was just a girl—the biggest one to ever live, but a girl all the same, with her own hopes and fears, all etched into her face.

Ever since the big Remnant attack, Carra Carre had retreated into herself. The usually grunt-prone behemoth had become almost entirely grunts and glowers, refusing to say anything during the leadership planning sessions. But there was a pain in the silence that even Swoo could see. Where they all felt cracked from the mystery of what they lost that day, Carra Carre seemed near shattered.

Swoo worried whether the girl's heart was ready for the mission into the Fault.

"Na good day, my Sis," Sis Dirt said as she reached the top of the ramp, clattering in her stone armor.

"Na good day," Swoo responded, as did Carra Carre.

They glanced at each other.

"Finefine," Dirt said, chuckling. "New Sis and old Sis. Where are na Bibi?"

Swoo nodded down toward the camp, where two tiny figures came up the central road. It wasn't long before they too reached the top of the ramp.

"How now, Bowers?" Nana said, a pale blue Adorner's bag slung over one shoulder and a larger canvas bag across her back. "Sorry we are late."

Beside Nana, Snore wore a tattered green cloth around her waist and nothing else. She stared forward, not at Swoo, but through her.

As much as Swoo had searched for Snore, she'd avoided the girl ever since she returned. Even she herself couldn't fully say why, though. Maybe it was guilt that Snore had fled again in the first place. Or maybe it was that she was afraid of the feral creature Snore had become, uncertain that their bond as sisters had survived their time apart.

"Na good day, sisters," Snore said.

Her tiny voice cracked from disuse, with a rasp, like a girl with a cough. Despite all she had been through, there was still a thread of innocence left in that voice. And in those big, weepy brown eyes. And in her chubby little body, leaner from her life among the cats, but still as pinchable as ever.

Swoo found herself crying again. The second time in as many days. Ridiculous.

She scooped Snore up and into her arms. These days, with the world the fractured mess it was, a hug was the only way to hold things together. Within the embrace, Swoo felt peace, security. Nana's little arms and Dirt's big arms wrapping around them only added to that feeling.

When Swoo looked up, she saw Carra Carre's head farther back, poking above Nana's. She felt a sudden wave of empathy for the girl. All the power of the Gods, yet no Fam to share it with. Swoo couldn't recall what had happened to the Vine Fam—she could still remember a few of the NoBe, but not much else. But she knew the warmth and joy the Mud Fam brought her, and a life without that was a life Swoo wouldn't wish on even her worst enemy.

"Come," Swoo said, waving one hand in invitation. "Join us, Carra Carre."

The other Mud sisters all looked over as well, with varying expressions. Snore's face took on a faint shadow. Nana's held uncertainty, Dirt's a hesitant hope.

But Carra Carre just stared at them for several long seconds before issuing an unmistakable scoff and turning toward the cave entrance. She put a hand on the giant boulder and rolled it aside, allowing in a stream of sunlight.

The rest of the camp had assembled to wish them goodbye. Swoo had come to know most of them, from the Bibi to the full Sis to the Flaggas and Pusher boys. And they had come to know her and to trust her leadership. Somehow, the Sis Swoo who hadn't been able to manage the fifty Bibi of the Mud Fam had brought together the hundreds of girls and boys of the One Camp. True, there had been failures, but as she looked out upon their faces, she saw far more love and trust than anything else.

As the Flaggas' drums kicked into rhythm and their algaitas blared a triumphant melody, Swoo's heart swelled with pride as they all sang together, voices deep and resonant, soaring and delicate, all the myriad tones of the girls and boys of the South melding into a single sound. A single anthem.

We are na One Fam, One Fam
We get better
by fighting together,
Na One Fam, One Fam.

We are na One Fam, One Fam
This Fam we choose
so we cannot lose
Na One Fam, One Fam.

The anthem skipped along like a pebble across water, a buoyant song, just what Swoo needed to hear. With a song at their backs, Swoo and her sisters turned away from their new Fam to face the open world.

The journey to the Fault had begun.

Useyi's Prayer

THEY DIDN'T talk much on their trek.

Dirt was at the rear of the column. Carra Carre led the way, with Swoo behind her and then the little ones. It was so much like the old days, yet so different. There was no Webba. Which meant no silly songs or epic stories or infectious grins. Swoo was different, too—on the old walks, she had forged the path ahead, cutting the branches in their way with her handaxe. This time, she seemed lost in thought, looking up only to scan the sky to see how many hours had passed. Nana was more reserved than she had ever been in the old days, though she carried herself with a confidence she had previous lacked, despite the occasional slip of her heeled shoes on the knotty jungle floor. Snore was still an unhealed wound, only just beginning to scab over. She didn't speak or sing or dance or wander off like she used to, but at least her spirit was lighter than it had been before she'd fled the Fam.

Around midday, they took a break to eat and drink. Carra Carre quickly moved away from the rest of them and found a spot beneath a tree, where she ate her portion of nuts, dried fruit, and chunks of boiled bushmeat. Dirt had been trying to let Carra Carre deal with her pain in whatever way she chose, but going into the most important fight of their lives, she needed to reconnect with the girl. The distance between them now could soon cost not just their lives, but the lives of everyone in the One Fam.

"My Sis," Dirt said as she walked over to Carra Carre, nodding toward the girl's half shirt. "What is that, eh?"

Carra Carre looked down at herself but narrowed her eyes when she saw nothing. "Eh?"

"Not your shirt," Dirt said, sitting down beside Carra Carre with a sigh. "Your heart."

It was bad enough to earn an irritated sniff of air, which was all Dirt had hoped for. "You think you are Webba now, eh?" Carra Carre asked.

Dirt chuckled. "If Webba cannot be here, then I am the closest you will get."

She'd hoped that Carra Carre would laugh along with her, but something about Dirt's words only forced Carra Carre back into a stoic stare.

"Do you fear you will forget her?" she asked suddenly.

"I cannot," Dirt replied immediately. "She is my sister. Then and always."

Only after she said it did she realize how it must have sounded to Carra Carre. Though Dirt herself couldn't remember any Vine sisters, she knew how unlikely it was that Carra Carre had been the Fam's only Sis. Some must have been taken by the Remnants. Sisters Carra Carre was struggling and failing to remember.

"I am sor–" Dirt began, but Carra Carre shook her head, halting her.

"I understand," she said.

Dirt felt like a fool. She'd come over to make Carra Carre feel better, yet all she'd done was make her feel worse.

"You are na good sister, Dirt," Carra Carre said. "In my memory, you are the best sister I ever have."

Then she stuffed a piece of meat into her mouth so large she couldn't speak anymore, and Dirt took that as a sign that their conversation was at an end.

"Up up," she called out, rising to her feet. "Finish your food. We must continue."

They reached Antie Yaya's just before sunset.

Or what was left of it.

As they emerged from the trees to overlook Antie Yaya's compound, they saw that the ornate hall of gray-brown limestone that stretched across one's view was a cadaver of its former self. The three plumes at the top had collapsed into the center of the hall, and with it, much of the building had come down. The grass plaza was in shambles, with chunks of grass churned up into dirt, bricks strewn all across it, and most of its trees bent and broken.

There was no longer any sign that anything lived there.

"No . . . ," Dirt said, sliding into her Godskin.

She leapt across the basin—the bridge was too damaged to use even if she'd wanted to—and onto the grass plaza. Then she made her way toward the ruins of Antie Yaya's palace, climbing up the remainder of the staircase and kicking through loose rubble.

"Antie Yaya!" she shouted.

The sound of a muffled human voice sent tremors down Dirt's spine. Suddenly, she was back at the Mud camp the day after the Vine attack, and Webba lay broken in the scattered remains of the Mud sleep hut.

She had to shake off the memory to charge toward the sound, which came from beneath an especially tall pile of bricks.

"Don't bother" came Antie Yaya's voice.

It had come from beneath Dirt. She looked around the ground, confused.

Then some of the rubble beside her slid away as a door opened up toward the sky. Antie Yaya emerged, poised and clean in a black blouse and wrapper with white floral patterns, a dress far more suited for a party than surviving a building collapse.

"Antie?" Dirt asked.

"Who else would it be? Come in, come in."

Antie Yaya disappeared down into the hole but left the door open. Dirt looked out toward her sisters, raising her hands to let them know she was okay. She was grateful that Carra Carre had waited with them, in case of Remnants.

Then she went over to the door and looked down. There were no stairs, just a poorly made step stool of nailed-together wood. Dirt didn't trust it with her weight, so she jumped down, landing directly on the stone floor.

It was a small space that could scarcely be called a bedroom. Its floor and ceiling were tilted at different angles, resulting in a space that was dizzying to stand in and full of the dust of crumbling brick. Two sleep mats woven from palm fronds lay in one corner and a wooden chest that Dirt could only assume was full of Antie Yaya's clothes sat in another, but that was all.

"It's humbling, eh?" Antie Yaya said as she sat atop one of the sleep mats.

The other sleep mat held Useyi. The man had his hands behind his head like he was watching the clouds drift by on a boring day.

"Welcome, Godskin," he said.

For a moment, Dirt felt a surge of rage well up in her. While they were fighting for their lives against the Remnants, losing friends they couldn't even remember, the man who had unleashed the beasts on the world lay peacefully on his back, watching the time pass.

But the feeling quickly fled when she realized that he was in the same position they were in. His whole world was gone. His family gone. His friends gone. He could still remember them, true, but Dirt wasn't certain that was a good thing. Was it better to lose things and know it, or lose things and not know?

"Na good day, Antie Yaya," Dirt replied, dipping her head in respect. "Na good day, Useyi."

"I would offer you tea, but . . ." Antie Yaya threw her arms up to gesture to the room.

"What happened?" Dirt asked.

"Those Remnants," Antie Yaya said with a sigh. "They came for my Butterflies. The girls thought to hide at first, which just led to those beasts tearing down my home to get to them. We lost dozens."

"Including Ebe," Useyi added.

The name sounded nice, but Dirt couldn't remember any girl named Ebe.

"Poor girl," Antie Yaya said. "She served me well."

Their words were horrifying—Dirt could only imagine the fear in the Butterfly girls as they huddled together, breaths held so that the Remnants wouldn't hear them, only to have the walls torn down around them, their spirits consumed. Yet Antie Yaya's and Useyi's faces were indifferent.

"Do you not care?" Dirt asked.

Antie Yaya shrugged. "We knew the Godskins were still alive to save us. That is why you're here, is it not?"

"Yes . . . ," Dirt began, confused as she always was when she spoke with Antie Yaya. "But na girls cannot come back. Even if we defeat na Remnants."

Useyi shook his head and, for the first time since they began talking, looked at Dirt.

"The magic is bigger than that." His voice was even and clear. And hungry. Beneath his otherworldly calm, Dirt sensed a desire as hot and persistent as the sun at noon. "There is nothing that is beyond its power. You all—you Godskins—touch just the surface of it and can crush mountains into dust. Flagga boys can run for days. Pusher boys can merge with all manner of animals. The thinnest tendril of this magic is in you, children, and you all are capable of incredible feats. Within the Fault lies far more than a tendril. There lies the entire beast." His face tightened; his gaze held fast. "Not only can you defeat the Remnants, you can change the world. Make it whatever you wish. Bring back whoever you like."

By the time he finished speaking, Useyi was no longer looking at Dirt. His eyes were unfocused, useless before the deluge of possibilities that seemed to be playing through his mind. If the magic was as he described it . . .

Can Webba return?

Dirt knew it was a selfish thought, to pull her sister back from the land of the Mamas and Papas. But Useyi described the magic as limitless. So Dirt wouldn't have to save only Webba—she could save everyone.

"How?" she asked.

Useyi's gaze returned to the moment, and he shook his head sadly. "That I do not know. The magic worked one way in my world, but it seems to be different here. I have no ability to use it here. I cannot even sense it anymore. That said . . ."

He trailed off as he returned to his thoughts.

"What is it?" Dirt asked.

"Well . . . for better or for worse, I am in part responsible for the design of this world. In the same way that I intended five people to use the magic, I intended that each of the five would have a role to play. A role that the others could not."

Dirt's confusion must have shown on her face, because Useyi put out his hands in a pacifying manner.

"Don't worry," he said. "You and your five will be able to use the magic when the time comes. The hard part will not be the magic; it will be overcoming whatever obstacles the Fault has waiting for you."

She looked to Antie Yaya, who pursed her lips apologetically. No more information was coming from either of them.

"Thank you," Dirt said, then turned to leave.

"Do you remember how I prayed for you before?" Antie Yaya asked, prompting Dirt to pause and turn back. "When you left my compound to fight in the arena?"

May the Gods grant you bravery, Dirt recalled. May they grant you strength. May they grant you certainty in who you·are.

"It would be redundant of me to offer the same prayers now," Antie Yaya continued. "And I suspect you're less expecting of the Gods now that you've actually met one of them . . ."

Antie Yaya looked up and away, searching for the words.

"Trust your family," Useyi interjected. He wore a thin, sad smile as he looked at Dirt. "Cherish them. Remember them. Whether you chose them or not, when the day is quiet and the night is long, family is the most precious gift you will ever have."

Antie Yaya stared at Useyi for a long moment before turning to Dirt. "I couldn't have said it better," she said, running a finger beneath her eyes as a tear fell. "Now go, young Godskin. The world needs you."

40

Carra Carre Sings

THE PATH TO the Fault was long and arduous, crossing miles of sweltering jungle. By the time they reached the abandoned Imperial Temple, Dirt could see that Nana's months away from Bowing life had diminished her endurance. Even with Dirt carrying her bags of armor and jewelry, the poor girl was exhausted, and they were forced to spend the night in the temple. They dragged several beds into one room and lay down to rest.

Then a sound awoke them. It was hours before the sun would rise, so when Dirt startled out of sleep to peer out the window, she couldn't see much. Only when Carra Carre appeared beside her and pointed into the trees, far past the sandy grounds surrounding the Imperial Temple, did Dirt see them.

Remnants.

A train of icy blue was just visible between the black leaves of the nighttime jungle, a smooth march of destruction heading . . .

"South," Dirt muttered, slipping into her Godskin, the power filling her.

Always South. The Remnants seemed to have an appetite for the One Fam. They could've gone anywhere else, but they always went South. The other Godskins barely even had to defend their regions—they should have been the ones going into the Fault.

The other Godskins.

Dirt frowned. Were there other Godskins? Who were they?

"We must stop them," Swoo said, joining them at the window and immediately climbing up the edge. "They are going to na One Camp."

Dirt placed a restraining hand on her shoulder. "We cannot," she said. "Na One Fam is prepared. They will defend themselves."

Conflict warred across Swoo's face. She knew Dirt was right, but it wasn't in her nature to avoid an enemy, especially one threatening the people she cared about.

"We must save ourselves for na Fault," Carra Carre added.

Her words did nothing to make Swoo feel better about abandoning the One Fam, but it was at least clear that Swoo was outnumbered. Brave as she was, there was nothing she could do to the Remnants by herself.

"When we use na magic, we will bring them back," Dirt said. "All of them."

With a frustrated sigh and a shake of her head, Swoo climbed back into her bed, as they all did. But Dirt found it impossible to go back to sleep. Instead, she watched the ceiling above as the night bled into day, all the while fighting off images of the One Fam being overrun by Remnants.

Then it was time to continue their journey.

×××

There were no trees. No water. Not even sand. In every direction, there was only the gray-black mud below, with great folds of it like frozen ocean waves and a sky above that was indecisive shades of blue and white.

As Dirt walked forward, each step punched through the mud beneath her like a finger poking into an empty cocoon. It was as if the land were infected with some strange plague, one that extracted all beauty and life, leaving it a corpse of itself. She heard the crunching steps of Carra Carre and the Mud sisters following behind her.

"Chaaaiii, what is this nonsense?" Swoo exclaimed. "Na ground is dead?"

Nana was silent, her nose scrunched in disgust at each step. Snore almost looked like her old self, her eyes wide and intrigued by the weirdness around them.

They continued on, and soon it was as if they'd reached the end of the world. Dirt froze midstride, one foot hovering over empty air as the earth plummeted suddenly into a pitch-black abyss. There was no other side to it—no narrow towers of land floating in the sea of emptiness, nothing. Just a yawning pit, a gash in the world that cut deeper than the eye could see. Dirt slipped into her Godskin and kicked a piece of the land into the chasm, listening for its impact.

It never came.

"Mama Eghi's teeth," Nana gasped.

Even Carra Carre grunted uncomfortably.

"We are going into that?" Swoo asked. Then she broke into laughter, doubled over in a mirth Dirt hadn't seen from her in a while. She righted herself, wiping her eyes. "So this is na end, eh?"

Though said with humor, Swoo's comment underscored the reality of their task. This was not an adventure from the stories. This was not a team of heroes taking on a mission they had trained for. This was five girls, only two of them with any power to fight off what they were about to face, and three others who were still children. There was a very likely chance that this would be where their lives ended, where they would be forgotten.

Before they continued, the younger girls took time to don their protection, each of them shielded by stones of a different color—Swoo in her fiery red, Nana in a sparkling white, and Snore in a mottled pattern of muted brown and black.

Dirt watched them prepare with a heavy heart. Useyi had said there would be other obstacles in the Fault. Perhaps things worse than the Remnants. Dirt was still First of the Mud, and the First was the one meant to fight for the survival of the Fam, not the other sisters. It pained her that they were preparing to fight alongside her.

"My Sis . . ."

Swoo's mouth hadn't moved—she was still tightening the straps of her armor. Dirt turned in disbelief to Carra Carre beside her.

"I do not know what we will soon face," Carra Carre continued. "But I am grateful to face it by your side. I will do all I can to protect your sisters as my own. And if we fall, we fall together. Sisters. Godskins."

Dirt couldn't find words to speak. Carra Carre had never called her "my Sis" before, despite all they'd been through. It took Dirt back to the days when she was not the Mud's First but Webba's Second. When she had a sister stronger than herself to rely on, to trust in, to carry half the world when its full weight was on her shoulders. Dirt realized that, in this moment before the most difficult endeavor of her life, she had that again.

She extended her hand, palm down, fingers half curled in. Carra Carre frowned in confusion, which brought laughter bubbling out from Dirt. With her other hand, she took Carra Carre's wrist and turned it face up, mirroring Dirt's from below. She wiggled her fingers against Carra Carre's palm and giggled when Carra Carre eventually returned the gesture with a shy smile, obviously a stranger to the girl's face yet so beautiful in its restraint and honesty.

It was a gesture Dirt had invented with Webba when they were Bibi. Now she shared it with another, someone who was not part of the Mud. A former enemy of the Mud and of Webba. Useyi's words returned to her mind.

Trust your family. Cherish them. Remember them. Whether you chose them or not, when the day is quiet and the night is long, family is the most precious gift you will ever have.

"Two bigbig coconuts," Swoo interrupted with a roll of her eyes. "Finish your nonsense and let us continue."

Dirt smiled, turning away from Carra Carre to look upon all her sisters. Swoo looked so fierce in her red armor, a young warrior. Nana was so pristine and fashionable in her white armor; the other Butterfly girls would no doubt be jealous if they could see her. And Little Snore, her armor nearly blending into the ground below them, not unlike the camouflaging fur of the jungle cats she had spent so much time with.

Dirt had always trusted and cherished them. But this was how she would remember them, whatever came next.

She took a deep breath. "We are na Mud sisters!" she sang. She knew her voice wasn't the best, but they didn't need the best right then. Just the song.

Her sisters responded immediately, by reflex. "We are na Mud sisters!"

We fight, oh yes, ooooooh!
We are na Mud sisters!
We are na Mud sisters!
We never quit, noooooo!

The second time, even Carra Carre joined in, her voice a low, mumbled roll beneath the others, her mouth tasting the song of her longtime enemies. She didn't sing it as if she were a member of the Fam, but the way the Mud supporters would in the Grand Temple, showing their respect and admiration for the girls before they went into battle.

When the singing was done, they approached the lip of the Fault, their toes peeking out over the edge of oblivion.

"Ripe?" Dirt asked.

"Riperipe," her sisters responded.

Then they leapt.

41

Into the Fault

THE FIVE OF them plummeted, rippling through the air as they descended into the void.

The blackness immediately rose up to meet and envelop them. Dirt couldn't see anything, not even her own hand in front of her. At first it almost felt as if she weren't moving at all but was stuck in midair. But then she opened her mouth to speak, and the wind rushed into her mouth, her nose, her eyes, blowing into every part of her face.

She slipped into her Godskin, then tucked in her arms so that her body was narrow as a knife and pointed her legs toward the ground. She felt her descent increase in speed, faster and faster, until she began to grow uncertain she would survive the fall even with the powers of her Godskin. So when she felt she was sufficiently ahead of her sisters, she began Whip Slapping, shooting spurts of air forward that propelled her away from the ground. She couldn't create enough force to stop her descent, but each Slap slowed her just slightly, ensuring she wouldn't hit the ground at full speed.

Luckily, she soon saw a point of orange light below her, and as she drew closer that one point revealed itself to be a tight ring of many lights that widened outward. Dirt aimed herself toward the center of the ring of lights, and once she could see the black stone ground she began Slapping furiously, slowing herself as much as possible before she crashed with tremendous impact, a cloud of pulverized stone bursting up all around her.

A few seconds later, Carra Carre lanced into the earth as well, cratering the ground with a force that sent Dirt stumbling.

The other sisters would be next. They'd decided that carrying the little ones during the descent would be too risky since they didn't know what they were falling into. But they had to think of a way to get the younger ones down safely. So Dirt crouched into a running position, then reached out to her side. Carra Carre, also crouched, took Dirt's arm. They ran in a circle, the momentum of one urging on the other until they had full control of the air around them, churning it into a cyclone that barreled up above them.

They kept their spinning until Dirt could hear Nana's and Snore's squeals above her. She looked up to see them caught on the swirl of air current, then squeezed Carra Carre's hand to let her know they could stop.

Dirt caught them each before they hit the ground, and then she set them down gently. Swoo landed gracefully beside them.

"Chaaaiii," both Nana and Snore cooed before dissolving into giggles. Nana got to work fixing both of their hair.

Swoo just stood in silence for a while, staring up into the dark. "We cannot go back," she eventually said in a matter-of-fact voice.

What was an endless gap up on the surface had narrowed down to a space that was no more than ten strides across. They stood amidst the ring of tall torches that held back the darkness, trying to make sense of their surroundings. Other than the impossible mass of stone around them and the torches that lit the space, the only notable aspect of their environment was the arched tunnel cut into the stone beside them that continued deep into the earth.

"We are here," Carra Carre said.

Dirt nodded. "Be watchful, my sisters," she called. "The way ahead will not be easy."

They broke the torches in half and carried the tops forward into the tunnel. The flames pressed back against the dark, but they couldn't stave off the growing tension as the girls continued deeper beneath the earth. It was surprisingly warm, Dirt realized. At first, she'd assumed it was the torches, but she soon realized it was coming not from the flames, but the walls themselves. She could see by torchlight that the stones around them were a shiny silver color, with slashes of faint red occasionally marring it. Those red spots seemed to be the hottest, and when Dirt stared at one long enough, she almost felt like she could see it moving, ever so slowly.

"Look," Carra Carre said, eyes forward.

Ahead the dark cave ended, and light began. The light grew toward them as they continued, and Dirt soon saw what looked like sand.

"Na desert?" Swoo asked.

Her question was answered when they finally escaped the tight darkness of the tunnel, which widened out into what seemed to be a bright new world. There were no walls that Dirt could see in any direction, no ceiling above. There was just honey-colored sand in every direction and a clear sky above that burned with a hot sun. It was indeed a desert.

"How can . . . ," Nana muttered. "Na desert in na ground?"

Snore picked up a handful of sand and seemed to think about throwing it into the air and letting it rain down on her. But she thought better of it and opened her hand, releasing the sand.

"I see no magic," Swoo said. "Only sand."

"Na magic is here," Dirt replied. "We must continue."

Dirt didn't feel any special magic, but she could tell there was something strange about the place. There was no breeze, no insects nor animal life. The sand was soft and seemed to suck at their every step, yet no stray grains clung to anyone's skin. Even after what felt like an hour of walking, the sun sat unnaturally in the same position, unmoved.

The sudden appearance of the door and statue only added to the strangeness. The door was a semicircle of gray stone five strides high at its center, its every inch etched with images too small to make out from afar but that reminded Dirt of the figures and stories that were etched into the walls of Antie Yaya's compound. Lush plant life was coiled all along the door's edge, leaves and vines and even what looked to be budding fruit.

As for the statue . . .

"Papa 'Duma . . . ," Dirt breathed.

It was taller even than the door, nearly ten times Carra Carre's height. The image was unmistakable—a powerful man with bulky muscles just beneath a layer of good, thick fat. Like a Bower. He even wore the Bower's casual clothing, but rather than a cloth half shirt and puffy pants, he wore a half shirt that appeared to be made of boiled crocodile leather, and his pants were strings of palm twine strung with thin stone plates. Dirt could almost hear the plates clattering against each other.

"Useyi's brother," Carra Carre mumbled, looking high up into the statue's face.

The door had a split down the center. Dirt walked up to it, ignoring the statue.

"We must continue. Our sisters depend on us."

The door had no handle, so she pushed on both sides and was unsurprised when neither moved. She slipped into her Godskin and tried again, but the door still didn't move. She tried shoulder-charging it, tried pushing on it with Carra Carre, tried jamming her hands into the center and prying it open.

The door remained closed.

"Obstacles . . . ," Dirt sighed.

"What can we do?" Swoo asked. "Must we sing na door open?"

Snore was sitting on the ground as she had been for minutes, siphoning sand from one hand to the other and back.

But Nana was staring intently at the statue of Oduma.

"What is it, Nana?" Dirt asked.

Nana glanced at Dirt with a distracted expression but didn't immediately answer. Instead, she walked toward the statue, one arm outstretched. She grabbed hold of one of the thin stone plates dangling from Oduma's legs and pulled.

To Dirt's astonishment, the plate came away. It was almost as large as Nana, but light and thin enough that she could carry it in one hand with no trouble. She turned to her sisters and held it in the air.

"Can we push this between na doors?" Nana asked.

Dirt was going to praise Nana for her brilliance, but her mouth sealed shut when the ground beneath them began to shake, this time more violently than ever before. Each of the girls was thrown off her feet as waves of tremors shot through the ground. Spurts of sand splashed across the air from the movement, and Dirt had to snatch Snore off the ground to keep her from being washed beneath it.

The shaking soon slowed, but it didn't stop. It lessened in violence, but increased in speed, changing from big, slow, heavy waves to small, quick vibrations.

Then the first chunk of stone crashed into the sand. Dirt watched it descend from the neck of the statue of Oduma and plummet far down to the sand below. Then another chunk from the fingers. Then another from the eyes. Stone rained down from the statue, and at first Dirt thought the statue was crumbling, that Nana had taken away a key part that would cause them all to be buried by sand and stone unless they fled.

But with each chunk that fell away, flesh appeared beneath it. An ebon cheek. Five thick, flexing fingers. Dark eyes set deep in the skull, regaining clarity and focus like those of someone newly woken.

In a matter of seconds, there was no longer a statue.

There was just Oduma.

The First of
the Vine

CARRA CARRE was nearly a woman, and she had seen much in her life. She'd seen the lowly Vine Fam rise to become the biggest in the South. She'd seen the storied Godskin come to life and had seen herself become one. In her youth, in her first year as a Bibi, she'd looked down into the River and seen the legendary and elusive carra carre, the largest crocodile to ever live. That day, she'd been filled with wonder as it passed below her with two hatchlings in tow, each of its scales as large as she was, its eyes black and glossy, its tail going on and on and on. It burrowed through the water at such pace, yet it was so long that it felt like a full minute before it had fully passed her view.

She'd told everyone, but no one believed her. They'd instead mocked the little Bibi for her grandiose imagination, naming her after the mythical beast she'd claimed to lay eyes on.

Still, nothing she'd seen in her life compared to seeing Oduma in the flesh. Not because of how large and impressive he was—he was still smaller than the carra carre. But because of how he widened his legs apart and lowered his stance and stretched out both arms, each one reaching out to Slap down upon an invisible waterline. His massive arms wheeled with such hypnotic grace that Carra Carre barely reacted when a heavy Slap came whistling down on top of her and the Mud sisters.

Thankfully, Carra Carre's combat instincts were too honed to be caught defenseless. She immediately entered into the power of the Godskin and braced herself, arms raised. She didn't know if she could stop Oduma Himself, but she couldn't let her young sisters be crushed like ants.

Oduma's palm tore through the air and slammed into Carra Carre's upraised hands. The impact jolted down her arms, into her shoulders, burning all the way to her toes, threatening to explode her from the inside out. Her armor hummed like a struck bell. Luckily, Dirt was beside her, her arms also upraised to absorb the power of Oduma's blow.

"Push!" Carra Carre shouted.

Together, both girls shoved upward. Were it anything else, they would have sent it into the sky. But Oduma's hand only flew back up to near his head before he gained control of it.

He looked down at them with empty eyes. There was no life behind them, no humanity or compassion or even anger. Just a complete void, as dark as the entrance to the Fault.

"Sis Dirt!" Nana shouted.

Carra Carre looked over to find the younger girls pointing at the gray door, which was already half agape and continuing to groan open.

With a short nod to Dirt, they dashed toward the door. However, Oduma was there first, stomping a massive foot directly in their path, sending up a wall of sand that blocked their vision. By the time the sand receded, another of Oduma's hands screamed down toward them, forcing them to scatter in every direction.

No matter how fast they moved, how well they misdirected, how ferociously they fought, they could neither hurt Oduma nor escape Him. Every time Carra Carre or Dirt attacked Him, the God didn't even seem to notice. And when she or any of the girls tried to escape through the gray door, He would plant himself in front of it.

Why? Carra Carre couldn't help but think. Her answer was in his eyes, she knew. Oduma had the body of a God but the eyes of an empty drum. He was under some other power, a power that was doing everything to keep them from passing through that door.

As the battle continued and Carra Carre felt herself tiring, hope began to drift away. But it wasn't the first time she had fought an opponent she could not overpower. The same thing had happened a season ago, in her fight against Webba. The girl had been faster, just as strong, with better, more unpredictable technique. Despite her best efforts, Carra Carre had come up short with every attack. But Carra Carre refused to lose just because she was overpowered. She'd resorted to trickery to win. Sometimes that was what it took.

"My Sis," she called to Dirt.

"Eh?" Dirt called back without taking her eyes from Oduma's form hulking in front of the door. She was just slightly hunched, breath heavy.

"You must go through na door," Carra Carre said. "You and your sisters."

"Thank you for your wisewise words, my Sis," Dirt responded.

She didn't understand. No matter.

"Do not hesitate," Carra Carre said.

She must have betrayed her intentions in her voice, because Sis Dirt finally turned her head, eyes wary.

Carra Carre crouched low before launching herself through the air. She sped directly into Oduma's face, directly into one of those giant, empty eyes, arms outstretched. She tried to make her body a needle, as thin as a Bower could be, aiming to pierce the god's eye and destroy his vision. A moment of blindness would be all it took.

"Carra Carre!" she heard Dirt scream.

Oduma's hand swallowed Carra Carre. She froze midair, a lunge away from her goal of the behemoth's eye, everything from her belly and below caught tight in his fist. She was a pebble to him. A baby bird. A curious but harmless little thing.

He squeezed her all the same.

Carra Carre felt a pressure in her body that had no rival. Her armor began humming madly, and she was grateful for little Nana's gift. If it weren't for the jewels covering her, Carra Carre knew her legs would have been immediately crushed, her torso mangled in Oduma's divine grip. Instead, she was simply constrained, pinned too tight to move.

A terrifying desperation began to seep through her. It was again like the fight against Webba, a feeling as if all the world depended on her success. Her plan to blind Oduma had failed. But *she* could not fail.

Below, she saw Swoo, Nana, and Snore sprinting for the open door. Oduma's foot was already midair preparing to smash them into bits. Dirt stood rooted in place, looking between her younger sisters and Carra Carre, the pain of indecision and loss already on her features.

Carra Carre knew who Dirt would choose if one side had to die. But she did not intend to allow her sister to make that decision. She looked from the girls running through the door to the coil of plant life along the door's edge. There were vines there. Vines like the ones she'd grown up among, like the ones she had wrapped around her head for most of her life, like the ones her Fam was named for.

And they *called* to her.

She reached her arms toward them, and even though she was dozens of strides away, she pulled them with her mind.

And they obeyed.

The vines uncoiled from their tangle along the door's arc and shot out in two directions—toward Carra Carre and toward Oduma's upraised foot. The vines spiraled up Carra Carre's arms, braiding so tightly around her forearms that they seemed embedded in her armor. The other end wrapped around and around Oduma's foot, and once Carra Carre felt the vines snap taut at full stretch, she yanked as hard as she could.

With all the power of the Godskin, she tugged. The explosion of power immediately shattered the jewels of her armor, frayed her muscles so completely that droplets of blood wept from the pores in her skin. She felt herself strain and tear all over. Even the most powerful girl in the whole Isle was not made for such things. She was built to throw around the bodies of other girls and boys, not the bodies of Gods.

Despite the instant destruction of her body, Carra Carre knew it was worth it. She felt the momentum of Oduma's foot reverse, felt its weight lighten and float up away from the door. She even felt the God topple to the side, hopping on one leg to regain his balance, kicking up waves of sand that covered the entrance just as Dirt, Swoo, and the little ones passed beneath its arch.

Oduma released his grip, and Carra Carre fell. As she did, she watched the two sides of the stone door come back together, closing so slowly that she felt every moment painfully, so quickly that she didn't consider for a second making it through herself.

As the stone doors sealed her fate and her broken body plummeted into the sea of sand, Carra Carre heard voices singing. She didn't know where the voices were coming from, but she knew who was singing—her sisters. Voices that she had forgotten, faces she still couldn't remember, coming together to sing the anthem under which she had achieved so many of her greatest feats, their voices so perfect and powerful.

It put a smile on her face.

43

The Adorner

THE RATTLING BOOM of the stone door closing brought tears to Nana's eyes.

Unlike Dirt, Nana had never fully forgiven Carra Carre for what she'd done. Nana had been there in person when the Vine Bower destroyed Webba and the Mud camp, and she'd seen the evil in the girl's heart. For days, Nana had flinched at every shadow passing within the trees. For weeks, Carra Carre had appeared in Nana's nightmares. Yet when Nana arrived at the One Camp, there seemed to have been some forgiveness between Dirt and Carra Carre.

More than forgiveness.

A sisterhood.

Nana hadn't really understood it nor fully believed it, and now she felt guilty. Whatever she had believed Carra Carre to be, the girl had changed. Nana, more than anyone, should have respected the possibility that a girl's heart could change.

Now Carra Carre had sacrificed everything. Not just for Dirt but for all of them, Mud sister or not.

"She was na True Godskin," Swoo said, her gaze fixed on the door closed behind them. "To na end."

Dirt didn't say anything for a long moment. She just stood silently, chest heaving from the fight. It was several minutes before she took a deep breath and spoke.

"We must continue," she said.

Useyi had warned them that there would be obstacles, but none of them had expected to fight a God, or whatever that was. Useyi said his powers didn't work here on the Isle, so he was just a normal man. Oduma had been different. He had been like a Godskin, but even more powerful.

What could be coming next?

The desert was gone, replaced by a wooden walkway that stretched forward over water in every direction. The walkway was sturdy, so there was no worry of falling, and after a quick taste, it was clear that the water was stream water, not seawater—good to drink. The air was cool and damp, a welcome respite from the heat of the desert.

Like the desert, though, there were no animals. No fish leaping across the water's surface, no birds wheeling overhead. The four sisters were the only living things in sight as they made their way along the path. Though the walk was long, the kind temperature and abundant water made it an easier trek.

All the same, the appearance of the door and statue filled Nana with dread.

They were still far enough away that the statue was just a stone torso on the horizon, the door a small sliver of its full self.

"Na swinging, sloppy, sodden, FOOL-SOAKED, STONE-CURSED BUCK!" Swoo howled at the sky. "We cannot fight another!"

Nana agreed. The first fight had cost them a member of their already small team, and they'd had two Godskins for that fight. Now they only had one, who still seemed to be suffering from the loss of her sister.

"We must find another way," Nana said, mostly to herself.

But Dirt looked at her and nodded. "Before, na Papa Oduma statue only attacks when we take something. We have time. We can think."

At Dirt's insistence, they continued walking, all the way up to the foot of the statue and door. She again tried pushing the door open to no avail. She tried wedging her fingers into the center line, but the space was too thin.

While Dirt searched for some opening to the door, Nana was absorbed in the statue. Whereas Oduma's had exuded an air of power and intimidation, this statue was delicate by comparison. Graceful. He wore fine, stilted shoes, not unlike those of a Butterfly. His clothes were the strange garments that Useyi wore, but appeared soft even in hard stone, extravagant even in all gray. He held one hand up, his wrist narrow and frail. The other hand was down at his side, his fingers half-dipped into his pocket.

Nearly every inch of him was covered in jewelry. Not stone jewelry, either. From the dual glint of sapphires and rubies in his ears to the jewel-laden bracelets at both wrists and ankles, there was only one God it could be.

"Papa Abidon . . . ," Nana said.

No, she'd made a mistake. Both ankles were ringed with bracelets, but not both wrists. The hand dipping into the pocket was bare.

That was when Nana noticed the jewels at the base of the statue, each one similar in size to the heavy rocks Nana used to lift back in her Bowing days.

"Sis Dirt," she said, but her elder sister was so intent on the door that she didn't hear her. Swoo was with Dirt as well, trying to think up a new way of opening the door. Both of them were distracted, and Nana didn't want to interrupt them if she was wrong.

But she didn't think she was.

Bowers believe all answers are fighting, she thought with an internal sigh.

"Bibi Snore," Nana said instead, turning to the youngest Mud sister. "I need your help."

As much as Swoo and Dirt seemed to be missing something since the loss of Carra Carre, Snore seemed to have gained some of her old self. Nana assumed it was a lingering hatred of the Vine. If there was anyone who hated the Vine more than Nana, it would be Snore, and the girl's wounds ran deeper, her forgiveness further from reach.

But even that didn't explain the way Snore jumped to her feet and nodded, displaying none of the vengefulness, pain, or fear that she had carried for so long.

"I will help you, Bibi Nana," she said with such Snore-like solemnity that Nana's face immediately split into a smile.

Mingled among the pile of jewels at the statue's foot were loops of good leather, of a better quality than anything Nana had ever worked with before. With Snore's help, Nana got to work picking the jewels she felt fit best with the existing color scheme of the statue's jewelry—just because she was doing it to open the door didn't mean it shouldn't look pretty. She and Snore tied them each with leather, then tethered one jewel to the next until she had a bracelet fit for the statue of Papa Abidon Himself.

Snore worked with a half-hearted distractedness that Nana was overjoyed to see. This was the Snore she knew. Not the rage-filled girl who pursued her goals at all costs. The Snore Nana had known was sleepy and mischievous and loving and unreliable—deeply, completely unreliable.

"You are you again, my sister," Nana said, smiling as she looped one leather strip around another. Snore had peeled a thin piece of wood off the walkway and was attempting to balance it on her upper lip. She shrugged at Nana but didn't seem to want to risk speaking and knocking the wood off.

"What changes, eh?" Nana asked.

Snore replied with the most minimal mouth movements she could manage. "Sis Dirr try to protecc me, but she fail. I try to protecc Sis Nubbi, but I fail. Same and same."

Nana stared at the girl as she teetered and slid side to side, her entire focus on a single, inconsequential piece of wood. What a marvel Little Snore was. She was not the most eloquent, but that didn't diminish her wisdom.

Ever since the Remnant attack that had reunited the Mud sisters, Nana had felt like part of her was missing. She'd thrown herself into making armor tirelessly, but as much joy as that brought her, she now realized that it hadn't closed the hole. Any moment of silence brought pain, which was why she had filled her days, rather than bear that silence and pain.

Yet Snore's words brought on a sudden and all-consuming silence. Nana felt the hole as acutely as she had when it was fresh, but she could finally see it for what it was—the pain of injustice.

Something had been taken from her that she didn't deserve to lose. It was cruel. It was unfair. So she'd created a hole where the world could make it right, fill her with something that made the injustice just.

Snore had learned sooner than Nana had that the world would provide no filling. An unjust thing had happened to her, and unjust things would continue to happen, to her and to others. The only way for the hole to close was for her to close it, to accept that her pain was not something new and terrifying, but just a stitch in the fabric of pain that all children shared, girls and boys, Butterflies and Bowers, Flaggas and Pusher boys.

"Thank you, my sister," Nana said, wiping the tears that were trailing down her cheeks, no doubt smearing her face paint.

Once Nana was finished with the bracelet, she and Snore held it up between them.

"Sis Dirt!" Nana called. "Sis Swoo!"

"Sis Dirr!" Snore repeated. "Sis Swooooooooo!"

The older sisters turned from their campaign against the door.

"Eh . . ." Sis Dirt didn't seem sure of what to say.

"You waste my eyes," Swoo said before turning back to the door.

"Look and see," Nana shouted, pointing up at the statue's wrist.

Understanding dawned on them both. Dirt smiled at Nana with such pride that Nana felt her face warm. Swoo grinned as well.

"Who has na sister more clever than I?" she said, hugging Nana's head and messing her hair.

Once Nana finished putting her hair back in place, they formed a tower, Dirt at the base with Swoo standing on her shoulders and Nana standing on Swoo's. From that height, Nana could comfortably reach the statue. They handed the bracelet up, and Nana looped both ends around the statue's wrist. Before she tied it on, she looked down at her sisters.

Dirt gave her a firm, reassuring nod.

Swoo looked up at her with a grumble. "I am no Godskin, Butterfly girl. My shoulders tire."

Little Snore stood over by the gray door, waving up at Nana as if one of them were about to leave on a journey.

Nana tied the bracelet on, then leaned back to admire her work. Though the statue's outfit had no colors, Nana was certain that her bracelet was the perfect adornment for it. It was that certainty that had made her leave the Mud Fam in the first place. It was a certainty she'd never known as a Bower, but one that she felt every day as an Adorner.

The stone door grated open slowly and loudly, earning a cheer from her sisters, and Nana's heart swelled at the sound, at the fact that she'd proven her value, earned the love that they gave so freely, protected her Fam not with her strength but with what she loved most—beauty.

Then she was gone.

44

The Jungle Bibi

SNORE HADN'T EVEN seen when Nubbi died. Not at first. She was doing something else—she couldn't remember what—and was very upset. It was only when they were inside the camp and the boulder was rolled behind them that she realized Nubbi wasn't with her. She'd cried so hard then that Sis Swoo had asked all around camp until one of the patrol Bowers remembered seeing Nubbi among the dead jungle cats.

So Snore wasn't surprised to see Nana disappear.

Sis Dirt was surprised. She looked around for a while in confusion, then began calling out for Nana. As time passed, she said Nana must be in the statue and began punching it so hard her fists bled. But the statue didn't break, and Nana didn't come back.

Sis Swoo was surprised. At first, she thought it was a joke. She looked over at Snore with a smile, asking how they did it. When Snore had no response and Nana did not reappear, the truth slowly reached her. She jumped off Dirt's shoulders and paced aimlessly back and forth, shaking her head. Eventually, she began crying. Her legs gave out, and she fell against the statue, shaking her head and crying for an hour before suddenly going silent.

But Snore wasn't surprised.

She knew that anyone could be hurt at any time. Could disappear. Could die. The Mud sisters were no different. They were just a group of girls.

"We mus' continue," Snore said.

Both big sisters looked at her. They were so tired, so defeated.

Snore didn't wait for them to respond. She walked straight for the door, ignoring their shouts, and crossed into the next room.

Home was the first thing Snore thought.

Trees that shot so high she could barely see the tops of them. Heavy fig and yaro tree branches dangled down their lengths, thick with broad leaves. Tropical flowers burst here and there like stars in the sky, in vibrant shades of scarlet, plump hues of cobalt, searing tints of gold.

She was back in the jungle. The place she was meant to be.

Snore didn't even wait for her older sisters. She walked forward, following a narrow trail between the thickets on either side of her. She strolled for hours, stopping to pee and climb and take a nap beneath a tree. By the time she reached the next door and statue, Sis Dirt and Sis Swoo were already there waiting.

"Snore!" they exclaimed when they saw her. She liked seeing her sisters happy. She knew they were still heartbroken from losing Nana, but they rushed to her and hugged her as if she were the most important thing on their minds.

When the reunion was complete, the big sisters looked back to the statue.

This one wasn't so tall as the one of Oduma or Abidon. It was a statue of a thin woman with a smirk on her face. She wore twin bands around her upper arms, and a long roll of stone paper spilled from her left hand. The big sisters were staring so hard at the paper that Snore had to go over and see it for herself.

"Mama Ijiri . . . ," Sis Swoo said with a morose tone.

Etched into the stone scroll were lines of characters and images that made no sense at all to Snore. But the way the bigger sisters were looking at it made her curious enough to stand around and listen to them guess.

"I see these"—Sis Dirt traced her finger along the lines of characters—"at Antie Yaya's."

"Na language of na Gods," Sis Swoo said, unable to keep the awe from her voice. "You can understand it?"

Sis Dirt shook her head. "Not the words. But na pictures . . . they must mean something."

Snore knew exactly what the pictures were the moment she saw them. She knew so few things, yet here one of her favorite things was written out before her.

"I know it," she said, but was immediately distracted because at the foot of the statue was a palm-leaf platter full of fruit. Papaya, honey melon, pineapple, banana, and more. A banquet of fresh food just sitting there, yearning to be eaten. Snore's mouth began instantly watering.

"Eh?" Sis Swoo said.

Snore waddled over to the bowl and reached down to snatch

up a banana. She would start with a banana, just because it was easy, then maybe move on to a mango, then enjoy some cherries.

"Bibi Snore," Sis Dirt called.

Snore stopped and turned.

"What do you know?"

Snore pointed up at the drawings on the statue's scroll.

"Na Gekko and na Guava."

Big sisters could be so blind sometimes. The first row of pictures were clearly the first verse of the song—a sleeping girl with a big belly, then with a small belly, then she's eating. And a big man watching her.

> *Papa 'Duma, my sister sleep*
> *She sleep until her belly shrink*
> *And when she wake, she go and eat*
> *Na Gekko and na Guava!*

Each line of the scroll was a different verse of the song. Snore used to play the game a lot with Bibi Nana. She'd even played with the big sisters once or twice, but they were very forgetful when it came to important things like that.

Snore returned to perusing the fruit offerings, but Sis Swoo peered hard at the statue's drawings, mumbling the words to the next verse of the Gekko and the Guava.

> *Papa Abi, my sister cry*
> *She cry until her eye go dry*
> *And when we ask, we no know why*
> *Na Gekko and na Guava!*

"She speaks true . . . ," Sis Swoo said in disbelief to Sis Dirt. "My Sis, Snore speaks true."

Snore heard Sis Dirt rise, her armor clanging. But she was only interested in the banana in her hand. She peeled the fruit out of its skin, then broke off a piece and tossed it into her mouth.

"But what do we do?" Sis Swoo wondered aloud. "If it is Na Gekko and—"

The grating sound of the mighty stone doors opening echoed through the trees. Snore looked over but didn't move toward it. She was enjoying the sweet taste of the banana, then she would wash it down with a juicier fruit. Then maybe, before they walked into whatever room was next, she would take a nap.

Before any of that could happen, though, Snore disappeared.

45

The One Camp's Last Stand

FOR ALMOST an entire day, the Remnants had been pounding through the boulders at the entrance to the One Camp. The sound echoed back through the entire cave, a heavy crashing that was as relentless as it was terrifying.

Crash. Crash. Crash.

Tiggi hated it. She and the other Mud sisters were seated with knees against chests, huddled deep in the cave inside one of the additional spaces that Sis Dirt and Sis Carra Carre had carved out from the interior walls. The space was large enough for all the Mud Bibi and a few Sis who were there to defend them. It was just a matter of time, Tiggi knew, before the Remnants broke in, and when they did . . .

"Bibi Tiggi."

It was Tempo. Throughout the defense preparations, while the other Mud Bibi worked themselves into a panic with rumored whispers about impending doom, Tempo had been a calm head. Though Tiggi couldn't tell if that was because Tempo was just a relaxed person or because she was simply too lazy to panic.

Crash. Crash. Crash.

"What is it?" Tiggi asked.

"Want to bet?"

Tiggi raised an eyebrow, but Tempo didn't seem to notice at all. She continued on.

"If na Remnants come inside in na hour, you owe me your chicken for na week."

"I bet," Tiggi replied without hesitation. If the Remnants entered within an hour, the likelihood that she would be alive to give anyone her chicken was beyond small.

Just then, the crashing stopped.

It had been so long since they'd been without the sound that Tiggi had forgotten how peaceful the One Camp was, how removed from the busy birds and frantic monkeys and rivers and wind and chaos of the outside world. They were all there together, their bodies warming each other, the Sis standing in front of them nearest the main chamber of the camp, their wide backs a comforting sight. The One Fam had built something truly special with that camp of theirs, and Tiggi, for a moment, had no doubt that the five would be victorious at the Fault.

Then the screaming started.

From where she sat, Tiggi could see almost the entire way to the main entrance. All along the central road in the distance, she could see the frantic scattering of the Bowers, Flaggas, and Pushers who had remained in the camp to defend it. From far away, they were so small. And so scared. An anthill scrambling after a Bibi's careless kick. Beyond them was the protective barrier that had been built, which stretched fully across the camp from wall to wall and was nearly twice the height of a full Sis. Girls and boys stood atop wooden ladders with stones for throwing, hot oil for pouring, and axes for chopping. None of them were expected to stop the Remnants, but they hoped to at least slow them down.

Beyond the wall, up the slope to the main entrance, were the tiny blue dots that had begun the screaming. The Remnants looked like ants from far away too. Harmless little things. Which only frightened Tiggi more. They had all seen what the Remnants were capable of. She knew they were anything but harmless.

A tremor of low, terrified mutterings shot through the Mud Bibi. The two Sis guarding them turned around and flashed confident smiles.

"Do not fear, young Bibi," one of them said. "Na Remnants are still far."

But over the course of minutes, Tiggi watched the blue ants grow closer and watched the other ants disappear. Watched the blue ants swarm over and through the barrier as if it weren't even there. Effortlessly, the Remnants burned across the camp, immolating everyone who stood in their way. Each time a Remnant grabbed hold of someone, the Remnant also disappeared, true. But there seemed to be no end to them. There were still dozens of Remnants pouring through the hole in the boulder that had blocked the entrance.

Soon they were no longer the size of ants. They were people-sized. Even bigger than people. Monsters. Giants.

When the Sis guarding the Mud Bibi began to shift nervously from foot to foot, the Bibi all at once realized the end was near. The first scream came from Wami, and it was like a roaring jungle cat, triggering the roars of its sisters. Soon they were all screaming. Not the usual reckless screaming of a group of children, but a horrified screaming that defied age.

Tiggi was too scared to scream. She clasped a hand over her mouth as the Remnants drew so near that their footfalls shook in her chest. Instead of the Gods, she prayed to her sisters. To Sis Dirt and Sis Carra Carre. To Sis Swoo and Nana and Snore. She prayed that they were safe and healthy and fighting their hardest to save them all. She prayed that the Fault had not defeated them. She prayed that Sis Dirt, especially, would save the Mud Bibi. Somehow. Some way.

Then there was no more time for prayer. The Remnants were upon them.

46

The First of
the Mud

SWOO HAD no more heart left to break.

She'd always been a practical person. She was a fighter, one who dealt with the hard reality of unarmed combat—there was no room for impracticality in a Bower's life. So she'd known from the beginning that they were risking their lives by going into the Fault. She'd prepared herself to see and experience horrible things. Leading the charge only to be crushed by stone, thrown off a cliff, torn apart by Remnants. She was prepared to suffer. To die.

But she'd never prepared herself to be the one watching others suffer and die. She'd never prepared herself to be the one left behind.

"What is happening?" she asked Sis Dirt in a voice so weak, she surprised herself. "Will all doors take na sacrifice? Is this why there must be five?"

Dirt didn't answer, but Swoo hadn't expected her to. The question wasn't for Dirt. It wasn't for anyone. There was no all-knowing older sister, no Antie Yaya, no Gods. There was no one left to answer anything.

"We must continue" was all Sis Dirt said when she finally spoke. "We can use na magic. We can save them."

She didn't look scared or pained or in need of answers. Her jaw was set, back straight. She looked determined. Swoo couldn't help but stare at her, wondering where her fearful and uncertain Dirt had gone. This girl—this woman—looked as if she had never feared anything in her life.

"Sis Dir—" Swoo began, but her sister was already continuing on, past the statue of Mama Ijiri and through the door.

Swoo took a pause to look at the half-eaten banana that remained where Snore had stood moments before. It was the third time she had failed to protect Snore. And it seemed it would be the final time. All she could pray was that, wherever Snore was, she would be able to forgive Swoo for her failures. Someday.

Then she was walking across the threshold, into a new world.

The first thing Swoo noticed was the sound of rushing water. The ground was all small, smooth stones, each one bearing a hint of wetness. They stretched for a few dozen strides ahead before plummeting downward.

At the edge of the cliff, right before the ground fell away, was a statue of Eghodo. Besides being the only one of the Mamas and Papas left, The Lawbringer was unmistakable for the torch she held upraised, to light the path of justice. Her forehead tiara shone gold beneath the sun's brightness overhead.

"Come," Dirt said. "Let us be quickquick."

They walked up to the statue, right to the edge of the cliff, where

Swoo looked down upon a waterfall bigger than she knew could exist. The cliff stretched long in a semicircle, and all along it waterfalls the width of rivers poured over the cliff face and fell down into the clouds.

The clouds.

"We are above na clouds," Swoo said, suddenly woozy from how high up she was.

"And above na door," Sis Dirt said, pointing.

Directly below them was the next stone door. It was facing up toward them, seemingly floating among the clouds, though it wasn't clear what was keeping it suspended in the sky. If they wanted to pass through it, they would have to jump. But first they had to open it.

"What can we do?" Swoo asked, eyes flicking between the door and the statue, searching for any sign that could help them continue.

When Dirt failed to respond, Swoo turned to her sister. She immediately understood her silence.

Remnants were emerging from the ground behind them, clawing their hard, grotesque bodies up through the stones until they stood fully and firmly in the world. They did not immediately attack. As each one emerged, it remained in place, waiting as more of its fellow monsters joined the assembly. Soon there was at least a dozen of them, and the number only kept growing.

"We cannot run," Swoo said.

But Dirt disagreed. "We must. We have no choice."

"We always have a choice, remember?" Swoo said with a bitter smile. "'All girls must choose,' eh?"

"What are you saying?" Dirt asked.

Swoo had known how this all would proceed once she realized Snore was gone. Useyi had made it so that five people were needed to use the magic of the Fault, intended for him and his siblings to heal the wounds that divided them. What better way to test their bonds than to see whether they were willing to sacrifice themselves for the others? The sacrifices were acts of love, acts of selflessness. The only way any five people would be able to reach the magic would be if they truly loved and trusted each other.

Carra Carre. Nana. Snore. Now, it was Swoo's time.

She drew her trusted hatchet from her waistband. She could not defeat all of the Remnants. In fact, it would be a miracle if she could defeat one of them. But she could keep them busy. Give Dirt time.

"Go, my Sis," Swoo said.

Unbelievable. She was crying again. The tears came too quickly for her to stop them. She watched through watery eyes as Remnants continued to climb up from beneath the earth, waiting for them to strike. Behind her, she could hear Dirt scrambling about the cliff face, frantic for a solution that would save them both. The knowledge that Dirt refused to give up what had already been lost only added to Swoo's tears.

Am I now na Bibi? Swoo thought.

She shook her head, tears sliding off her face, and took a deep breath.

Once Swoo attacked, the Remnants pounced on her from all angles. She did her best to keep from being surrounded, dodging and ducking and diving out of the way when necessary, grateful for Nana's armor, which kept the Remnants from getting a solid grip on her. She wasn't strong enough to do much damage, but she hacked away a paw here and there, severed the backs of a couple of knees, rammed her axe handle into a few eyes. Any Remnant that roamed toward Dirt, Swoo intercepted, and after a few minutes of fighting, she'd even managed to kill two of them, their bodies turning to mist before her eyes.

As much damage as she delivered, she also received. The armor on her chest was smashed from a heavy blow, and she was almost certain one of her ribs beneath was broken. She had blood in her mouth from an injury she didn't remember taking, and two of the fingers on her axe hand were so swollen they looked like they might burst.

But still the Remnants came. Three charged her at once, wide enough apart that Swoo couldn't slip around them. Her only choice was to back away, ceding ground in an instant that she had fought for minutes to maintain. She backed up more quickly than she realized and was stunned when she slammed up against something behind her, her armor humming from the impact. She was immediately consumed by fear—what if she had brought the Remnants right to her sister?

She risked a quick glance over her shoulder and saw that it wasn't Dirt she'd backed into.

It was the statue.

Swoo had always taken pride in the quickness of her mind. It was the mind that had made her the elite NoBe Bower she'd once been, the mind that could see a subtle shift in an opponent's weight and know exactly what attack was coming and from what angle.

At that moment, however, she cursed that mind. Because as soon as she saw the statue looming up behind her, tilting ever so slightly from the impact of her bumping back into it, Swoo understood everything that was about to happen. The statue would fall, as it was supposed to. It would plummet over the lip of the cliff, top pointed down. That torch Eghodo was holding, its stone flame bulbous at the bottom but gathered into a single point at the top, would be like an axehead, falling falling falling and crashing into the door. *Through* the door. That was why the door was as it was, floating face up among clouds.

Dirt wouldn't have put it all together yet, Swoo knew. She might not realize until it was too late. Swoo couldn't fight the Remnants off any longer.

"Remember, my Sis?" Swoo called out, turning and running to her left, drawing the Remnants away from Dirt. "When I am too afraid to jump?"

It had been when Dirt first became a Godskin. They'd taken their usual morning run to the Rock territory. Dirt, emboldened by her newfound power, leapt from the high cliffs into the water. Swoo had been too afraid of the rocks below, too afraid she wouldn't be able to jump far out beyond their jagged teeth.

That was the first time the roles had reversed between Swoo and Dirt. The first inkling of the fearless leader that Dirt had become.

As Swoo led the Remnants away from Dirt around the curved edge of the cliffs, the statue toppled. It fell just as Swoo had predicted, its torch exploding against the stone door, both of them shattering, a shower of stone chips falling through the door and disappearing.

Only then did Dirt begin to put things together. Her face swung between Swoo and the open door, her confusion plain as she tried to figure out what Swoo was doing and how to get her before jumping through the door.

"My foolish sister," Swoo said with a smile.

They didn't know what was in the next room. They couldn't risk Dirt fighting Remnants and being too injured to continue. But Swoo knew that if Dirt could choose, she would chase Swoo down and fight a thousand Remnants to save her.

So Swoo didn't let Dirt choose. She made the decision for them, the only decision that would both preserve the mission and keep Swoo out of the Remnants' hands, keep her from being forgotten.

She leapt.

47

The Last of the Mud

DIRT WATCHED from afar as Swoo plunged off the cliff. The Remnants followed after in a scatter, like grains of rice discarded. They all fell, and the clouds swallowed them, and it was done.

Dirt inhaled a long, slow breath, filling her chest, raising her shoulders. Then she let it out slowly and wiped the tears forming in her eyes before they could fall. They were immediately replaced by a new set of tears. Then another. No shoulders shaking, no shortness of breath, no contorted face or throbbing head or dripping nose. It was just the tears in a never-ending stream. No matter how much she wiped them away, they continued, so she just let her hands fall and let the tears flow.

When she felt fully emptied, she turned to the cliff edge and looked down into the open door. Like the others, it was black and blank. There was no view of the other side, nor a reflection of this side. It had been difficult to walk through each door, not knowing what she was walking into. Now she would be diving—who knew what she would be plummeting into?

Dirt leapt. It should have been harder to go through this door than the previous ones, but it wasn't. It was easier. Because the Fault had already taken her sisters. Her Fam. Everything she valued in the world. There was nothing through this next door that could be worse than what she'd already suffered.

She was grateful for the wind as it buffeted her. It wicked the remaining moisture from her face and was so heavy against her eyes that she was forced to close them, giving her a moment of peace and allowing her to refocus on the mission. Carra Carre. Nana. Snore. Swoo. Her sisters were not gone forever, not yet. If the magic of the Fault was as powerful as Useyi claimed, then she could bring them all back. She could remake the world to be as it had been, before the Remnants came, before Useyi. A world where she lived in peace and joy with all her sisters.

Even Webba.

As Dirt plunged through the black divide and into the next world, her thoughts went to Webba. Such thoughts had become her place of comfort. In some ways, she was grateful that Webba had left before having to suffer what they had all suffered over the last few months. In other ways, Dirt couldn't help but feel that, with Webba around, things would not have raged so completely out of control. That Webba's presence would have somehow been enough to hold all of reality together, Useyi and the Fault be damned.

When Dirt opened her eyes, the first thing she saw was the ground. She landed surprisingly softly, the passage through the door somehow slowing her descent. Unlike the previous world, this was a room. Or more of a cave, actually. Made from the same dark stone of the One Camp, but less than half the size.

The second thing she saw was Webba.

All the air rushed out of Dirt's lungs. She suddenly felt outside of her body, like she was witnessing Dirt from a numb, floating void just beside herself. There was no sound but a thin and consistent buzzing.

"W . . . ," Dirt couldn't finish the name.

This is na dream, she thought.

It had to be. She must have fallen asleep passing through the doorway. Or she was so exhausted she was hallucinating.

Yet Webba seemed so real. As large as ever. Her powerful body layered with good fat. Her skin nearly blending into the black rocks around them. She stood with the boundless confidence and mirth that Webba had for so long, her heavy legs somehow healed of their paralysis.

"Na good day, my Sis," Webba said. She grinned.

The grin. The voice. Dirt didn't know what to do. She was afraid that if she did anything at all, she would wake up. The hallucination would end.

"Come, my Sis," Webba said, turning and walking toward the back of the cave. "Let us speak, eh?"

They sat across from each other, legs crossed. Judging from the faint but amused smirk on Webba's face, Dirt suspected her own face was as shocked as it had ever looked. In order to avoid simply staring at Webba, Dirt glanced about the room, taking in the moist stone and lack of vegetation.

But inevitably her eyes returned to her sister. She looked the same, but . . . different. Mostly in the color of her skin. She was her dark, beautiful self, but there was a blue sheen to her skin. Dirt suspected it was a trick of the lighting. The room had no torches, just hot red veins in the walls that held a dull glow.

"I am different, eh?" Webba asked. "Speak true, my ever unripe sister."

"You are . . . ," Dirt replied. "But also you are not. I . . . My Sis, how can this be?"

A knowing smile leapt into Webba's eyes.

"You ask me?" she said. "It is I who should ask *you*. How are you here? What happens after I leave na Mud?"

Dirt told her everything. Flagga Day and Useyi's appearance, the Isle God Bow, the Remnants. The last few months had flashed by so quickly that she was surprised to recall all that had happened. The day Webba left, Dirt's entire world had been Bowing. She'd been looking forward to coaching again, to helping Swoo succeed in her first year as a full Sis and overseeing the growth of all their new Bibi.

Those days felt like they were a hundred years ago. They felt like they were yesterday. That was the scary thing about life, she realized. It moved so fast and so slow, and there was no way to know which it was doing until long after.

"Chaaaiii," Webba said when Dirt was finished, absently drumming her belly. Rather than the usual round hollowness, the sound was flat and firm. "Look at you, eh? How far you have come."

Dirt smiled. She just couldn't get over how good it felt to be in Webba's presence again.

"And what of you, my Sis? You are here before me. . . . How?"

Webba shrugged, grinned. "I must be somewhere. Why not here?"

Dirt rolled her eyes. She'd forgotten how much Webba treated conversation like a game. Like a dance. She enjoyed leading, forcing Dirt to follow.

"I do not miss you as much as I think," Dirt said.

"Na liiiie," Webba responded. "Imagine you do all you do to come here, and it is not I. Just rocks. You will cry."

"Joyful tears," Dirt shot back.

Webba tilted back like a rocking chair, laughing her great big laugh with her face to the ceiling. Then she slowly calmed, her expression cooling from unrestrained mirth to an almost sorrowful calm, her face suddenly drooping.

"What is it?" Dirt asked, concerned.

"I do not choose to be here," Webba said. "I am here because of you."

Dirt frowned. She didn't understand.

"Do you know what are na Remnants?" Webba asked.

Dirt shook her head.

"They are us," Webba said. "All na Mud sisters of na past. All na Bowers and Flaggas and Pusher boys and Mosquitoes."

"Butterflies," Dirt interjected.

"Eh heh," Webba confirmed before continuing. "When we leave our Fam, we come here. When we are forgotten, we become Remnants. Our spirits go into na bodies of animals. So when I leave na Mud, I go to Antie Yaya, and I wake up here in na Fault. Now I must serve na Remnants."

"But you are not na Remnant," Dirt said.

"Not yet," Webba said. "But I am on my way."

Dirt slowly began to see it. The blue tint to her skin. The firmness of her belly. She was turning into the blue crystal of the other Remnants.

"Almost all those who remember me are gone," Webba said. "Once they are no more, I will be na full Remnant. The only one keeping me as I am . . ."

She trailed off, but Dirt understood. "Me."

Webba grinned.

"I will never forget you, my Sis," Dirt insisted, desperate.

Webba nodded, then climbed to her feet and walked away, deeper into the room.

"Come, my Sis," Webba said.

They didn't walk far. Webba stopped after a few moments and gestured to the back wall.

"You see it?" she asked.

Dirt had to peer closely to notice any difference. The wall was all stone, black in the dim light. Yet there was a slim cut in it, not much longer than an arm and barely wide enough to stick her head in. Within the cut was what looked to be a river of black fire, slowly moving, flames licking at the edges.

Dirt instinctively reached up to touch the Scar on her face. She rarely looked at it these days, but she remembered its appearance—it was exactly the same as the cut in the wall.

"What is this?" she asked.

"Na Fault," Webba said. "Na magic. If you put your hand inside, you can change this world."

Dirt nodded, bit her lip. She already knew the world she wanted. Now she could make it.

She reached her hand out toward it, bracing herself for whatever feeling she would suffer—whether burning or something else.

But before her hand could slip into it, Webba's shot forward and gripped her wrist.

"I am still na Remnant, my Sis," Webba said apologetically. Her eyes were full of sorrow and regret. "Na Fault makes us protect na old world. It knows you are na danger to it, and so . . ."

Webba's grip was like iron shackles, far tighter than it had ever been before.

I am brave. I am fat. I am Dirt.

From within her Godskin, she was able to shake her wrist free and pull away. She stepped back, looking her sister up and down in disbelief.

"What is it you are saying?" Dirt asked. She would not accept this. Never.

Webba just shook her head. "I am saying . . ." She squatted down and extended her arms out wide, preparing to do the Bowing salute. "Our final Bow must begin."

48

Sis Dirt vs. Sis Webba

DIRT DIDN'T salute back. She stood in place, her body slack, her face frozen with a sick expression. None of this made sense. Even as Webba finished her salute and rose into her Bowing stance, Dirt didn't move. Even as Webba began Slapping, approaching ever so slowly, Dirt remained as she was.

Then Webba Rode in, low and fast, Trapping Dirt around the waist. In their years together, Dirt had sparred Webba more times than she could count. She knew the feel of Webba's body as well as she knew anything in the world.

That was not Webba's body. It felt alien as it crushed itself against her, as hard and lifeless as the stone all around them. Webba had been fleshy and strong, her fat thick, her arms relaxed and delicate one moment, then a lung-sucking vice the next, a level of control few had mastered as well as she. This lacked the flesh, lacked the thick fat, tense instead of relaxed and bone-grinding rather than lung-sucking.

It was *wrong.*

Dirt defended herself instinctively, lowering her weight to keep from being Bowed. Webba tried again, using a high Trap up under Dirt's armpits. Dirt started to defend again, but she didn't need to—Webba released her Trap and jumped back, putting distance between them.

It seemed that Webba had disengaged for no reason. Then Dirt felt the leather straps of her armor sliding off her skin. She clasped the chest piece against her, but the armor along her waist fell away, and she knew that as soon as she let go of the chest piece, it would fall as well.

Then Webba was Riding in on her again, giving her no choice but to let the armor fall so she could defend herself. The targeting of her armor sent a clear message—Webba wasn't just trying to beat her. She was trying to hurt her.

No, not Webba.

As they fought through a series of Traps again, more and more Dirt felt that this wasn't her sister. This was a different entity. The Fault, maybe. Or the magic. Whatever it was, it had taken over her sister's body. If Dirt destroyed it, she could use the magic to bring Webba back. The real Webba. If this fake Webba won, Dirt would be gone, which meant Webba would become a full Remnant, a mindless monster in search of life to destroy.

Dirt had to win. A goal that was easy to think, but difficult to do. This Webba had all the strength and speed of a Remnant, enough to rival any Godskin. But she seemed to have Webba's tactical mind, her incomparable Bowing technique. Within seconds of fighting for Traps, Dirt felt herself tossed head over heels, flying across the room and slamming hard against a wall. Jagged juts of stone dug into her back, scraping painfully against the bones of her spine. Were it not for her Godskin powers, she was certain the impact would have broken her back in a dozen places, killing her instantly.

As Dirt climbed up to one knee, a tendril of doubt crept into her.

"Sometimes, my Sis," Webba said, approaching calmly, "Fam unites. Sometimes Fam fights. You are my sister." She stopped a stride ahead of Dirt, looking down at her. "Fight me, eh?"

Dirt took a long, calming breath, centering her mind. She rose to her feet.

"I understand," Dirt said.

Webba had never begged for anything in her life. She was a girl who earned what she needed through strength or—when her strength was not enough—her kindness and generosity. Begging was not dignified for anyone, but especially a Bower. Better to suffer in silence.

Dirt finally saw this attack for what it was: a plea. Webba was begging to lose, to be freed. Dirt could only imagine the pain of the life she was living, a slave to the will of the Fault. Webba had told Dirt where the magic was and how to use it. She wanted Dirt to succeed.

But Dirt would have to take the final step. That had been what Webba was saying: sometimes the only way to save your sister was to hurt her.

"Come, my Sis," Dirt said, squatting and clapping her hands together in the Bowing salute. She was proud of herself for holding back the tears. "Let us end this."

><><

There was nothing Dirt could do. Webba was always five steps ahead, tossing Dirt all about the cave. Even when Dirt used the Whip Slap, Webba just sidestepped, closed the distance between them, and grabbed Dirt for a Trap. Then she was getting thrown again. Perhaps, in the expanse of the Grand or Imperial Temples, Dirt could have used speed and space to claim an advantage, but in the confines of the cave, there was nowhere for her to run, so their fight was restricted to the basic techniques of Bowing—and no one was better at Bowing than Webba.

Even worse, Dirt was tiring faster. Webba had always had far superior endurance, and now that they both had the power of the Gods coursing through them, that superior endurance was clear again. While Webba was still bouncing from one foot to the other, light and fresh, Dirt's steps were becoming a labor, her mouth open as she tried to suck in more air.

"Tired, my Sis?" Webba asked.

She attacked again. Slap, Ride, Trap, Bow. Dirt hadn't felt so defeated since before she had returned to competing, back when she was still just a coach training with a young and merciless Swoo. Each time she returned to her feet, Webba was smiling, undaunted.

Dirt tried to go on the offensive, only to be countered into the floor. She was grateful there was no timekeeper keeping score—she would have been dozens of points behind already.

I am brave. I am fat. I am Dirt.

The words she normally sought for reassurance felt strange now. She couldn't help but think immediately after: *But this is Webba.* Webba had fought the South's elite Bowers for years, thrashing them all. She was the only Bower Carra Carre had feared.

Webba had fought off a dozen Vine Sis. One Dirt was simply not enough.

So maybe she needed more Dirts.

Dirt reached out and touched the wall beside her. It was warm, hard, nothing surprising. There was not a drop of mud within it that Dirt could use. So she reached *deeper*. She mentally burrowed into the rocks, up toward the surface, feeling for what her eyes could not see. Thankfully, Webba ceased her attack, watching with curious amusement.

"What is this, my Sis? Na power?"

Then Dirt found it. It was far, and it wasn't much, but hidden among the infinite weight of the world, she found a thin vein of mud. She began pulling it toward her, feeling it trickle over and between pockets of earth in a narrow stream, a snake through thick bush. Soon it emerged from the red veins in the walls, forming into another body, a Bower of the same size and proportions as Dirt herself, but made entirely from the red-brown mud.

"Chaaaiii!" Webba shouted. "Two and one, eh? This power is strongstrong."

"As you will see," Dirt replied.

Webba laughed. "Eh heh! This is my sister Dirt. Fierce and proud. Let us Bow, eh?"

Though she couldn't control it, Dirt could feel the mud version of herself like an extra limb. She circled away from it, the two of them approaching Webba from opposite sides. Dirt faked a Ride, drawing Webba's attention, which allowed the mud clone to Ride in fully.

Webba anticipated it, of course. She countered the clone, tossing it to the ground then stomping on its head, squishing it from its Bower form to a shapeless mound of mud. Webba raised her foot and shook off some of the mud, looking at Dirt with an apologetic expression.

"Not so strongstrong, eh?"

Dirt almost laughed. She'd had the wrong goal from the start. She should have known there was nothing she could do to defeat Webba. No one could defeat Webba, at least not in Bowing. The only way Dirt was getting anywhere near that magic was if Webba was out of the way.

But that didn't mean defeating her.

Dirt reached out to the wall again. She sought out not just the first mud she could find, but a bigger pool, her mind delving in every direction to pull together every drop she could.

This time, however, Webba didn't allow it.

"Not again, my Sis," Webba said, speeding toward her.

Dirt dashed away, escaping Webba's lunging grab. With space between them, she again touched the wall, pulling in mud. Webba was relentless, though, and Dirt had to continually flee from her attacks, sneaking in opportunities to summon more mud toward her. Even when she had enough mud for a full-sized clone, she did not make one. She continued drawing on more and more, and the effort sapped her, draining her energy as much as she drained at the Isle's mud.

As Webba lunged toward her again, Dirt bounced to the side—but the lunge was a fake. Webba quickly changed direction, Trapping Dirt and hauling her into the air. She carried her to the center of the room, away from the walls, and slammed her to the ground.

"No more mud, eh?" Webba asked, sitting atop her. "What can you do?"

Dirt had no choice. She was nearly at the end of her energy anyway. Her muscles all burned, even through the Godskin. This was her last chance.

She could still feel the mud through the ground. With the last of her energy, she pulled all the mud she'd been drawing in out of the walls. It came in large streams, far thicker than before, splashing onto the floor in gobs before forming up into clones of Dirt.

Not one. Not five.

Dozens.

All around Dirt and Webba, full-sized mud clones rose. Dirt felt her power in each one, her desperation. Her own body had lost the power of the Gods. If Webba so much as sneezed on her, it would be the end of her life.

Before she could, the clones dived in, swarming Webba. They dragged her by every limb, carrying her away. Once she was separated from Dirt, even more of them piled on, molding into each other atop her body. Webba fought viciously, thrashing left and right, flinging their mud bodies into explosions against rocky surfaces.

But there were too many. They forced Webba against a wall and completely enveloped her. They started with her feet, then her torso and arms, before covering her head. Just before Webba's face was drowned in mud, the former First of the Mud grinned.

"You do wellwell, my Sis," she said. "See you soon."

Then she was hidden entirely beneath mud, all of which immediately hardened into unyielding rock.

In the sudden silence, Dirt realized that Webba's voice had been the only thing keeping her going. Now she was alone. So, so alone. Every girl she'd ever called sister was gone from this life.

Trust your family. Cherish them. Remember them. Whether you chose them or not, when the day is quiet and the night is long, family is the most precious gift you will ever have.

Now her family was gone. And the only way to bring them back was an ancient magic she didn't understand. The last people to use the magic had failed, destroying their own family and creating a flawed world they didn't recognize. How could Dirt be sure she would do any better? What if she used the magic and nothing changed? Or, worse, she forgot the sisters she'd already lost?

Dirt fell to her knees, sitting for minutes in silence and dark, the weight of her decision increasing by the second. Eventually, she realized that she had no choice. She could not live in the world she was in now. A better world was worth risking a worse one.

She stood and approached the Fault. Looking into its flickering black felt both uncomfortable and mesmerizing. She had a desire to look away, yet also a desire to look deeper into it, to delve its properties until she fully understood why it so resembled the scar on her face, her mark of adulthood.

But she didn't have time for all that. Instead, once she reached the back wall, she stretched one arm forward.

"Dirt, wait!"

Dirt spun around, her defenses up. She could muster her Godskin for seconds, at most. Whatever the new threat was, she prayed it wasn't strong or fast enough to stop her from plunging her arm into the Fault and using the magic.

Across the room, rising to his feet, was Useyi.

"Please," he begged. "Listen to me before you use it."

49

NoBe Tiggi

TIGGI STOOD in a sea of madness. Her fellow Bibi ran in every direction, crying with a deep terror that she had never heard before. They did not know where to go. They did not know what to do. All they could think was a simple mantra: survive.

Tiggi herself felt no different. She didn't want to die. She didn't want to be forgotten. But the Remnants had reached them. In an instant, they dispatched one of the Sis. The other had decided to run instead of fight. To lead the Remnants away from the defenseless Bibi. To Tiggi's astonishment, she succeeded. As the Sis fled around the edge of the interior, back toward the camp entrance, the Remnants followed.

All except one. One of them had drifted closer to the Bibi, and its mind shifted its target. It turned toward them and faced them coldly, its contorted snake head and eyes atop a small canine body with the talons of a hawk.

"Stop!" Tiggi screamed.

Most of her sisters ignored her, but a few of them near her froze, listening for any solution that Tiggi, the sister they'd never truly loved, might have had. If they continued to scramble in fear, they would all die. Only one of them would fall to this Remnant, but the main host of Remnants would circle back and take each one of them. They had to work together.

"With me!" Tiggi shouted, and she immediately turned and ran toward the back wall of their alcove.

Sis Dirt and Sis Carra Carre hadn't been able to finish the construction of a new camp. But they had started. They'd intended the alcove to just be an entryway, and they'd taken out chunks of the wall high above the ground, the beginnings of a tunnel to another camp. Once Tiggi reached the back wall, she looked up at where it bent into the short tunnel. It was above the ground by at least five times Tiggi's height. There was no possible way that any of them, individually, could reach it.

But as a group . . .

Tiggi turned just in time to see the lone Remnant run into the alcove, take a Bibi into its jaws, and disappear into a spill of blue mist.

"Come, my sisters!" Tiggi screamed frantically. It was just a matter of time now. The Sis would fall. The other Remnants would return. "Come, please!"

Again, some heard her while others didn't. But no matter. She had enough to begin. She stood directly under the tunnel and turned to face the sister beside her. It was Tempo. Trusted, kind Tempo.

"Climb me," Tiggi said.

The way Tempo stared at her, she must have looked truly mad.

Tempo obeyed without another word, and once her feet were settled on Tiggi's shoulders, Tiggi called out to the next girl.

Soon, five Bibi were stacked. The next one, Tiggi thought with relief, would be the first one saved. As a few sisters began climbing, the others began to take notice, the orderliness of the human ladder cutting through their panicked minds. They redirected themselves toward Tiggi and the others, scrambling over and immediately forming into a surprisingly civilized line. There was jostling as some sisters glanced repeatedly over their shoulders in fear and urged on those ahead of them, but the procession was overall peaceful.

At least until the Remnants returned.

The Bibi near the top of the ladder was the first to see them. "They are coming!" she howled.

Then the panic renewed. Tiggi watched her sisters' faces grow hot with that terror again, and as much as she also felt it rising in her, she was more consumed by heartbreak. Over their shoulders, a blue tide rolled in from the middle of the camp, closing the distance with impossible speed. They had two or three minutes, at most, before they were wiped out.

That was when Tiggi made a decision.

Her sisters had never loved her the way she felt she deserved. But that didn't mean anything. They were her Fam. Fam was not shown in the love that was returned, it was shown in the love given. They were all good people. They just didn't understand her. She thought of Useyi and the Mamas and Papas. Their inability to love each other had destroyed everything. Tiggi didn't want her Fam destroyed.

Last season, in the God Bow finals, Tiggi had decided she wanted to become Sis Dirt. She'd thought that meant climbing the ranks of the Fam until she was First, enjoying all the respect that came with that. Now she realized the title didn't matter. What she had so admired in Sis Dirt was not her title, but her love of her Fam, shown in how much she sacrificed for them. In all her time as a Mud sister, Tiggi had never seen Sis Dirt demand respect or love. She didn't have to. Because she was always willing to step forward to face danger, always willing to venture into the unknown, to sacrifice everything if it meant protecting the Fam.

So Tiggi did what she knew Sis Dirt would have done.

"Song!" she called to her sister beside her. Song was the only Bibi who looked like a true Bower, her belly already growing in. "Come and take my place."

Song left the line, moving to Tiggi's side. "I do not understand," she said.

Tiggi didn't have time to explain. She simply began moving gradually out from the base of the ladder. The sisters above yelped from the sudden imbalance, but Tiggi continued. Song eventually realized what was happening and crouched low, sliding into the spot as Tiggi evacuated it.

"What is this?!" Song bellowed.

But Tiggi was free, her shoulders grateful.

She walked up the line, smiling at each of her sisters as she strode past. They returned her gaze with ones of total bewilderment or even indifference—they were too focused on escaping to think about what their ever-strange sister was doing.

Tiggi reached the lip of the alcove, looking out across the camp. The Remnants were almost there. Behind her, a dozen of her sisters had yet to climb up. After that, there would still be the five sisters who formed the ladder, unable to get up. Tiggi prayed that at that very moment, Sis Dirt was about to use the magic, about to change the world.

But Tiggi couldn't rely on that.

As the Remnants closed in, she jumped from the alcove and ran away as hard as her legs could carry her. The Remnants pursued her, and it made her think of the time when she'd first joined the Mud camp, when some of the sisters had played "Torture Tiggi" by chasing her through the jungle. Those games, as bad as they were, had made her fast. Faster than any other Mud Bibi.

Still, it wasn't long before the Remnants caught up to her. And there was no Bibi Snore to save her.

50

The Magic of the Fault

DIRT WATCHED Useyi approach. He looked haggard. His clothes were torn up, and he was smeared all over with sand and grass stains and splotches of a half dozen other colors and textures.

"How do you come here?" Dirt asked.

"I followed you all," Useyi said.

"So you see my sisters fall," Dirt said with suppressed anger, "and you do nothing?"

Useyi continued advancing as he nodded. "I deserve that. I am sorry. But you understand there is little I can do."

No, Dirt didn't understand. He had been the one to cause all this mess, yet he always insisted that he had no power to fix it. Dirt was tired of the excuses. Four of her sisters had sacrificed themselves to fix the problem he had created.

"Stop," Dirt commanded.

He slowed, but he did not stop.

"Dirt. Godskin," he said in a low, careful voice, as if he were trying to talk down a hungry jungle cat. "Please hear me. You must be careful when using this magic. It is risky."

"And so?"

"So you are a novice. I'm here now. I can do it."

Dirt was shaking her head before she even said a word. This all felt wrong.

"You say before you cannot use na magic. And I say stop."

Still, he continued forward. "Forgive me that lie. I did not have the power to make it down here on my own. But I still have enough to use the Fault. Just tell me what world you envision, and I can create it for you."

He was just a couple of strides away, and Dirt's discomfort was reaching its peak, something within telling her to stay ready, stay defensive.

"I say stop!" she boomed.

He froze, the authority in her voice undeniable.

"You lie before," Dirt said. "And you lie now."

Useyi took a deep breath, never taking his eyes away from Dirt's. For a long while, he was silent, just watching, his body stuck in a disarming curl.

Then, finally, he spoke. "You want to restore the world as it was, yes?"

Dirt hesitated before answering. "Yes."

Useyi's face broke at that, fear taking over his features. "Dirt, please. In the world you enjoyed, I had no family."

"I will restore your Fam."

"How? You do not know them."

"You will tell me."

"Tell you what?!" Useyi spat, and a sudden rage flared up in him—a rage fueled by desperation. "How can I tell you what a person is? All their great loves and private fears. All their triumphs and failures. What can I tell you so that you can bring them back to me as they were? Eh?! Do you want to know how Oduma would beat us when we were late home from school? Or Abidon's addiction to palm wine? Or the time Ijiri killed a neighbor's dog and blamed me? Or Eghodo's lost pregnancy? Eh?! Are these the details you need to bring my brothers and sisters back to me, you nonsense child?! You are not *real!* I made you all, and now you are telling me that you will wipe away those I love? I cannot allow it!"

For a second, Useyi seemed to realize the insanity that had taken control of him. But then, as Dirt stared at him wordlessly, his face screwed up again, completely consumed by the desperate madness he had shown moments before.

"I will not allow it!" he wailed, charging Dirt.

Dirt had faced down many foes in her time as a Bower, but always a foe who had a clear aim. Even the Remnants, as wildly powerful as they were, always wanted to grab her with jaws or claws—they were predictable.

Yet she had no idea what it was Useyi intended to do to her. He used no Bowing stance, had no teeth or pincers to clamp her with. He just threw himself at her with unrestrained emotion, and in the chaotic light of his eyes, Dirt saw herself.

He was alone in the world, just like her. His mistakes and failures had led to him losing his Fam, and now he was doing all he could, with his limited power, to fix it. She wanted to hate him, but she understood him now, and she could only find in herself a mix of pity and admiration.

Still.

She could not risk losing her sisters forever. And the world he sought to restore would do that.

Dirt turned toward the Fault and plunged her arm into it.

I am brave. I am fat. I am Dirt. We are na Mud sisters. We are na children of na South. We are na children of na Isle.

She didn't know the magic of the Fault. Those thoughts were the only magic she had ever known.

Then Useyi appeared right beside her. From so close, she could see the tears rolling down his face as he thrust his arm into the Fault as well, and Dirt only had time enough for her eyes to widen, to feel the worry deep in her gut that the magic would fail and that this would be the end of her and everything she loved.

Then everything went black.

51

The Mud Fam

DIRT AWOKE on a rough floor, staring up at flat wooden slats. The sunlight filtered through the trees above, which shuddered in a breeze, setting the shadows of leaves playing and whispering like a troop of Bibi.

Everything hurt. Her muscles, her skin, her bones, from her face to her chest to her toes. They all burned so bad, they were almost numb, swimming so deeply in a sea of pain she no longer noticed she was wet.

She rolled to her side and realized that she was in a cramped wooden space, just long enough for her to lie down fully, just wide enough for a few girls to sleep side by side.

The sleep hut.

Dirt sat up in shock, immediately regretting it as her pain flared anew. But she didn't have time to nurse her wounds. She climbed to her feet and went to the sleep hut's wooden door. It was just as it had always been, dangling from its twine hinges. She pushed it open.

When Dirt stepped out of the hut, eyes squinted against the early morning sun, the first thing she saw was Webba. She was seated in her chair with the big wheels to either side, and she wore a grin that made Dirt pause in the doorway.

"Na good day, my Sis," Webba said.

Behind her were the dozens of Bibi, each with a small and hopeful smile on her face. Some of them were giggling.

"Na . . . ," Dirt began, but she stopped herself, taking in her surroundings.

It was the Mud camp. The same Mud camp Dirt had spent so much time in. Yet to her right was the sleep lodge, that long hall that she and Swoo had built for the new Bibi. She looked back at the sleep hut and saw that it was the original construction, not the version they had remade after Carra Carre and Verdi destroyed it.

Verdi.

She could remember Verdi.

"What is this?" Dirt asked, holding her head as a headache bloomed.

A voice came from along the tree line, irritation clear in its gruffness.

"Are you so blind?" Swoo grumbled. Her handaxe was slipped into her waistband, and over her shoulder was a large pig, dead and ready for cooking. "Use your eyes—it is na Mud camp. Sis Dirt na Godskin saves us all."

Swoo was the only one moving. She continued through the camp like it was any other day, slapping the pig onto a stump for cutting.

"But . . ." Dirt didn't know what to say.

Everything was right, but wrong, too. It wasn't clear to her if she had turned the world back to how it used to be or created a new world or something in between.

"Sis Swoo speaks true," Webba said.

Sis Swoo . . . Dirt thought. Not NoBe.

"You save us all. As we know you will." Webba beamed with pride.

"Do you all remember . . . ?" Dirt asked.

They all nodded. In her own memory was everything from the last few months. All the triumphs and failures and hopeless moments. Even though these seemed to have been undone, they still remained. It was the same for the others.

Dirt looked Webba over, her eyes settling on her thin, shriveled legs.

"I . . ." She shook her head in disbelief. "All that is better . . . yet I cannot fix your legs?"

Webba laughed. "My Sis, you cannot fix what is not broken," she said. "And what better place for na lazy oldold one like Sis Webba than na chair?"

Dirt smiled. Webba was a special girl. No, woman. Yet her face held no Scar.

"Where is . . . ?" Dirt pointed to Webba's face.

"Your Scars are no longer," one of the Bibi noted, making all of them devolve into cooing wonder.

Dirt reached up to feel her own face. They were right.

Swoo grumbled, walking right between Dirt and her Fam to pick up spices from the other side of camp. "So we are all here, eh? There is work to do. Let it be done." She strode back to the pig with a pestle full of spices.

"Sis Swoo is rude!" a voice cried from among the Bibi.

It took Dirt a moment to locate Snore in the front ranks of the Fam. She was . . . smiling. That radiant, innocent smile that had been so rare for so long.

Snore broke rank with the other Bibi—another good sign that she had returned to her old self—and approached Swoo.

"Ruderude!" she cackled, hopping into a Bowing stance and Slapping at Swoo's thighs.

Swoo looked down at her with a mix of annoyance and confusion. Then, ever so slowly, her features morphed. The tucked lips of annoyance wobbled into pursed lips of sorrow; the frowned brows of confusion dissolved into the bunched brows of grief. Suddenly, Swoo collapsed, wrapping her arms around Snore and burying her face in the little Bibi's shoulder.

Dirt had never seen Swoo cry like that. Never. Not even in her time as a Bibi. The outpouring of pain brought tears to Dirt's eyes as well, and she saw several Bibi suffering the same.

"It is fine, Sis Swoo," Snore said, patting Swoo's downturned head. "You and Sis Dirt save me now."

When the crying was finished, Webba declared a celebration. A feast was prepared, with Swoo's roasted pig as the centerpiece. They ate in small groups surrounding the ring, enjoying a warmth and sisterhood they had been deprived of for so long. Dirt was speechless for most of the night, sitting in silence as Swoo told stories of the last few months, embellishing each of them in her favor, despite the fact that they'd all been there to witness everything.

"And when na Remnants attack na Imperial Temple," she was saying, "I go and call na other Godskins. 'Come!' I shout. 'Come and defend na Isle!' And all come and—cham!—jump to listen and I tell them where to go. 'You, bigbig girl, go and fight here. You, East sister, go and fight here.' Without me, who knows how we survive?"

Dirt rolled her eyes but couldn't help but smile, allowing the stories to continue.

Just over Swoo's shoulder, Dirt saw a pod of Bibi she had never seen sit together before. Tiggi, Tempo, Bubu, Wami, Song, and Little Snore were sharing their portion of the feast, enjoying the food and being silly and laughing the way young girls deserved to. Dirt had no memory of what had changed among the Bibi, but she was happy to see the other girls had finally come to accept former Butterfly girl Tiggi as one of their own.

"Finish quickquick," Webba said hours into the feast. "We must go somewhere soon."

Dirt raised an eyebrow, curious. "Where?" she asked. "All of us?"

Webba didn't respond. She just bounced her eyebrows in amusement then wheeled herself away to go hurry the Bibi along.

Dirt looked around for answers, but all her sisters shrugged.

As always, she just had to trust Webba.

52

The Vine Fam

THE LAST THING Carra Carre remembered was being crushed. The statue of Oduma had ground her bones until she passed out from the maddening pain. But before she did, she saw Useyi scurrying across the desert, following the Mud sisters through the stone gate.

Her last moment was full of pain and confusion, wondering what possible reason Useyi could have for being there. Then the world went black, and she woke up just outside her camp, leaning against the wall of woven vines.

She didn't know what was happening or how she'd gotten from Oduma's grip to the Vine camp, but she was able to remember everything. *Everything.* Her mind was a torrent of memories, many of them ones that she knew she hadn't possessed before. She had hundreds of her own sisters, girls as small as Snore and as big as Webba. She knew all of them by name, considered many of them close friends, had bled and sweated and shared meals with so many of them. The Remnants had taken them, but they were back now, just on the other side of the vines.

Carra Carre moved aside the wall of woven vines that camouflaged the camp entrance and strode inside. It was the same as Carra Carre remembered, shoddily built wooden huts in a wide but well-hidden clearing. It was simple, but it was enough, and in some ways Carra Carre preferred it to the beautiful camp that Swoo had burned down. The old one had been a camp for a Fam in power. This was the camp of a Fam in need of growth—that was how Carra Carre viewed the Vine.

Sisters roamed the camp, some going about chores, some doing their early morning stretches. When one of them saw Carra Carre, they hollered in glee.

"Na First is here! Sis Carra Carre is here!"

Vine sisters came running from every corner of the camp and surrounding jungle, cheering wildly. Whatever anyone was doing was dropped, their attention turned fully to Carra Carre. In normal circumstances, she might have thought the display to be too much. There were more important things to be done than greet her.

But not long ago, she had felt so lonely, it was unbearable. So she could only stand in appreciative silence as her sisters assembled in front of her, jumping and dancing and cheering just from her presence.

Then Verdi emerged from the central hut.

Her sister was in good health, the best Carra Carre could remember seeing her in a long while. Her arms were still thick and strong. Her belly was firm. She walked with proper balance, unlike the way she had after Dirt smashed her ears.

Just the thought of Dirt sent Carra Carre's mind hurtling through memories. Dirt must have done it, she realized. Dirt had used the magic of the Fault to restore the world.

"My Cee Cee," Verdi said, her purple orbs peering out of her vine mask.

The last time they'd seen each other, Carra Carre had come to understand how her newfound friendship with Dirt had felt like betrayal to Verdi. Carra Carre had apologized, but they'd had no time to come to a full reconciliation before the Remnants attacked.

"My Sis," Carra Carre said, striding to meet her near the camp's center.

For a second, they just stared at each other.

Then, as Carra Carre opened her mouth to speak, Verdi said, "I am sorry."

It was all Carra Carre needed to hear. In that "sorry" was an apology for everything Verdi had put her and the Fam through over the years, from her mad campaign to control the South to all the needless violence against the other Fam. She was apologizing for being inconsiderate, manipulative, and an overall poor sister.

It was so much in so few words. But it was enough.

Carra Carre wrapped her sister in a tight embrace. How long had it been since they'd hugged like that? They enjoyed a moment of peace in each other's arms, their bodies saying things their words failed to convey. Then the other sisters swarmed them. The hundreds of other Vine sisters giggled madly as they charged toward their First and Second, forming a mass of girls. In all her years as a Bower, Carra Carre couldn't recall a time they had all hugged like that. The life of a Bower was a hard one, and the Vine had always viewed softness as something that could weaken them.

That was before they'd all lost each other. Forgotten each other.

Carra Carre vowed to appreciate her Fam more. Not just as fellow competitors, but as people. As sisters.

And if that softness weakened them, so be it.

53

The One Fam

EVEN WHEN the Mud sisters went away from their usual path and turned toward the water, Dirt wasn't exactly sure where Webba was leading them. Then they reached the foot of the cliffs, near the Rock territory.

"We are going back to na One Camp?" Dirt asked.

Webba gave her a secretive look but ignored the question. "Help me up na cliffs," she said instead.

Dirt ducked down beside Webba's chair.

I am brave. I am fat. I am Dirt.

A peaceful calm still descended upon her, but there was no surge of power. No steam cleansing her mind and body.

She was no longer a True Godskin.

"My Sis," Dirt said. "I cannot . . ."

"Na Gods truly leave," Webba said before chuckling. "But I am not so fatfat as before. I do not think I need na Godskin to lift me. Sis Swoo!"

Between Dirt and Swoo, and taking a couple of breaks, they were able to get Webba's chair up the cliffs. Then it was a short trek along the seaside before their true destination became clear.

"Flagga Day?" Dirt asked.

Webba grinned.

Once again, the South's boys and girls had come together, Butterflies in their finest dresses and high-heeled shoes, Pusher boys grilling enough meat for everyone, Bowers casually sparring. But it was of course the Flagga who owned the day, their sticks proudly upright in the air, multicolored flags streaming from them.

For every Flagga Day before, it had been a collection of strangers, their only bond being the desire to celebrate the holiday. But now, it wasn't just a holiday. It was a reunion.

As Dirt and the Mud came into view, the One Fam—all the boys and girls of the South—roared in celebration. Dirt couldn't help but smile, especially as Webba reached out to raise Dirt's arm and wave it toward their audience, drawing a round of laughter.

The Mud Fam joined the assembly, greeting old friends, snacking on sweets and meats, partaking in any games or dancing they passed by. After so many months of misery, it felt good to be joyful, without fear or apology. Dirt felt lighter, so much so that she didn't mind at all the loss of her Godskin powers. That part of her life was over. The days ahead would be full of food and dancing and watching her sisters grow. Not fighting for survival.

"Bibi Nana!" Snore shouted, running into Nana's waiting arms.

Beside Nana was the boy, Ekko. Dirt could remember him now. She was grateful that he was back and appeared to be healthy. More importantly, she enjoyed seeing the light he brought to Nana's eyes.

When the Vine arrived, there was a moment of silence.

It was soon broken by a reverent applause, one that swelled into a sincere crush of cheers and shouted praise. Whether by memory or rumor, they all knew that Carra Carre had gone down into the Fault to save them. They knew what she had risked, and for that, she and the Vine were forgiven their wrongs. Verdi walked through the assembly sheepishly, keeping her gaze down. But even that changed over time as more and more people greeted her, showing her that the past was being left in the past.

When everyone was assembled and the time came, the Flagga tossed their sticks into the water. They drifted slowly toward the horizon, the sky turning from blue to yellow to orange as the sun danced across it. This time, the slowest stick belonged to the Sand Flagga, who were singing out their anthem as the algaita blared for the day's ending.

Yet, just like last time, as the final stick disappeared across the horizon, another stick came toward them.

The children of the South were stunned into silence.

"How?" Swoo asked. "You have no Scar. No Godskin. Na Gods are gone."

Dirt couldn't provide any answers—the very same thoughts were running through her own mind.

The stick drew ominously closer, resolving itself into the same wooden vehicle that Useyi had appeared on.

Fear began creeping slowly back into Dirt, and she had a painful image of going through it all over again: Useyi, the Remnants, the Fault. She thought she'd won, but now she recalled Useyi sticking his arm into the Fault as well. Maybe she hadn't. Maybe she'd just doomed all of them to another cycle of the same misery.

This time, the vessel didn't crash against the rocks. It steered itself around them, drifting all the way to the shallow beach at the foot of the cliffs.

Dirt knew she should have steeled herself for a fight, but she couldn't. Her fighting days were over. If Useyi wanted war, he had come to the wrong place. The children of the Isle were finally at peace, and Dirt wouldn't let that be broken by being dragged into violence.

They could place guards to ensure he never made it up from the cliffs. Or they could erect a barrier at the top, keeping him from ever stepping foot on the Isle. Even a human chain, each of them holding hands and demanding he leave, might have been enough.

Anything but another fight.

Useyi appeared, climbing up from the depths of the vessel, clad in his usual strange garb. And he was smiling. A big, sincere smile that split his face in two.

Antie Yaya followed behind, drawing coos from hundreds of the children atop the cliff. How Antie Yaya had come across the sea with Useyi, none of them could say, and nor could Dirt. It was strange and difficult to understand.

The next people to emerge made it all clear.

Oduma the Defender. Abidon the Liberator. Ijiri the Trickster. Eghodo the Lawbringer.

One after another, they emerged, each of them smiling like it was their first day. They were unmistakable, even to those who hadn't seen their statues. Yet their demeanor was relaxed, happy, unlike the cold threat of their statues in every way.

Dirt remembered that last moment before the black, when Useyi had plunged his arm into the Fault. Somehow, they had both remade the world. Dirt had brought her sisters back, recovered everything the Remnants had taken. But Useyi, too, must have found a way to rebuild his homeland and restore his family. They'd sailed across the sea not for war—judging by the way they were all waving up at the children joyfully—but for peace. To celebrate the reunion of families of every size and type on both sides of the world.

"Na good day, Children of the Isle!" Useyi shouted up.

"Na good day!" they all shouted back, prompting both sides to collapse into laughter.

All of Dirt's fear dissolved. It was indeed a good day, she thought. And with her friends and sisters at her side, every day after, whether they faced the end of one world or the beginning of a new one, would be a good day as well.

Acknowledgments

THIS BOOK would not have been possible without so many lovely and hardworking people. First and foremost are Jim McCarthy, my agent, and Reka Simonsen, my editor. In the literary world, agents and editors make the world go round, and my world is only kept spinning by these two—thank you both immensely. Thank-yous as well to the brilliant cover art of Laylie Frazier, and to Greg Stadnyk and Irene Metaxatos, who designed the jacket and interior, respectively. To the entire production and management team at Atheneum—publisher Justin Chanda, managing editor Kaitlyn San Miguel, copyeditor Brooke Littrell, proofreader extraordinaire Clare Perret, and production manager Elizabeth Blake-Linn: thank you. Writing is just dreaming without you all to make it into something real.

A final thank-you to all those who inspired this series. The women in my life, the students I've taught, the beautiful places

I've visited and lived in. Nene Nwoko, whose brilliant work on the audiobook for *Daughters of Oduma* rang in my mind as I wrote this book. The Dream Nurture Initiative, which takes in and provides for children not so different from those of the Isle. The Senegalese wrestling community, whose passion and generosity of expertise are invigorating. All my YA fantasy contemporaries, who paved the way for this book to sit on bookshelves, and all the readers who support us across libraries, bookstores, book clubs, social media, and more.

There are few feelings better than reuniting with old friends, and I'm so grateful to be able to return to the Isle and reunite with the Mud Fam. Though their story on the page ends here, Snore, Nana, Swoo, Webba, and Dirt—and all the friends they made along the way—have become such a part of my life that I can't imagine a future in which I don't visit them in the little sleep hut in my mind, trading stories and playing Na Gekko and Na Guava and reminiscing about the times we shared together.

I wish the same for each and every one of you readers who accompanied me on this journey. I hope this series has given you the ingredients to make each day a little better than the last. If nothing else, I hope it gives you a life philosophy that will always serve you well: Eat. Dance. Fight.

Love you all!